ZENITH

A Lake Prophet Mystery

The Lake Prophet Mysteries
Book 3

ELI EASTON

RJ SCOTT

Love Lane Books

Copyright

Zenith

A killer haunts Prophet and this time it's personal

The discovery of a body at the Thompson Cabins sets off a chain of events that hits too close to home for Sheriff Gabriel Thompson. When his brother Sam becomes a prime suspect in the murder investigation, Gabriel is forced to keep secrets from Tiber and call in outside help as he fights to prove Sam's innocence. It's a nightmare that becomes all consuming.

Tiber Russo, animal whisperer, is dealing with problems of his own. A stalker threatens him and his entire menagerie of pets. With Gabriel wrapped up in the new case, Tiber tries to solve the mystery on his own. Who in the sleepy town of Prophet wants to do him harm? But when the threats turn lethal, Tiber finds himself in over his head.

Tiber and Gabriel have solved two murders together and started a deep relationship. But this time the forces ranged against them are personal, and the target is on them and the backs of everyone they love. With each of them isolated trying to protect the other, their strength is diminished. Even with the love they share, can they make it out of this alive?

To Lola. who taught me how to talk to animals
~Eli Easton

Always for my family
~RJ Scott

Zenith

Chapter One

Gabriel

I woke, startled, my heart racing, shivering with cold from where I'd shoved the covers away. Lost in panic, I rolled over to search for Tiber, my fingers grazing his sleep-mussed hair. His steady breathing should've been comforting, but I'd woken filled with a sense of dread.

From the familiar shadows in the room, I guessed it wasn't much past dawn as, yet again, I'd been forced out of sleep by a nightmare, pulled deeper into memories that never made sense. The familiar, insistent nudge of a cold, wet nose at my hand was a reminder of why I wasn't still asleep. I leaned over to look down at the side of the bed. Duke was there, whining low in his throat, his tail wagging dust bunnies along the floor as he stared up at me. I'd been gripped in a nightmare, and our yellow Lab, Duke, had pulled me out before the pain and memories became too much for me to control.

Before I hurt Tiber.

"Thanks, buddy," I whispered, scratching behind his velvety ears.

He licked my hand before padding to the bedroom door and curling up in the bed we kept there. I lay back on my pillow, closed my eyes, torn between wanting to remember what I'd been dreaming about, and wanting to find some kind of dreamless sleep. Tiber shifted next to me, rolled my way, and I opened my eyes to get my fill of the gorgeous man who'd invited me into his life. I gently tugged him closer, and he murmured and tucked his face into my neck, the spill of his dark hair across my shoulder. His deep, rhythmic breathing almost lulled me back to sleep. Almost.

I'd never felt the kind of love I had for Tiber with anyone. He was the other half of my heart, whether we talked, we sat in silence, played with the pack, or watched movies, I was at complete peace with him, and I could hold him like this forever.

When sleep evaded me, and my bladder insisted I get up, I lost any hope of more rest, climbed out of bed, careful not to wake Tiber, and went into the bathroom. The splash of cold water on my face worked wonders, but the shower helped chase away some of the final shadows, and I almost felt ready to face the day. Wrapped in a towel, I headed back into the bedroom, but Tiber's side of the bed was empty. I found him in the kitchen, rubbing his eyes sleepily, staring at the coffee pot.

"Morning," he mumbled, leaning in to plant a soft kiss on my lips. "You okay?" he asked.

I hesitated before sighing. There was no point in hiding

what happened in my sleep when Tiber understood nightmares.

"Either Duke or my nightmares woke me up, but I'm sure it was Duke."

Tiber ran his fingers through Duke's fur. "Good boy," he murmured. "Get dressed; coffee will be waiting."

I hugged him from behind, inhaling the scent of him, all warm and sleepy. "I could be late if you wanted," I suggested with a leer and a nibble to his shoulder.

"I have a client call in exactly thirty minutes." Tiber eased himself away, and I swear I pouted, because he snorted a laugh. "If the town could see you now." He reached up and straightened my damp hair, then skimmed my cheeks before resting a finger briefly on my lower lip and smiling. "Big bad sheriff, all damp, naked, and pouty."

I couldn't help kissing his smile, because jeez, he was my Tiber, and he was *everything*.

As I dressed, he began recounting his schedule and talking to the animals when he let them out, but my concentration went back to trying to pierce the fog to recall that elusive dream. It was frustrating, knowing why I had the nightmares, but never getting to the point where I could resolve the things that caused them. As it was, the resolution was back in the city with the feeling of something lurking out of reach.

The scent of freshly-brewed coffee began to waft from the kitchen—Tiber had a way of grounding me, always knowing what I needed even before I did. "...I said I'd fit him in at ten, and he seemed good with that," he finished, pouring two cups of caffeine, and sliding one toward me along with a plate of toast.

"Huh?"

"My new client, at ten."

I groaned. "Sorry, I *was* listening." I nibbled at the toast and jelly, and Tiber shook his head, although he was still smiling. Thank goodness, I hadn't let the nightmares take me so far away that he would give up on me. "New client, you fitted him in."

"Yeah, so wish me luck."

Patch took that moment to jump onto the counter, but Tiber shooed the calico down, and got an armful of purring and fur for his troubles. Something inside made me want to stay right here with him, with the dogs and the cats, and Renfield, and maybe, we could even invite Frank the tortoise in from the yard. Then, we could cuddle on the sofa, and I wouldn't have to move an inch.

I didn't do any of that. Instead, I hustled out of the door, ready for the day, and then, headed straight back to steal one more kiss. Just to keep me going.

"Can you pick up milk on the way home?" Tiber asked as he broke away with another smile, then leaned down to organize bowls of food for the various pack members.

"Sure."

I waved, he grinned, and I left.

And, at last, the effects of the nightmare had slipped away.

We lived fifteen minutes from the sheriff's office, but I had the new Beach Boys album that Tiber had gotten me for Christmas to keep me company. I was singing along with "California Girls" as I turned out from Tiber's lane to the main road when my radio crackled.

"Sheriff Thompson?" Devin sounded stressed already,

but given he'd lost his focus over the case of a missing file only yesterday, I wondered if he was carrying that over.

"Go ahead."

"There's been an incident at Thompson Cabins."

A cold prickle of dread ran down my spine and my chest tightened. "What?"

I pressed my foot to the pedal for more speed, swerving to avoid potholes, and considering the best way to get there as fast as I could, as if I could beat time and get there to stop whatever was wrong. Was it the kids? What about my brother? What about his wife, Lori?

"There's a body, a tourist called it in."

"Is it my…" I couldn't think. "My family."

"Shit, no, sorry, sir, I meant, it's not your family." He went quiet.

I flicked my turn signal to get off the road to town and take a back road to the cabins. "I'll be there in two, lock down the scene."

When I arrived, I landed in chaos. I sought out Sam, who was by the stables, his hands under his arms and Lori standing by him, holding onto him. I couldn't see the twins, but this was a crime scene, and my brother wouldn't do anything that stupid. Right?

"You both okay?" I asked him, and he nodded as I gripped his arm. "The kids?"

Sam blanched, wordless, and it was Lori who answered.

"I dropped them at daycare, found the body when I came back."

"You found the deceased?" I asked her.

She shook her head, and pointed at a woman who was being comforted by a grim-looking Devin.

"Stay here," I told my brother and his wife. "Right here."

Next up was the woman and the crime scene, and fuck, how had this happened in Prophet again?

"Sir." Devin nodded.

"Ma'am." I stopped in front of the tourist, in a heavy coat, the hood pulled up, her hair wet under there— probably from the rain I'd woken up to—and her blue eyes red with tears.

"There's a... there's..." She gestured behind the stables, to an area cordoned off with tape.

"She was booked in for the early ride," Sam said from right by me.

I sent him a glance of disapproval. "Jeez, Sam, you need to stay back," I said.

He winced. My relationship with my brother was mending slow and steady, and maybe I could have couched the order in pretty words, but this was a crime scene, and after a moment he stepped back.

Devin held the crying woman awkwardly and patted her back, inclining his head toward whatever was behind there, and I steeled myself for whatever it was. When I'd left the city, I thought I'd left murder behind, yet in a short year, I'd been faced with two murders, and now... maybe three. Maybe there was a reason for this body to be there, an old person who'd died of natural causes, or maybe it was an animal, and the tourist and others had exaggerated what they saw.

"What have we got?" I asked Devin, but he couldn't ease himself away from the tourist.

He was grim. "One male, multiple wounds. I didn't look at them too closely."

I nodded, processing the information. "Witnesses?"

He inclined his head toward the tourist, then at Sam and Lori. Great. That didn't help much given the tourist claimed she'd found a body, and Sam and Lori lived here.

Okay then.

I stepped around the corner, lifted the tape, and then, stopped in my tracks.

This wasn't the lifeless ritually displayed body of Mike Bressett, or the goriness of Billy Odette's corpse, this was a silent sprawling death. If it wasn't for the blood, the man on his back, his legs and arms sprawled, would look as though he were asleep. Blood soaked his white shirt, smart pants, a tie hung loose around his neck, and he was still wearing both shoes. His eyes were closed and one of his hands was curled into a fist, the other open, and there was no need to check for vitals because this was death at its most real. The overhang of the stables had protected the body from the rain, and by his foot there was a soft leather man bag, the strap snapped.

Taking a deep breath to steady myself, I radioed in. "Dispatch, this is Sheriff Thompson."

"Go ahead, Sheriff." Hen's voice was professional, but I could hear the question in her tone.

Shit. Shit.

"Dispatch." I took a deep breath. "We have a homicide at Thompson Cabins. Get forensics here."

Chapter Two

Tiber

"You said in your application that Bruno is having anxiety issues?" I peered at the man and dog on my computer screen, a polite, non-judgmental expression on my face. Or my best attempt at one anyway.

I was getting weird vibes from this new client, and I'd only been on the Zoom call for sixty seconds.

"Anxiety. Yeah, that's it." The man awkwardly patted the head of the dog seated on the couch next to him. With the other hand, he slipped a treat that was in his palm. It was done sneakily, as if I wasn't supposed to notice.

Was the guy—Jim Smith, according to his application—thinking I'd judge him for spoiling the dog? Or was he worried the dog wouldn't stay seated on the couch if he didn't bribe him?

The dog, Bruno, was a large boxer with the breed's typical brown coat and white muzzle. He sat upright and stiff, his alert gaze off-camera as if looking at someone or something else. I made a note.

"Tell me about the anxiety," I said. "What in Bruno's behavior makes you think he's anxious?" Though he seemed pretty anxious to me right then.

Jim Smith gave me a half-smile. "Before we get into that, tell me about yourself, Tiber. I'd like to know who I'm dealing with."

I hesitated. "You can find my bio on my website."

"I know that. But I wanna hear it from you." He gave me what presumably passed in his mirror as an encouraging smile. It had the legitimacy of a three-dollar bill.

I was puzzled about Jim Smith. He was not my usual caller. My pet consulting clients were often, though not exclusively, women. If they were men, they tended to be older; Jim Smith appeared to be in his late-twenties, close to my age. They included people who were worried about their pets, obsessed with their pets, and people who were at the absolute end of their rope. Some of my clients were desperate—their dog hated their new love interest or was about to be tossed by their landlord. Some simply wanted to communicate with their furry friends. But, whatever their issue, they were *always* people who loved their pets. If they weren't, they wouldn't have sought me out or willing to pay my consulting fees.

Jim Smith didn't strike me that way. His pale skin was flushed, as if he'd been exerting himself or was angry. His face was plain, his physique too thin, his blue eyes dull, and he was dressed in a black turtleneck, black slacks, and —perhaps a personal quirk—even black gloves. But it wasn't his sartorial choices that made my skin crawl. I got the vibe he was someone with a hair-trigger temper.

"That's fine," I said easily. "I have a Master's in Animal Behavior from the University of Washington. It's a field that combines zoology and psychology. I've been working with private clients for four years, and I have reviews and references on my website if you'd care to take a look."

"I know all that," Jim said. "I can read. I want to know about you as a person. What are your hobbies and interests? Are you married? In a relationship?" He raised his eyebrows and half-smiled again.

"Mr. Smith, you're paying for my time. I think we should focus on Bruno." Sweat gathered under my arms, tickling my skin, and I felt lightheaded. I hated it. I hated that it was so easy for me to get thrown off on a call. Or by any human interaction, really.

Unlike animals, humans often had hidden agendas, ulterior motives. I was shit at dealing with those.

"But how can I trust your advice if I don't know anything about you?" Jim pushed, his tone impatient. "I don't think that's too much to ask. I'm not asking anything you wouldn't put on Facebook."

"I'm not on Facebook," I shot back. It was the *social* in *social* media that tripped me up. But this call was going off the rails. I tried to change the subject. "Is there someone there with you? Bruno is very distracted."

"No, he's not." Jim grabbed Bruno's black and metal-studded collar and yanked, trying to get the dog's attention.

My fists curled on my lap. That was abusive. But

Bruno didn't even glance at Jim. He started to get down off the couch, but someone off camera must have given him a command to stay put, because he lowered his haunches back down with great reluctance, his eyes worried and locked on that off-camera person, his body rigid.

Everything in his posture said he didn't want to be there. Everything about him screamed…

"That's not your dog," I said with surprise.

Jim huffed out a gasp. "What? Of course, he is." But his skin flushed pinker.

"He doesn't even like you." It wasn't the most diplomatic thing to say, but it was true.

"He's my fucking dog, all right?" Jim gritted out. "This is just… he's anxious. As I said! We'll get to that. But first, I need to know more about you, Tiber Russo, than a fucking sanitized two-paragraph résumé on a website. Are you into sports? Vegetarian? You look like one."

"I'm sorry, but I don't give out personal details. Let's focus on Bruno or—"

"Do you like scary movies?" His smile turned nasty. "Do you suck dick? Do you fucking scream in bed?"

I gasped and slammed the lid of my laptop shut. That wasn't good enough. I could still see his leering face, imagined he was watching me. But I didn't want to open the lid to close the Zoom app because he might be there, waiting. I jumped up and paced in my office for a few turns, trying to figure out what to do. There was no phone line to unplug. But I went to my wireless router and turned it off. That would for sure kill anything using the internet.

He was gone. I shuddered, wrapped my arms around myself, and tried to slow my breathing.

Jesus, it was my worst nightmare. I always got stressed about having to face a new client. But it usually turned out fine. Normally, my consulting calls went well. If nothing else, I could connect with the animal on screen. But Jim Smith had been seriously creepy.

I tried to calm down. I told myself he was just some whack job. It wasn't personal. Maybe he got off on disturbing people on Zoom calls. Maybe he was laughing his ass off right now.

My address wasn't on the web, and I didn't have to take another call with him. It was fine. It was all fine.

I went into the Venmo app on my phone and refunded his payment. In the notes portion I typed *consultation cancelled*. Sent. It was the smallest revenge and cold comfort. But it was all I had.

I texted Gabriel, needing to feel his reassuring presence. But he didn't answer. Maybe he was busy doing sheriff stuff. I felt a pang of unanswered need, and turned to option two, which was the door to my office. I opened it and the pack surged in. I sat on the floor to receive their wet kisses and exuberant affection.

Leo, Gracie, Ferdinand, and Duke—the dogs all knew when I was upset or on the verge of a panic attack. They crowded around me, trying to lick the megrims out of me. I had to laugh. "Okay. Okay."

Duke barked.

"Yes, I know I promised you a walk after my call. Guess we can go."

Leo grumbled.

"It's not lunchtime yet, buddy. When we get back."

I got up and gathered the leashes, having to hunt because Fudge, the cat, thought it was great fun to drag them off. While I was in the front room, I checked out the window to see if I needed my raincoat. It was raining pretty good. About a six on the Pacific Northwest one-to-hell scale. I was just turning away when my gaze snagged on a figure.

Someone in a hooded rain slicker stood near the tree in my front yard.

I turned back, heart tripping, gaze searching.

There was no one there. A thrill of dread ran down my spine. There *had* been someone. Or…? There was no one by the tree now, and no similarly shaped object I might have mistaken for a person. Nothing but wet green foliage in that direction.

And the trunk of the tree was thick enough to hide behind. I clutched the leashes and stared. Waited. I'd only gotten a flash of the person, but it was seared on my retinas. Dark olive green raincoat, the kind that was heavy and thick, hood up, and the silhouette of the figure tall with wide shoulders. I'd guess it had been a man, a grown one. It had been there—unless my imagination was crazy inventive.

Nothing moved.

Duke brushed against my leg. *Are we going or what?*

The dogs would have barked if someone was out there, wouldn't they? Maybe not if the person was across the yard and quiet. The rain would cover sounds—and scents.

I was freaking myself out. It was that call with Jim

Smith, that was all. I was on edge. There was no one in my yard. Still.

"Okay, guys, change of plans!" I said. "Lunch now, and maybe a walk later if the rain lets up. Come on. Kitchen." I hustled them out of the front room, ignoring the sense of being watched.

If the pack knew I was bluffing about why it was I didn't want to go outside, they were kind enough not to mention it.

Chapter Three

Gabriel

I APPROACHED THE BODY CAREFULLY, then crouched low, examining the deceased. The air was damp from the rain as I scanned the scene, trying to absorb every detail, every hint that could give me a clue. The position of the body, the spread of the limbs, the expression etched into the face —everything was a potential piece of the puzzle. I could almost hear the panicked breaths, the desperate struggles. Were there any last words from the victim? Something maybe Sam and his wife, or the kids, could have heard? A plea, maybe a shout for help? Did this happen last night, or more recently? I closed my eyes, attempting to transport myself to an exact moment in time, feeling the terror, the surprise, the final realization that he was going to die.

Each piece of evidence told a story. There were wounds to his chest, blood; the torn fabric at the bottom of the victim's shirt spoke of a struggle. The slight discoloration around the wrists suggested that maybe he'd been restrained or had tried to defend himself. Small indentations in the ground hinted at a scuffle. He hadn't been killed and dumped—with this much blood, the murder had happened here.

My mind raced, constructing scenarios. Was this a random act or something premeditated? Was the victim familiar with his attacker? Every detail was a whisper, a nudge toward understanding. As I tried to piece together the last moments of the victim's life, my phone vibrated, interrupting my thoughts and I glanced at a text from Tiber asking me to call when I had a minute. I hesitated, torn between replying and dealing with the scene before me. In the end, there was no choice to be made, and I had to ignore it, hoping Tiber was all right, and knowing I'd call him back as soon as I could.

Devin approached; his expression serious. "Gabe, do you want me to interview the witness here or back at the office?"

It was obvious she was in shock. "We can have a chat here, and also book a time for her to come in if we need more." I tapped my chest where my camera was, as a reminder for Devin not to block it as he asked questions.

He nodded. "She just came here for some horse riding." He sounded bleak.

Then, it was my turn to nod. I stood and brushed off my pants, turning a slow three-sixty, then pulling the tape loose and winding it around trees some twenty feet out so the scene covered a larger radius. Devin had followed the rules, but instinct told me there was more to this than met the eye, and we could never be too careful. If someone had thrown a weapon into the undergrowth, it might have traveled some way, or if there was another body…

I couldn't even imagine that. I was still reeling that there'd been another violent death in Prophet.

With nothing else I could do until forensics arrived, I took some final scene photos and went back out to Devin, who'd taken the witness to sit at a small table and was talking to her in a low and compassionate tone. I'd ask any questions he missed when I checked the footage, but he was showing competence, which had developed on in leaps and bounds in the last year. I spotted Sam and Lori hovering near one of the cabins, one of the group of cabins plus stables that the Thompson brothers —, Sam, me, and our little brother Ezra—owned equally. The weight of it all fell on Sam. I dumped money into it, tried to help where I could, which was too little, too infrequently, and stayed out of Sam's way. Ezra just never stayed in the country for one reason or another, be it college or some random backpacking trip.

Lori was distressed and bewildered, and, as I approached, Sam stiffened, then ran a hand through his hair in a gesture all too familiar when he was overwhelmed. "Gabe, the fuck?" he said. "Why would someone dump a body right here? Jesus, the kids were in bed just there!" He waved toward the family home, no more than sixty feet away, with windows facing the scene, although most of it was blocked by the barns.

I laid a reassuring hand on his shoulder and squeezed. "I don't know, Sam. Do you recognize the victim?"

He blanched. "I haven't looked properly. Jesus, is this

another Billy situation? With the throat torn out and…" He stopped talking, swallowed as if he was going to be sick.

"Can I ask both of you to take a look?"

Sam gripped his wife. "You can't make Lori—"

"For god's sake Sam, I'm a nurse; I've seen these things before." She gestured for us to walk, and we went to the corner, just outside the perimeter, but it was difficult to get a good look from here, and it was against all kinds of protocol for Sam and Lori to go inside the tape.

"I can't make him out," Sam said after a while. "Why would a guy dressed like that be out here? He's not staying in the cabins; I checked everyone, and he's not exactly dressed for a trail ride." He scrubbed his eyes, and peered through the misting rain, which created a thin barrier between us and the body. I scrolled to a photo I'd taken, and held it up to them both, enlarging the face, and thankful the vic looked so serene, as if he'd fallen asleep, albeit with his face streaked with dark mud and slightly turned from the camera.

"I swear…" Sam deflated, "there's something about him, okay, but I don't know."

"I don't recognize him," Lori added.

"Okay, let's step back and away." I corralled them to where Devin and the witness stood, catching half an answer where the woman explained she'd arrived from Forks an hour ago. I wasn't an expert, but the vic had been dead longer than that, so if her story checked out, then she wasn't going to be any help.

There was a small group of townspeople who'd decided a walk out to the cabins and stables was what they should be doing this morning. I could disperse them, but what was the point of that?

"We'll take care of everything," I reassured Sam and Lori.

"What if I hadn't been here?" Sam asked. "Lori and the kids were here alone until late last night because I was in Forks—what if they'd been the ones to find the body, or what if…" He went pale, and my instinct as Sam's big brother—to hug him and reassure him—collided with my duty as a sheriff to get him away from the scene. "Can we get maybe some coffee out here or something?"

Lori stepped away, realized Sam wasn't following, then turned back to collect him and tug him to the house, and I was relieved to see him go. The thought of this happening so close to my family, to the niece and nephew I was only just learning to love, and to a brother I was working hard to reconcile with, shook me.

Life is too short.

Shouldn't I have learned this lesson already?

I moved to the tourist. She was talking in a soft tone, between sniffles, to Devin, and when I grew closer, I could see her hand on Devin's arm.

I introduced myself. "Sheriff Thompson."

"Margot Farrier. Mrs. Margot Farrier," she replied, and we shook hands.

"Could you briefly walk me through what you saw?"

"Again?" she asked and leaned into Devin.

Given the stiff way Devin held himself, it was obvious he wasn't sure how to handle a witness who needed physical comfort. "I've already told Devin."

Devin winced at the familiarity, probably imagining I'd

criticize him for giving her his name, but he'd done the right thing to form a connection with the witness.

"Someone else to hear your story would be good," I said, to encourage her.

"I arrived just after nine this morning and parked over there." She pointed at her Toyota, the only car in the parking area. No sign of another car that could belong to the victim. "I'm early, way too early actually, so I'd stopped off at this cute little shop in town, Grounds for Joy? Then, I decided to sit in the car and eat my bagel, and finish my coffee, and then, went looking for a garbage can." She inhaled and pressed her free hand to her chest. "I went around the corner, and he was there. Just. There." She pressed her lips thin. "Dead."

"And you didn't see any other cars? Or people in the general area?"

"No, apart from the owner. I think his name is Sam. He was over by that truck, uhm, cleaning the inside of the truck, and he heard me scream." I glanced at the Thompson Cabins truck, an '86 Dodge Ram with a towing hitch—the truck our dad drove, which Sam had never replaced, kind of scruffy, but solid as a rock. Sam had always loved that truck as a kid and spent a huge amount of time on her—every moment he had to spare—but judging from the scuffs and dents, he hadn't had much of a chance lately.

Okay, so Sam had been outside with the truck. I filed that away. Maybe he'd seen something he didn't even realize he'd seen. Hell, I'd take any hint I could right now.

"Did you touch anything at all?"

She shook her head. "God no. I just backed off. I mean, it's still there, right?"

I nodded, and she slumped against Devin who, to his credit, kept her upright. We exchanged glances.

He inclined his head.

"Ma'am, can we call someone for you?"

She blinked at me, and it was Devin who answered instead as he checked his watch. "Her husband is on his way, ten minutes out now."

"Would you like us to call the paramedics?" I asked.

She shook her head, tears collecting in her eyes. "I just want my husband."

True to the timing, a tall, slim dark-haired man drove up, crossed to his wife, and gathered her into a hug. There wasn't much more to ask her. She'd already thrust her phone under my nose, and her husband backed up that she'd been at home with him and their children last night, and in fact, there was proof in the form of time-stamped photos they'd taken of the four of them playing Monopoly. Add to that a receipt from Grounds for Joy, our small town coffee shop, and my instincts said she was an innocent bystander unlucky enough to find the victim.

Sam and Lori arrived back with coffee, which I didn't even want, although I took one to underline that the job I'd sent them to do was important. Devin crossed to the gathering onlookers, his tone low, disgruntled answers; I even heard the word *wolf* mentioned several times.

It was as if no one listened in this town.

Around eleven a.m., a Clallum County coroner's van parked up, and the official team—one coroner in charge and two techs—stepped out, ready to scour the crime scene. Leading them was a sharp-eyed woman I recognized, the head of the forensic team, Amelia.

"Morning, Sheriff, where do you want us?" she asked with enthusiasm, opening the back of the van. She put on the white coveralls the forensic team wore and took out what she needed, including the pop-up shelter to protect them from rain. I pointed to the body, then one flick and the large tent popped up as one of the techs opened out a folding table. She peered around the corner and nodded.

"Morning, Amelia," I answered, and hovered by her as she went through the formalities of what she was seeing and how she was handling it. She spoke into a recorder, and her observations matched mine; although, she also noticed one of his shoelaces was undone. What that meant I didn't know, but it seemed an important point for her.

Once they'd had their turn with the scene, they cleared the man bag for evidence and passed it to me. Donning gloves, and with evidence baggies to hand, I searched the contents—paperwork in folders and a roll of antacids. No sign of a phone or laptop. Only, as I rummaged through its pocket, a driver's license caught my eye.

"John Melchet, twenty-six, a bank employee from Forks." I announced.

Behind me Sam gasped. I rounded on my brother, and his mouth had fallen open.

After a moment, he collected himself. "I know John Melchet. He was the loan officer at my bank." He paused, confused. "What was he doing here in Prophet?"

"He was your loan officer?"

"Sure. Mine and others. Hard-nosed fuc—man, but fair." He shrugged at that last thing, and I noted that Lori hugged him in support. "I was due to see him later this week."

About a loan? I wanted to ask, but it wasn't the right moment. If Sam was hurting for money, I had money, courtesy of all of my years undercover and salary mounting up in the bank.

The coroner, having completed her preliminary examination, joined us, stripping off her gloves and the rest of her gear, and giving Sam a pointed look. He and Lori wandered away to give us privacy, and she spoke. "Okay, so your victim has multiple stab wounds to the chest and stomach. Cause of death seems open and shut, a couple of the stab wounds would have punctured his heart. Bruising on the wrists, suggesting he was bound at some point. I'd guess zip ties, but I'll need to run tests to be sure. I'd suggest time of death was approximately eight to twelve hours ago, but I'll know more when I get him back to the office. Surprisingly, no animal disturbances on the body."

"Thank you, Amelia." I shook her hand, and she gripped it hard.

"One murder is an accident, two makes the place weird, now you have three. It's like, since you moved here, everything's gotten serious." She was joking, but I felt that as if it were an accusation. Whatever. It wasn't because of me people were dying, it was just that the darker side of city life was creeping into the mountain wilderness. It was inevitable that even Prophet would be swallowed up one day.

After the forensics team left with the body, Devin and I did a thorough search of the area, and it was Devin who found the gleaming silver-handled butcher knife covered in blood discarded among fallen leaves. He bagged it immediately, but he and I both knew this was most likely the murder weapon. We left the cordon in place, and Devin took on the duty of keeping an eye on the scene. I headed back to the SUV. I had to get the knife into the forensic chain of evidence, and I placed it with care on the seat.

We needed to check for the loan officer's car, but Prophet wasn't that big and a stranger's car would stick out like a sore thumb.

I flicked through the folders from the man bag, loan applications, most of them with addresses in Forks, but my heart stopped at the final one, the single address in Prophet. A balloon payment due soon. Interest payments missed. A default notice for Samuel Thompson.

My brother's name was on the paperwork.

Chapter Four

Tiber

By the time I got a return text from Gabriel saying he'd be home for dinner, I'd convinced myself I hadn't seen anyone in the yard. Lunch, and then a long walk down to the lake with the whole gang, had cleared my head—even if I had been on the look out for a lurker in the vicinity. I'd seen no one, and the dogs' antics on the quiet lakeshore had banished the last tendrils of unease from the day's events.

I'd been freaked out by the weird client session, and that was all.

February in Prophet was usually wet and chilly, but snow came to visit now and then, and it was always a treat. As the dogs romped on the pebbled lakeshore, the temperatures dropped, and the wind across the water made me hunch my shoulders and tug on a wool beanie I carried in my coat pocket. But the extra cold was worth it when the rain turned into fat, fluffy snowflakes. The scene turned magical with the gray lake, the dense green evergreens crowded around, and white coins dancing in the air.

The dogs thought so too. Leo, my little fifteen-pound mutt, chased his tail, while Duke snatched snowflakes out of the air. Ferdinand, the basset hound who preferred the term "senior" to "elderly", wanted to sniff every snowflake that landed on the ground to see if it might have a trace of food. And Gracie, the wolfhound from an abusive background, sat and stared up into the sky with wonder.

This little beach—I thought of it as *our* beach—was always deserted. As far as I knew, the only access to it was the game trail that led past my house, which deer, elk, and other wildlife used to get to the water. The town of Prophet was out of sight around a woody curve in the lake shore, and no boats bothered to stop here, nor were any out on a day like today.

It was so private, I dared to express my gratitude for the snow, and maybe release the day's dread too. I started to move, simple steps left and right at first, then the dance I'd learned for the powwows at the rez in Arizona. It made Grandmother happy when I participated in the powwows, even though some of the other kids on the rez thought they were hokey.

Maybe it *was* hokey, dancing this ancestral dance on the shores of Lake Prophet. I'd never have done it in front of another living person in a million years, not even Gabriel. There was still part of me that felt as if I wasn't native *enough*, only a quarter Navajo, to lay claim to that heritage, that I was an imposter, even if I did look as Navajo as my full-blooded grandmother.

Don't worry about that. Leave it all behind. Just dance.

I danced and I chanted. The dogs danced around me, filled with joy. And together, we welcomed the snow.

By the time we got home, the snow was falling thick and starting to stick on the branches of the evergreens and birch, and in the indentations of the paw prints frozen in the muddy ground. The dogs were as happy as I was to get inside where it was warm. My little house had central heating, but I started a fire in the woodstove just because. I answered emails and had two more client calls, both with regulars. They went fine. Afterwards, I puttered around in the kitchen, making spaghetti. I texted Gabriel to see when he'd be home. He didn't answer. Instead, as I was draining the pasta, with happy yapping and scuttling, the pack let me know he'd come in.

"In the kitchen!" I called out.

He walked in, all rosy-cheeked, dark-hair mussed, and that five o'clock shadow that drove me nuts. Hell, he was hot in his sheriff's uniform, period. He put his arms around my waist and nuzzled my neck.

I laughed and squirmed. "Your nose is an ice cube!"

His chuckle was a low rumble against my back. "Wait 'til you feel my hands."

One slipped under my shirt, and I shrieked. "Ai! Why don't you go warm up by the fire while I plate this. Are you hungry?"

I turned to get a good look at him. He had shadows under his eyes.

"Yeah. I didn't have lunch, and shit, I forgot the milk."

His tone was rough. "It's all good, we can make do and I'll get some tomorrow. Let me get you some food."

"Thanks." He bussed my cheek and left the kitchen, followed by the pack. Well, except for Ferdinand, who sat at my feet staring at me.

"Don't give me that look, Ferd. You can't have pasta sauce," I told him. But I slipped him a bare spaghetti noodle.

"Were you busy today?" I asked Gabriel after we were seated at the kitchen table with our food.

He took a bite, chewed. Maybe he was hungry, but it felt like he was avoiding an answer. I studied his downcast eyes, the tightness in his shoulders. He wasn't just tired. It was something else. Something dark.

"What is it? What happened?" I asked, suddenly alarmed.

He raised an eyebrow. "You and your mind reading."

"I'm not reading your mind. I'm reading your body. But don't change the subject. What happened?"

He put down his fork and wiped his mouth with a napkin. "What would you say if I told you there was another murder in Prophet today?"

"What?" I gasped. I hadn't heard anything. Then again, I hadn't left the house except to walk the dogs. "Why didn't you tell me? Text me? Or—what happened?"

He shook his head, his jaw clenched. "A body was discovered at Thompson Cabins this morning."

"*What*? Oh my God! Are Sam and Lori and the kids okay? Why didn't you let me know?"

"They're fine."

I got the story from him, though it felt like coaxing toothpaste from a near-empty tube. A body near the stables. Some stranger in business attire. Apparently,

Gabriel had spent hours standing guard over the scene so forensics could do their work. And fielding endless inquiries from townspeople.

He was unsettled and upset—as he should be. But I could tell there was more he wasn't saying. It was as if his story was a donut, and the center hole was missing.

"You said the victim wasn't someone from Prophet. Do you know for sure who he was?"

"There was ID on the body," Gabriel admitted.

"So who was he?"

His hazel eyes shifted away from mine. "I can't say. Anyway, it's no one you would know."

I frowned. "But… you always tell me. It's not like I'm going to gossip about it. Who do *I* talk to?"

Actually, I did talk to a few people in town now, despite my hermit ways. One-Eyed Jack at the mercantile. Libby Smith, the wildlife painter. But still.

"I know you don't gossip." He gave my hand a quick squeeze. "But you don't know him, so his name wouldn't mean anything to you. Like I said, he's not local."

If it wouldn't mean anything to me, I wondered what his hesitation was. But I let it go. "Do Sam and Lori know him? Was he a guest?"

"No."

"Then what was he even doing there? I don't get it. It wasn't an animal attack, right? Or—"

"*Tiber.*" Gabriel's tone was strained.

I blinked at him. "What?"

He rubbed his face in frustration. "Look, I don't want to discuss this particular case. All right? Because it's Sam. It's *my brother.* And I can't… I have to be there for him."

"Of course."

"And I'm already too close to this thing. I'm already… Do you understand what I'm saying?"

There was a touch of frost in his tone. Or maybe I just heard it that way. His eyes locked on mine but refused to give up any warmth.

What *was* he saying? There'd been two murders in Prophet in the past year, and I'd been heavily involved in both of them.

He didn't want me involved this time; that was what he was saying. And it hurt.

"If you think I'd put myself in danger again, I promise I—"

"That's not it," Gabriel said.

"Then what?"

He pressed his lips tight. "Sam is involved in this. Maybe Lori. They're family. I can't have you messed up in it, too. I can't worry about you, too, and I can't be seen to… Christ. I just need to handle this on my own. Please."

"Fine."

Yes. It hurt. I stared down at my plate and twirled spaghetti around my fork. We ate in silence for a while.

Funny how Sam and Lori were *my family too* when it came to the holidays. But apparently not when there was trouble. I told myself I was being too sensitive. But I couldn't help it. Being sensitive was my freaking job.

"So how was your new client call today?" Gabriel asked, his tone determinedly chipper.

I opened my mouth, closed it. I'd intended to tell him all about it. Get his reassurances, and his hugs. But I no longer felt the need or desire.

Besides, it was no big deal, and Gabriel already had enough worries on his plate.

"It didn't work out. I refunded him," I said. Then, because I didn't want to fight: "Hey, I got some peppermint bark for dessert. Hen sent it home with you at Christmas, and I just found it in the freezer."

"That's okay," Gabriel said. "I should get back to the office. Just wanted to come home and have dinner with you."

"Oh."

He pushed his plate back and stood, pulled me to my feet. He held me tight. He was warm and solid, and I closed my eyes, letting his essence seep into me.

"I love you," Gabriel said.

"I love you, too," I answered.

And for now, it was enough.

Chapter Five

Gabriel

I KNOCKED to warn Devin I was coming in, otherwise he might end up with a concussion from the door. "It's me."

"Come in, sir."

The tiny office door creaked open, revealing Devin sipping coffee and sitting in one of the two chairs we could fit in. The incident room smelled like old papers and coffee, and the incident board was back up, with a tub of pins to one side. I'd really hoped we wouldn't be using the space again as anything more than storage. The last time there'd been a murder in town—before I got here—had been 1963, and that had been a hit and run solved the next day when the driver turned themself in.

There'd been no need for a private space to work through theories, and even though I'd thought about extending the space after the Mike Bressett case, and then the Billy Odette murder, it hadn't been pressing. I mean, what were the chances of there being another death in Prophet?

I'd seen boards like this many times before back in LA, but somehow, this time, it felt personal.

Devin had pinned what few photos we had, plus some brief notes on the board. His focus was sharp, scanning each piece of evidence, trying to make connections as he finished one coffee, then moved onto another one lined up next to a half-eaten muffin.

"Left you coffee, and a muffin," he said and gestured outside to the main office.

I went to the station's small kitchen and helped myself, taking a few moments to get my head out of the guilt swirling in my mind that I'd been an ass to Tiber, and the worries about the whole Sam thing. The body had been on Sam's land, and the victim had Sam's name on papers in his bag, not to mention it hadn't escaped my notice that Sam mentioned he hadn't been home until late the day before.

Obviously, it wasn't Sam. But I didn't like the smell of it one bit.

My cell vibrated, and I checked it, seeing a message from Tiber and wincing before I clicked it. I'd probably come across as a closed off asshole, but I couldn't let Tiber in on the case. He'd sent me a photo of Gracie and Duke sleeping muzzle to muzzle, and I couldn't help but smile, and for a second, I wanted to tell him everything just because I'd promised I would always be honest with him —only this was Sam, plus Tiber did have a tendency to put himself in danger, and sue me, but I was over protective. I sent back a message of my own.

. . .

GABRIEL: Sorry about not being able to talk to you.

　Tiber: All good. You have to work, and I know you can't tell me everything that might be confidential. It's not like we're married so I'm covered by law not to have to take the stand.

　Tiber: Ignore I said that.

　Tiber: Come home soon. Love you. xx

　Gabriel: I won't be too late xxx

THAT MIGHT BE A SMALL LIE. I needed to go over Devin's progress with the incident board, and then, pay a visit to my brother. God knows how I was going to ask him about the money situation, given the cabins were a third mine, and a third Ezra's. Then, I realized I'd left Tiber hanging.

GABRIEL: Love you, too xx

FUCK. Had I left it too long? Did sending love sound like an afterthought? Messaging was a shit medium. I hesitated to write more though, even to dig myself out of a hole that was a result of me overthinking. Stupid phones.

I headed into the incident room, tugging the door shut behind me and taking my seat. I wasn't hungry—dinner had been enough—but I ate the muffin out of habit, and also, they were Hen's special muffins, breaking it in small pieces as I ran through what we had so far. To his credit, Devin didn't say anything as I stared, waiting for me to get my head into the room properly, and then, with the muffin finished and caffeine helping me fight last night's sleeplessness, I cleared my throat.

"Anything new I need to know on our victim?"

Devin gestured at the board. "Other than that, no. Nothing from the coroner yet; of course, the knife has been sent for testing. Our victim, John Melchet, aged twenty-six, joined Clallam Mutual Bank straight from college. No criminal record. No partner, no children, lives with his mom in Forks. I have a call in with Forks PD for anything they can add to what I found on the socials, but we'll get a better picture when we talk to his mother and the bank."

"I'll drop in on her when I go to the bank to talk to employees. What was Melchet doing in Prophet?" I mused and leaned forward in my chair.

"Well, none of the client paperwork connected to town apart from the file with the unsigned default notice for your... for Sam Thompson." He glanced at me, and I met his gaze steadily. I would do this by the book. "So, chances are, he was here to talk to Sam. Probably not, I mean, would a bank send someone all the way out here for that?" Unspoken was a typical suggestion we might make at this juncture, that maybe our vic was here to give a client bad news, and said client reacted by murdering him.

I paused a moment. "We need to get Sam and Lori in for a chat in the morning."

Devin looked surprised, but didn't ask why; instead, he spoke carefully as he attempted to understand why I'd said that. "In order to get more background on the scene, sure."

"No." I placed my mug on the desk and turned in my chair to face Devin. "If this wasn't Sam, if you were presented with this location and evidence of connection, what would you do?" The words burned like acid in my throat. The murder was nothing to do with Sam, and I would prove that, but Devin needed to take point, and he needed to do this by the book until Sam was in the clear.

Fuck me, this shit was a teachable moment.

"I'd ask them in for an official interview," Devin offered after a moment. "But…"

"There is no but here, newbie. You follow the facts and take the case where it needs to go."

"Sure."

"And you'll be leading the interview."

He swallowed. "Me."

"You."

"Okay, I'll call him in the morning." He stared back at the board.

"I've never seen such an empty crime board, but still, tell me what direction you'd go in with this."

"Find out as much as I can about the victim, cross-reference the databases for similar deaths and scenes to rule out a serial, wait for word on cause of death, fingerprints on the knife. Sam said he was in Forks, which I'll get more detail on. You said you're going to Forks to carry out interviews with employees who worked with him. You should talk to the bank about their security cameras to see if we spot any suspicious interactions with Melchet." He counted each one on his fingers.

"I'm impressed."

He smiled at me, and yeah, I was proud at how far he'd come. "Thank you."

I hesitated a moment before the next thing I said,

because it was unthinkable we'd need this information, but I had to say it.

"Sam's reason for not being at home, for being in Forks, make sure you don't drop the ball on any other sources for locating Sam's truck, okay, check ANPR, rule him out."

"Yes, sir. What about Sam's phone, will it have tracked his location?"

"He uses an old flip phone. I doubt it even works very well, let alone geo-locates anything."

"Okay, but if he made calls, they might have pinged off towers."

I wished everything was as simple as the TV cops made it look. "A long shot. But do what you can. Now, the only thing you missed is you need to imagine the scene in the context of the town, and what I mean by that is, who might walk that direction? Dog walkers." I thought of Tiber at the shore, and I missed him. "Runners," I added. "Is there anyone in town who saw a car, or is observant enough to notice someone out of sync with the normal town rhythm? Useful approach in small towns, and also in larger towns in the more tight-knit communities. That's what you'll be doing while I'm in Forks tomorrow, okay?"

"Got it." Devin dutifully entered it onto his encrypted note app, nodding as he typed. I wasn't that much older than him, but while I was in the camp that had paper backups of everything, he was happy in the electronic world, able to see links on random pages that I would miss. Still, he'd built the picture of the case on the board with paper and photos.

This was going to be a long night.

. . .

I LEFT the office a little after eight, late enough that my niece and nephew would be in bed, and early enough that my brother would still be awake. Maybe it wasn't strictly protocol to interact with a potential suspect—and on paper that is what he was—but the personal side of this niggled at me.

He answered the door on my first knock, but didn't automatically invite me in. We'd reconciled enough to exchange invites to each other's houses, and he'd hugged me and told me he was there if I needed him, but there were limits.

Cautious parameters to our social interactions.

"Did you find something?" he asked, keeping his voice low. Was that because of the sleeping kids, or so that Lori didn't hear?

"Can I come in?"

He hesitated a moment, and then, let me in. I stepped into the kitchen that held so many childhood memories. Even the huge kitchen table was still here, scarred and marked by all three of the Thompson brothers in their time. If I looked hard enough, there would be a carved set of initials from a time when I thought I was in love with my seventh grade English teacher. I'd scrubbed it as best I could after that embarrassing interlude ended with a letter home to Dad, but still, I knew it was there, marking the wood.

"Drink?" he asked.

I glanced at the counter where a bottle of Jack Daniels stood, and next to it a simple kitchen glass, half full.

"On duty," I lied.

His face fell. "You're here on official business then?"

"Sure." Whatever he thought, I wasn't going to correct him. "Where is Lori?"

"In the bath. Do you need me to get her down?"

Actually, I was way too relieved it was only the two of us—easier that way. "We need to talk about the paperwork we found in the loan officer's bag." He blanched, and I forged ahead. "Thirteen thousand, Sam. And an unsigned default notice."

"Shit. They were actually going to call in the loan?" He was shaky, then, as if I'd just shocked the hell out of him.

"Was our murder victim due to visit here to discuss this with you?"

Sam blinked at me. "No. We had an appointment next Monday to discuss an extension. He's never come to the house. I don't think they even do that."

"And was it likely, when you had this appointment, that you'd get an extension?"

He crossed to the counter, picked up the Jack in the glass, plus the bottle, then sat down opposite me, slumped almost, as if his strings had been cut.

"I don't know. Maybe not."

"When were you going to tell me?"

He sipped at the drink, more like swallowed a mouthful, then covered the cough with one hand. "This weekend before the meeting. I was going to ask..." He scrubbed at his eyes. "I was on my own here," he said, as if to remind me I hadn't been here when things went to shit for him.

"Well, I'm back now," I murmured, not wanting to open old wounds when we'd been doing so well to patch over the hole by trying to connect with each other.

"You have to understand it wasn't deliberate."

"Of course—"

"It was a combination of things. We had issues with two cabins, then with the pandemic, and the economy taking a hit, we didn't get families booking in, just one-night stays, and all the larger bookings fell off a cliff, then with Billy's death, and vet bills for the horses on top of the regular upkeep, it all spiraled. I tried my hardest to dig myself out. I work long hours, but fuck, I don't even have enough money to fix the goddamn truck, and I have to rely on secondhand parts." He sighed. "You know, Dad said I'd do this, run the place into the ground, and I'm just proving—"

I placed a hand over his and got straight to the point. "Leave Dad out of this. You work damn hard, and no one can weather a perfect storm of crap without letting things go. It's what happens to all businesses. You're no different from anyone else."

"Gabe—"

"Look, I'll have the money in your account tomorrow." I'd worry about how that might look in an investigation later, and I made a mental note to file paperwork with Devin, at least if anyone dug into the issue further.

He opened his mouth as if he was going to tell me not to bother, almost defaulting to the anger from when we'd been estranged, and he'd wanted nothing to do with me. But he was a husband and father—a good one as far as I could see—and instead of reverting to being defensive, he nodded, then tipped his chin. "I'll draw up some kind of agreement for the loan."

"No need," I said. "This is me investing in the cabins and stables, for Sarah and Aaron and their future, and it means something to me. So, no, this isn't a loan, this is family doing the right thing for family. Okay?"

"Fuck," he muttered. "Thank you." He downed some more whiskey, but I took the glass off him when he went to put it down, then slid it out of his reach.

"Please don't," I murmured, and he scrubbed at his eyes.

"I fucked up."

"No, you didn't. And Sam?"

"Yeah?"

I gripped his hand. "We're brothers; we're there for each other. Okay?"

He glanced up then. "Okay."

He squeezed my hand, and I hoped that the stress of it all had lifted enough for him to stop worrying.

"Have you told Ezra about the money?" I asked, and my chest was tight just with asking the question. I hadn't spoken to Ezra in so long, he never answered any of my messages, never came home, always out there saving the planet, or whatever calling he had.

"No, I kept it all in here." He tapped his temple. "Anyway, you know Ez, he's never around." He brightened. "He said he'd come back for Christmas next year the last time he messaged."

We sat in silence a while, and I pushed all thoughts of Ezra aside and focused on the case again. I tried not to sound as if I was interviewing him, but I felt compelled to get ahead of what might be happening to this case.

"Sam, why were you late back here last night?" I asked. Should I be asking? Was I crossing an ethical line by giving him any kind of heads up.??

He didn't do anything.

I'm his big brother. I need to get ahead of this. I'll do it carefully.

"As I said, I got a call from this online garage in Forks about a carburetor I'd bought from them on eBay. I went to pick it up, but I must have had the wrong address, and I couldn't track them down on Google Maps. Now they're not answering emails. Assholes. Like I can afford to spend two hundred on nothing."

That sounded okay, as if it was a real reason for him to not be here, and thus, have a solid alibi, as if people other than just his brother would believe that. He'd have been caught by road cameras.

"Do you have receipts for gas?"

He shook his head. "I didn't stop for gas."

I really wished he had, then it might have put him out of the line of fire. Keeping disappointment from my tone, I carried on.

"Just a heads up. Devin will call you in the morning, suggesting you come into the office. Crossing the Ts, dotting the Is. Me investing the money might be a thing. Just be honest and upfront about it."

He flushed red, probably at the thought of other people knowing his business, but I didn't detect fear or concern when he nodded. "I'll be there."

I headed for the door, cast one look around the

counters, smiling at the cookie jar I remembered from childhood, and he saw me out, tugging me into a hug before I left.

"Thank you," he repeated.

"It's nothing."

We bro-hugged, and I went down to my car, opening the door, but he called after me and I turned.

"Gabe?"

"Yeah?"

"You're wrong about it being nothing. It's everything."

Before I could respond, he shut the door. By the time I'd gotten home, back to Tiber's place—our place—I was feeling back on an even keel, and when I walked in to find Tiber on the sofa reading with the entire family gathered around him, well, all apart from Frank of course, who'd be outside by the pond, I went to my knees in front of him and buried my head in his lap, right next to Patch, who batted at me with a black paw.

"Sorry I had to go back to work," I murmured.

He stroked a hand through my hair, then tugged me up to pull me close for a kiss. One by one, our little family melted away, until only Duke remained, curled up next to Tiber.

"You never have to say sorry," Tiber said against my lips.

I cradled his face. "Tell me more about your day? Was it good? What happened with the new client? You said it didn't work out?"

Something passed over his expression, the merest hint of a frown, and he pulled me in for another kiss. I somehow got the feeling he was using the whole if-we're-kissing-we-can't-talk thing, but eventually, he moved back.

"Just didn't work out. But I had a few other good sessions today. The kids and I enjoyed the snow."

I sensed there was more to the story, but I wasn't going to push. Instead, I squeezed between him and Duke, who snuffled his displeasure at being moved, and then, Tiber curled into my arms.

I'd tried to keep the case and my private life separate, and it was hard, but for now I was home, and everything was good. Part of me wanted to tell Tiber about Sam and the money. Keeping things from him was so hard when he was my sounding board. But I knew I was doing the right thing.

I'd worry about tomorrow when I woke up.

Chapter Six

Tiber

I PARKED down the street from the Merry Maids Preschool and turned off the car, taking deep breaths.

This was fine.

They were kids. Little ones at that. Not yet the age where casual cruelty or epic boredom and disinterest became a thing. And I had Frank. Focus on Frank.

I got out and opened the back hatch of my Subaru Outback. Frank looked up at me worriedly.

"It's okay," I told him. "I'm not going to leave you here. This is just a short visit to meet some kids who need to know about tortoises. You're an ambassador for your species, buddy. But right after this, we'll go home and have a whole iceberg lettuce for lunch, I promise."

Frank was mollified, but still grumpy as I fixed my backpack to my back to free my hands, then hauled him off the blanket and into my arms. He was over two feet long and fifty pounds, so it was a load. He tucked his head and legs into his carapace due to the cold.

"I know it's nasty," I said. "We'll be inside soon."

Ugh. My stomach flipped over. Inside was where I didn't want to be. But there was no way out of this, so the only escape was forward. I marched up to the school with Frank in my arms.

At Christmas, Sarah and Aaron, Sam's four-year-old twins, had visited my house with Gabriel and had met the whole pack. They'd been fascinated by Renfield, the rabbit, and especially by Frank. They'd asked if they could take him to school to show the other kids.

I agreed under the condition that I take him in and out. It seemed the least I could do to make sure Frank was safe and not over-handled. It had been an easy promise to make on Christmas Day when that show-and-tell was *someday*. But then Sarah and Aaron's preschool teacher had emailed me, and it had become a whole thing. With everything else going on, I'd managed to block it from my mind until six a.m. this morning when I got a text reminder I'd set for myself. It was mother-fricking today.

Ugh.

It's fine, just get it over with.

Sometimes being an introvert made life so difficult.

Samara Rafferty, the woman who ran the preschool, was a pretty and perky woman in her thirties with a big afro she wore natural and tamed by a Mary Jane headband. Her figure was slim and elegant, her skin an autumn brown-gold, and her nose slightly upturned. Whatever her heritage, it had done her many favors.

"Tiber! I'm so excited to meet you," she enthused. "And this must be Frank. He's amazing!"

Frank's head emerged a half-inch or so, and he glared at her.

"Hi, sweetie!" she cooed, and Frank obviously approved because his head came all the way out. His legs too, paddled in a request to be put down.

"Just a minute, bud. Where do you want me…"

"Come on in and meet the kiddos!"

The kiddos included eight children. I guessed they were all between three and five years old. They were playing with various toys, spread out across the play room, when we entered.

One boy looked up and said, "Whoa!"

Then Sarah saw me. "Tiber!"

She ran over to hug my legs, followed swiftly by Aaron.

I was touched at the reception but couldn't return it with a tortoise in my arms. "Hey, guys! Let me put Frank down."

"Frank, Frank!" the twins chanted as I followed Samara's gestures and placed Frank on a table. The table had short legs and little chairs around it, all built for munchkins. I knelt beside it and held on to Frank's carapace lest he crawl right off. His legs and head were fully extended as he raised himself to his maximum height. It was both a show of strength in a strange environment— the way cats will puff themselves up to appear bigger —, and a sign of curiosity.

The children crowded around.

"Now, remember," Samara said, "don't touch unless Tiber invites you to. We don't want to scare Frank."

I gave her a grateful look. "How about I tell you guys about Frank, and then, you can take turns checking out his shell and legs."

"Is he a Mutant Ninja Turtle?" asked one little boy, demonstrating a ninja karate chop.

"Nope. He's an African sulcatas tortoise. The sulcatas are not endangered, but they are considered a vulnerable species. That means there aren't many of them in the world, and we need to protect them and help them so they can—er—" I hesitated, realizing I was going down a path that was probably not ideal for toddlers.

"Make babies!" Samara said brightly. "So, there are lots more of them."

"Exactly."

"Can Frank have babies?" asked a little girl, clutching her doll.

"Uh… Right now, Frank is the only sulcatas living anywhere around here. So, I don't think he'll be having babies. Anyway… this type of tortoise comes from the Sahara Desert and can live to be seventy years old."

"That's sooo old," said Aaron. "But Frank isn't that old, right, Tiber?"

"No, Frank is about thirty. So, he has a long time to live yet, if we take good care of him. Can anyone guess what Frank likes to eat?"

We went through all the Frank things. The kids were surprisingly gentle with him, taking turns touching his carapace and legs to feel the texture. Frank was a trooper, and even mildly curious about the kids. But he reached his limit before they ran out of questions. After spending twenty years in the front window of a reptile shop before he was dumped at a rescue, and being handled and poked and stroked by everyone who came into the store, he had definite boundaries these days. Just like me. I could tell when he started trying to crawl to the table edge in earnest that he'd had enough.

"Frank is tired. I think he needs a nap." I glanced around for Samara for help, and she stepped right in.

"Okay! Let's say goodbye to Frank. Maybe Tiber can put Frank away, and then, come back and talk to us for a few minutes about what it's like to be an animal behaviorist. You guys remember I told you that Tiber's job is to figure out what animals are thinking?"

"Yes, yes!"

"Ooh, please!"

"I wanna do that job!"

"Can you talk to dogs?" asked a little girl. "My dog's name is Bobo."

"Animals don't talk!" Ninja boy scoffed.

"Tiber can talk to them!" Aaron insisted hotly.

"Tiber is my uncle!" Sarah beamed.

Gah, that was so sweet. I had about reached my limit, just as Frank had, and I'd been hoping to make a quick exit, but saying no to Samara and the kids felt a bit like kicking a kitten. And Sarah and Aaron were so cute with their liking me and all.

"Okay. Just for a few minutes," I agreed.

"Great!" Samara smiled. "I have questions myself."

"Let me go put Frank in the car."

Outside, the air was frigid. I hugged Frank's underside

against my chest, arms around the top of his carapace as I gingerly walked to the car. He stuck his head out to peer at me from an eye-crossing close distance, so I kissed his head. "You were a gentleman and a scholar. Thank you."

Frank blinked as if to say it was nothing, all in a tortoise's day.

At the car, I put him on the blanket in the back, tucked the ends around him, and added another blanket on top. Sulcatas did not like the cold, although they didn't hibernate like California desert tortoises. They could tolerate some low temperatures, but they couldn't be allowed to get chilled or wet. I'd installed a large dog house with a hen house heater out at his pond last winter, which was stuffed with lots of fresh, loose hay, and I brought him in on cold nights or anytime he pawed at the back door. He loved lying by the wood stove. So, the cold in the car, even though it was about forty degrees, and well above freezing, wasn't his jam.

"I'll be super quick," I told him. "Hang tight."

I locked the car and hurried back inside.

My hope for a five-minute spiel became ten. Samara wanted me to tell the kids how one became an animal behaviorist and how that was different from being a vet and what types of places an animal behaviorist could work. I thought the kids were a little young to be thinking about careers, but I complied. I figured they might retain a general idea or two.

Then, the kids wanted to know what animals had to say, and I described some of the things certain behaviors told me. In truth, a not insignificant part of how I talked to animals had to do with intuition and with my role as a Go-

Between, as Stone Whiteplume had put it—a messenger between the human and animal worlds. But that was too woo-woo for me to voice out loud, even to preschoolers. So, I stuck to behavioral science.

Before I knew it, I glanced at my watch and fifteen minutes had passed.

I stood up from where I'd been perched on a desk. "Sorry to cut this short, but I need to get Frank home. It's pretty cold out in the car."

"Okay, we don't want Frank to catch a cold!" Samara said brightly. "Say thank you to—"

"What's that smell?" Ninja boy asked, wrinkling his nose.

As soon as he said it, I smelled smoke.

Samara looked around and her face went ashen. "Oh god!"

I turned to follow her gaze. Through the open doorway, the hall was hazy. Gray, shifting tendrils spiraled in the air. *Fire.*

"Stay here with the kids!" she barked.

She ran out of the room.

"It's okay," I said, though it was anything but. "Everyone gather around me. Come on! In close!" All I could think was that I didn't want kids running out into the hall, scattering, their little persons impossible to find in the smoke.

Fortunately, they obeyed, all huddling in. They seemed more curious than scared.

"Is this a game?" Aaron asked.

"Are we going to play hide and seek?" asked the little girl with the dog named Bobo.

I looked around the room. The door to the hall was the only door in, but there were two windows, and we were on the ground floor. The smoke in the hall was thick now. Why hadn't a fire alarm gone off? Surely a preschool would have them.

Samara raced back to us; her entire demeanor serious as sin. I could see the fear behind the brave face she put on for the kids. "Okay, listen up! We're going to have a parade. Everyone line up, holds hands, and don't let go! Hurry now! Fastest one wins."

"We could use the windows," I suggested in a low voice, as the kids scrambled.

She shook her head. "Storm windows are up. They're hell to open. There's a clear path to the carport door if we hurry. I'll lead. Can you take the back of the line?"

"Done."

The next thirty seconds or so were surreal. Samara led the way from the room, holding Ninja boy's hand. The smoke was suffocating in the hall. I was at the back of the line, holding Sarah's hand, and Aaron was in front of her. And all I could think was that Gabriel's *niblings*, as he called them, were in mortal danger, and it was my job to get them, and all the kids, out safely. Because if not... I didn't even dare think it.

I couldn't see. I felt the heat of, saw the red of flames to my right. Somehow, a serious fire was raging in the rear of the house, however that had come to be. I didn't know where I was going and couldn't even see Sarah. I let the line pull me along, clutched Sarah's little hand. Kids were coughing. I was coughing.

"Don't let go!" I heard Samara call out in a choked voice. "Hold on tight!"

And then, I was pulled through a doorway and found myself outside in a carport. The fresh air was tempting, and I sucked in a lungful before realizing there was still some smoke here. I coughed and hacked, but managed to keep hold of Sarah's hand as Samara led us away from the carport and out into a big yard with playground equipment, a safe distance from the house. She dropped to her knees, hugging the kids as they crowded into her.

"Good job, you guys!" she said through tears. "You did so great! Way to follow the leader. I'm so proud of you."

Sarah still held my hand, crying now. Without thinking, I picked her up and held her tight.

Aaron peered up at me, lip quivering. "I got Sarah out of the fire."

"You sure did, Aaron. You're an excellent brother."

I looked behind me. The little ranch house that housed Merry Maids Preschool was an inferno.

THE FIRE CREW SHOWED UP. Prophet didn't have a paid fire department but Lucas, the chief of the volunteer brigade, shouted orders for his crew. By the time the parents came to collect their kids, all of them badly shaken, at least another hour had passed. I was hoping to see Gabriel, but Devin said he'd gone to Forks.

Lori huddled beside me with Sarah and Aaron. She was white as a sheet and kept asking what had happened. I didn't know what to tell her—or anyone. We'd been talking in the playroom when we noticed the fire. How the little house had come to be ablaze, or why smoke alarms hadn't alerted us earlier, I had no idea.

Surely, no one would deliberately set fire to a house full of children. What kind of maniac would even think of such a thing? It had to be an electrical problem. A stove burner left on. Something. Though Samara didn't seem the type to make dangerous mistakes. Whatever had happened, I was sure it wasn't her fault.

The house was a complete loss, though. I hoped she had good insurance. Ugh. What a horrible thing to have happened.

No one was hurt. That was the main thing.

I suddenly remembered Frank. I hugged Lori and the twins, accepted her thanks for the tenth time, and hurried around the house to the side street. I jogged toward my car, my gut churning. Frank was probably fine. Tortoises could withstand colder temps than these if they had to. I was maybe ten feet from my car when I saw that something was wrong. The back passenger window was dark and... fuck, it was shattered. I could see lumps of safety glass on the sidewalk.

Someone had broken into my damn car.

I ran. How could this day get any worse?

I reached the car. Yes, someone had smashed the rear passenger window, and the door locks were up. Panic whelmed up inside me, and I glanced through the open window into the rear of the vehicle for Frank. All I could see was a heap of blankets.

I rushed around to the back. "Frank?" I opened the hatchback. No carapace greeted me, no scaly head, no fathomless eyes. I searched through the blankets, anyway, probing and shifting. "Frank! Frank!"

I backed up and dropped to my knees, looked under the car, then over at the lawn. "Frank!"

But it was no use. Frank was gone.

Chapter Seven

Gabriel

I PULLED my car into the parking lot of the Forks Police Department and waited a moment as my engine ticked. There was a coffee shop just across the road, and part of me wondered if I could sneak in a coffee, but I'd said I'd be here by ten, and I was only four minutes early.

So much for coffee.

I liked Forks, and even though it was bigger than Prophet, it wasn't a huge place, spread out and nestled between forested hills and lush greenery, the hub to a lot of smaller satellite towns. It was big enough to have many of the national retail chains and fast-food joints, sprawling commercial areas that could be like any off-ramp in the country. But the downtown area retained a bit of quaintness. Railroad Park with its old steam engine had been a favorite of mine—and Sam's and Ezra's—growing up. The police department was in City Hall, a modern white structure situated in the center of town. The bank where John had worked, which was my main point of interest, stood about a block away. As a courtesy, I was connecting with a member of Forks PD, and in this case, the name I had was Officer Elisa Dowden. She was waiting in the lobby for me, a tall woman with long dark hair in a ponytail, wearing a frown.

"Officer Dowden?"

"Sheriff," she acknowledged with a sharpness in her tone, and I waited for the usual speech about how I wasn't to step out of line in *her* town. Instead, it threw me when she smiled. "Sorry, I need coffee first, and not the shit they have here." She thumbed over her shoulder and grimaced, then guided me out of the station and across the road, chatting the entire way about the weather and football and carrying the entire conversation.

Coffee in hand, we walked over to the bank, through the well-lit lobby, and straight over to a woman waiting to one side.

"Bernice," Elisa acknowledged, then gestured at me. "Bernice Lerner, manager of this branch. Bernice, this is Sheriff Gabriel Thompson out of Prophet."

We shook hands but didn't waste time on chitchat. Instead, Elisa and I were shown into a room with no windows, and Bernice took the facing seat. She looked stressed, or maybe she was grieving. She'd lost a member of her staff, and that had to be hard in a hundred different ways.

Bernice straightened her skirt, moved her coffee a couple of inches to the right, and then nodded, her expression serious. "How can I help you?" Her tone was cautious, and we wouldn't get anywhere if she didn't relax.

"We're just here to get background on your employee," I said, and offered an encouraging smile.

"John, of course." She swallowed, and shut her eyes, as if she needed a moment to compose herself, and then, she opened a file in front of her. "Exemplary record. He joined us as a teller four years ago, straight from college; local man, lived on Oak with his mom, Trudy Melchet. Diligent, he was the kind of person who made sure every element of a transaction was audit-proof, and by that I mean, he made copious notes on every decision a customer came to after his advice. The last we saw of him, was February fourteenth, and we have him on our security cameras getting into his own car and leaving at seven minutes past two p.m. He was scheduled to visit a longstanding customer on the outskirts of Forks at three p.m."

Shit. So, he *did* go out on visits? Had he been on his way to visit Sam? An unscheduled visit to a small town. I doubted it, but I had to be certain. "Is it bank policy for loan officers to visit clients at their homes and businesses?"

"No. The client is one of our…" she paused "… more complicated and um… it demands the personal touch," she finished and looked embarrassed, and I guessed whoever this client was had to be on a rich list. "As a rule, we don't visit clients."

I scribbled the information down. "And the customer's name?"

The manager didn't answer straight away, but Elisa gestured for her to carry on.

"The customer is Joel Robertson, you might have

heard of the Robertson Dairy brand?" I hadn't, but she didn't appear interested in my answer anyway. "I've written the address here for you, but only after I checked with him that it was okay to do so. I have his written authority, . ." She slid paperwork toward me, and I twisted it to see the details.

"Thank you."

"Mr. Robertson called the office at three thirty-eight, and spoke to one of our tellers, Cara, enquiring where John was, but when Cara checked in with John, he wasn't answering calls. She tried again at three past four and four-thirty, but then, the business day was ending, and Cara imagined that John had somehow mixed up appointments. It wasn't a concern to us, not from a professional point of view; after all, these things happen, but it wasn't like John to mess things up. And then," she stopped, swallowed, "this morning Officer Dowden called to say that there'd been an incident. In Prophet! What was he doing in Prophet?"

I wish I knew the answer to that.

"Are you able to let me have a list of other *prestigious* clients John may have been asked to visit?"

Her face pinched as if she'd sucked a lemon. "What I can tell you," she began primly, "is that I would need a warrant to release bank information."

"Of course, we can get that," I said. "Meanwhile, if you could suggest a reason as to why he should be in Prophet potentially on the bank's time?"

Bernice considered her words carefully. "We have five business clients in Prophet, many others with personal accounts, but John was our loans officer, and as

I said before, we do not do business outside of the bank itself."

"Apart from the um…" I pretended to check my notes, "Robertson Dairies?"

"Apart from them."

"I'd like to speak with anyone who worked closely with John," I began, my voice gentle.

She was happy to shift the spotlight from herself. She called in three staff members—her assistant manager, plus two tellers—one after the other. The narrative was consistent: John was methodical. He bordered on arrogant, often rude, and wasn't well-liked among his peers.

"Not part of the team," Clara, the youngest teller, summed up, and that seemed to be the general narrative. "But good at his job."

I asked her the same as I had all the others, "Do you know of anyone who might have a grudge against Mr. Melchet, or have an issue with the bank?"

She paused, then snapped her fingers as if something had just occurred to her. "I heard him arguing with someone last week," she hesitated. "The man was tall, dark hair. I only caught a glimpse, but he kinda looked like… well, he was tall like you, same hair color as you, but not you, if you know what I mean. Actually, looked a lot like you." She chuckled, nervously.

I pasted on a reassuring smile even as I felt the weight of her words. Was it Sam? Had he been here and argued with John? Why wouldn't he have told me that? My heart raced, but I needed to remain calm.

"Do you have a name for this customer?" I pressed. *Please don't let it be Samuel Thompson.*

"No." she replied and cast a look at the closed door as if she was checking in with Bernice, who I knew was hovering. "Sorry."

Elisa glanced at me with a raised eyebrow, but I gave her a slight shake of my head. I know they weren't supposed to give names, and I shouldn't even have asked that, but... what if it *was* Sam?

Leaving the bank, I had no real answers to anything, and the clouds seemed to press in on the town, matching my mood, worse when it started to rain.

"The mention of the argument was interesting," Elisa murmured. "You think someone got turned down for money, or defaulted, and killed John for it?"

"Seems thin, but we can't say for sure. We'll need to get a warrant for records," I said.

"I know a local judge. I'm on it."

Our next stop was John's mother's house. Mrs. Trudy Melchet, a short round woman with blonde hair, opened the door, her eyes red with crying, a small group of people gathering behind her; family, I assumed.

"Officer Dowden," she said.

Elisa placed a hand on her arm and lowered her voice, offering a sympathetic pat. "How are you, Trudy?"

She lifted her chin. "I don't know." She was honest in her grief, her whole body weighed down with the loss.

"This is Sheriff Gabriel Thompson from Prophet."

She extended a hand, which I shook. "You found him then?" The tears started again, and I was lost as to what to say.

"May we come in?" I asked instead.

"Have you found the person who killed my boy?" Her voice cracked.

Elisa side-hugged her as we went inside. "Not yet, Trudy, but the sheriff is working hard to make sure we do." She shouldn't be promising that, but I was too focused on the wall of photos, some of them of the man I'd seen dead. I assumed it was a dedicated space for him, as there were photos from a chubby baby, up until graduation.

"It's okay," she said to the group behind her, and the three of them backed away into the kitchen. "Friends," she explained as we settled into the living room.

"John was always so stressed," she began. "He had such a thankless job. People would get angry at him when he denied their loan applications. They would yell and threaten him." She paused, wiping her tears. "Last week, someone fought with him. John came home, and he was just… broken. Why can't people understand? He was a human with feelings."

Elisa put a comforting hand on Mrs. Melchet's shoulder. "We're doing everything we can to find out what happened."

"Do you know if John had any specific reason to visit Prophet Wednesday afternoon or evening, Mrs. Melchet?"

"He was supposed to be home at five, and we were going grocery shopping. He helped me. He was a good boy. He would have told me if he wasn't going to be there."

That was pretty much how the interview went. He was a paragon of virtue according to his mom, an awkward, sometimes arrogant man to his colleagues at the bank. But in none of what I'd heard today, was there any reason why he'd broken off from his normal schedule to hare off to Prophet.

"Do you know of anyone that might have reason to hurt your son?"

"No. Everyone loved him."

Given our talk at the bank, I wasn't entirely sure *everyone* loved him, but a mother's love was boundless.

Someone out there had waylaid him, tied his wrists. Whoever had done this had planned it ahead of time. I was sure of it.

I handed her my card. "You can call me at any time if you can think of anything else you want to add."

As we left her home, the weight of the day's revelations bore down on me. A potential argument with a man as tall and dark-haired as me? A man who lived by his diary, but who'd broken his routine? There were just more questions, and nothing in the answers I'd been given had helped me, or exonerated Sam, or... God, this was shit.

"Everything okay, Sheriff?" Elisa asked, breaking my train of thought.

"Just thinking," I replied.

"I'll get the warrant, then follow up on the client he was due to see. I know Robertson well enough in town to casually chat to him, but I'll check phone records as you asked. We still don't have his car," she added. Then, she glanced at me. "Is it in Prophet?"

"We haven't found any trace of it in town." Although finding one dumped or abandoned car in the back roads of the forest would be like looking for a needle in a haystack. As we drove back to the station, I couldn't shake the thought of Sam mixed up in any of this. I needed answers. And I was determined to find them. Whatever the cost.

THE CALL from Devin hit when I was twenty minutes outside Prophet, there'd been a fire at the preschool, everyone was okay, but he'd like it if I hurried my ass back to town. He didn't exactly use those words, but it was close enough. The fact he mentioned Sarah and Aaron was enough for me to head straight there to find Lucas Quinnel, our chief volunteer firefighter, standing with his colleague staring at what was left of Merry Maids Preschool.

Not much at all. I could see straight through to the back, only one wall remaining, and somehow some of the kids' paintings were still there, flapping in the wind.

"Started in the back," Lucas said, in lieu of a hello. "Rain helped us with controlling it. Arson will be taking a look, but there was a gas can out back near the shed that Devin has taken into evidence, not that this means it was used in the fire, but the burn patterns... I think accelerant was used. Also, the fire alarms inside didn't go off, and the lady who runs the preschool swears they'd been tested recently." Sticking to the facts, he summed up what I needed to know.

But, what the fuck? Who would burn down a preschool when there were kids inside? No, scratch that, who would want to play at arson at all?

"The kids? The teacher? Any TA's?"

"All out, safe. The teacher, Samara Rafferty, is with Devin, and they're at the Diner handling the parents of the kids. Nothing else we can do here except secure the property. It's gonna be a long one, which is gonna play hell with my love life." Lucas sighed. "What kind of asshole does this?"

The same kind who might murder someone?

Nah, that was just… ridiculous. I mean, Sam wouldn't…

I pressed fingers to my temples, the headache that had been threatening all day, due to over caffeinating and not eating, was a band around my skull.

"The fucking awful kind," I answered after a pause.

"Lucky that Tiber was there."

My heart stopped—hell it was already working overtime at the thought of my niece and nephew being in there, but what was this?

"Tiber?"

"He was doing some kind of show-and-tell with that freaky-ass turtle thing he has."

"Tortoise," I corrected. How could I have forgotten the show-and-tell? He'd been so nice to agree to it when Sarah and Aaron had begged, even though I knew he hated any form of public speaking. I should have remembered.

"Yeah, that."

I fought my instinct to get in the car and check in on my niblings and Tiber—I needed to do my job, and I was in a freaking daze. Instead, I assisted Lucas in putting up the cordon, and by the time I made it to the diner, it was just Devin there, making notes on his tablet and drinking coffee. He stood immediately when I stepped in.

"Sir."

"The scene is as secure as we can make it," I said. "We

can't guard it; the firefighters have done their thing; we need to…" I massaged my temples. "The kids…"

"Sarah and Aaron are fine. Aaron was a little hero. They're excited, not at all scared now. Your brother and Lori took them home."

"Okay."

"Only, sir, Tiber was there."

"But he's okay; Lucas said he was okay." Oh fuck. My chest was so tight.

"Yeah, but there was an incident, with his turtle—tortoise—and he's at home. He's very upset and uhm… you'll probably want to check in."

I was in the SUV so fast I swear I left a trail of smoke, and after calling Lori to check the kids were okay—they were, and she didn't call me on the fact I'd phoned her and not Sam—I headed home, slamming on the brakes at the house and running inside.

What the fuck had happened?

Chapter Eight

Tiber

"SOMEONE TOOK FRANK! And, I think, they started the fire. It has to be Jeff!"

I knew I was bordering on panic—no. Already there and settled in for the long haul. I needed to be calm. I needed to be in battle mode. But as soon as Gabriel walked in the door, I was venting and shaking as if I had no control whatsoever. Because I didn't.

"Wait." Gabriel looked tired and shaken. "Take a breath, babe. I talked to Lucas at the scene, and he said they haven't determined the cause of the blaze yet. Let's not get ahead of the ball."

"Can't you see it?" I demanded. "Last fall, Jeff tried to burn down my fucking house, with my animals inside. It's obviously him. And then, he took Frank. Frank! You know he hates my animals." I paced back and forth in the living room. My face was wet with tears, but they were angry ones. I couldn't believe my gaslighting psychopath of an ex-boyfriend was back and screwing with me again. I'd thought that was all over. "Oh my God, what is he going to do to Frank?"

"Honey, calm down." Gabriel stepped closer and wrapped his arms around me.

I appreciated the gesture, but I was too keyed up to stand still. So, I gave him a quick hug back, then pulled away, pacing again. "If he hurts Frank... I can't stand it."

"It's okay. We'll find Frank," Gabriel said in his best reassuring cop voice.

But I wasn't buying it. "How? Jeff could be miles away by now. He might have hurt Frank already." A thought occurred to me, and I wiped my face with my sleeve, hope sparking. "Can you put out an APB on him? Do a check to see if he's rented a car anywhere in Washington State? Or try hotels?"

Gabriel nodded; his expression weary. "I can do that. First thing in the morning."

I just blinked at him dumbly.

His jaw tightened. "Right. I'll do it tonight. But before I go back to the office, I need some facts. Please, just sit down for a minute and breathe."

The idea that he might be able to trace Jeff to a nearby hotel, and find Frank, did make me feel a little less like a mini-explosion in progress. Anything I could do to help the process along, I'd do. I sat on the edge of the sofa, hands in my lap, and looked at him expectantly.

He started to sit next to me, but paused, glancing at the windows overlooking the back deck. I followed his gaze and saw a row of worried faces staring at us. They were so cute; it startled a laugh out of me.

"Want me to let them in?" he asked.

I shook my head and sighed. "No. I was so upset; I was freaking them out. Let's just get through this first."

"Okay." He sat beside me, and took out his notepad, all business. "The school fire…" he began. "That's serious business. If it was started deliberately—"

"It was. You know Jeff poured gas around my house! I bet he did the same thing at the preschool." Even the memory made me so angry.

He held up a hand. "I know. And I'm going to locate Jeff, believe me. But I'm just trying to get the facts straight. How would Jeff have known you were at the preschool?"

"He must have followed me." I took a shaky breath. "I didn't tell you before, but a few days ago, I thought I saw someone in the yard."

Gabriel's back went stiff, and his eyes flashed. "Here? You saw someone here? Was it Jeff?"

"I don't know. I thought I saw someone standing in a dark slicker, like with the hood up, near the tree out front. I didn't see a face. It was just a glimpse. But when I looked back, he was gone. I thought… I thought maybe I'd imagined it."

Gabriel made a note, but I could tell he was upset. "Did it strike you as being Jeff at the time?"

I had to be honest. "It didn't even cross my mind. But I didn't get a good look."

"Did you go out to check? Did you see a strange car? Footprints? Anything?"

I shook my head, feeling stupid. "I was too freaked out to go out and check around. And it was, um, raining."

"Did the dogs bark?"

"No. But—there's more. Just before that happened, I had that call with the new client I told you about. And he was super weird. Like stalkery. He obviously didn't even know the dog he was claiming was his pet. Like he'd just made it up to get me on the call. And then, he asked personal questions. About sex."

"What?" Gabriel flushed. "Why didn't you tell me about this before?"

I squirmed. "I texted you at the time to tell you about it, but you didn't answer."

Gabriel winced, and I realized I was acting as if I expected him to be there for me twenty-four seven. Of course, he was the town's sheriff, and he wasn't always available, nor should he be. "It's fine. Just saying that, by the time you got home, I was over it. And there was the body at Sam's. It didn't seem important."

"What was this client's name?"

"Jim Smith. But I have no way of verifying that."

"How did he pay you? Do you have an email address?" There was an edge to his voice. I was pleased at his protectiveness, but at the same time, his worry only ramped up my own.

"He paid on Venmo. There should be an email in there, I guess. Hang on." I got out my phone and checked the Venmo receipt in email. The one I'd refunded. "The money was sent from dogbody1330@gmail.com." I looked up at Gabriel, confused. "Guess that's not much to go on."

"No. It's hard to track a generic email like that." Gabriel rubbed his chin. "And you didn't recognize the guy?"

"Never saw him before."

"Do you have any reason to think that call was related to Jeff?"

My heart sank. I really didn't. Jeff didn't have a lot of friends, much less ones who'd torment me just for fun. "No. Okay, so the weirdo on the call isn't related to what happened today. Or, probably, the person I saw in the yard, unless he could teleport. If I saw anyone at all. Still. The *fire.*"

Gabriel put away his notepad, a frown etched on his brow. "Believe me, if that fire was set deliberately, someone's gonna pay. I still can't believe you were in the preschool with Sarah and Aaron. Thank God, you're all okay."

"I know." I wrapped my arms around myself, suddenly feeling cold and empty.

"Did you see anyone lurking around the preschool at all? Or take note of any vehicles parked nearby?"

I thought back. "No. But I was pretty focused on getting in and out. And on Frank."

At the mention of his name, I got a flash of carrying him out of that school, his body heavy in my arms, of kissing his scaly head. My eyes burned, and my throat closed up. I covered my face with my hands. "I s-should never have l-left him in the car."

I'd regret it until the day I died. I'd promised Frank he had a safe home with me, forever. *I'd promised.*

"You couldn't have known. I've been to that preschool a dozen times. It's a nice, quiet street. Oh, babe."

Gabriel pulled me into his arms, and this time, I took the comfort, shifting onto his lap. I let out hours' worth of frustration and grief. And I knew there was lots more where that came from. All I could do was pray that Frank was okay. That he hadn't been taken by some evil person like Jeff, but someone who thought he was cool and wanted him for a pet. At least, in that case, he'd still be alive somewhere.

"I swear to you, we will find Frank," Gabriel said, as intense and serious as I'd ever heard him. And there was the rough edge of tears in his voice too.

He held me a few minutes. But I felt the shift in his body, in his energy, even before he gently pushed me off his lap. "I'm gonna go check on Jeff right now. I'll swing by the motel first, see if he's there. If not, I'll drive to the office and start calling around. I'm sure Devin and Hen will help."

I nodded. "Please. And if you find him, *call me*. Hell, even if you don't."

"I will."

He stood, but hesitated, looking around at the animals, at the house. "I don't want to leave you here alone. Maybe you should come and stay at my place?"

It was a new worry, but it didn't feel real. I shook my head. "I'm not going anywhere. I'm not leaving the animals. He's already got Frank, and I know him. He'll want to make me suffer for a while worrying about him. I doubt he'll do anything more tonight."

Gabriel sighed. "Okay. But keep your phone on your

person. If you hear or see anyone, call me immediately. I'll touch base soon."

Then that man, who'd been working all day, left to go back out there and find Frank.

I knew neither of us would sleep until he did.

Chapter Nine

Gabriel

I HEADED BACK to the office, and I had no idea where to start because my head was too full of everything. Devin was at his desk, even at just past 7 p.m., the lamp burning in the dark, his head on his clasped hands, staring at a report.

"What are you doing here?" I asked and startled him so bad he pushed back from his desk, his chair hitting the wall.

"Sir," he said, and then, didn't know what to do with himself.

"Sit down, sorry to startle you. Shouldn't you be at home?"

"Too much to do, sir," he replied, and shuffled some papers on the desk. "The fire, the murder, the kids…" All the energy drained from him. "Who would do that? With kids for fuck's sake. Sorry for the cursing, but…"

I slumped to my chair, and the enormity of it all hit me. "Someone took Frank from Tiber's car."

"The tortoise. I know."

"Tiber is convinced it's his ex, Jeff Strickland, somehow messing with him again, and then, with the fire at the school, after what he tried to do to Tiber's place, I don't disbelieve him."

Devin sat upright and stared. "Strickland? Fuck, shit, sorry, I'm trying not to curse so much, but Jeff Strickland. For real?"

"I stopped by the motel, and Daisy hasn't seen him. I've put in a call with Portland PD, they've said they'll check his whereabouts, and the only thing I can do is put out an APB on him. I'll do it, if they can't locate him, but for now, I'm going to hunt for Frank."

Devin stood and shrugged on his heavy coat. "I'll help."

"You don't have to, it's not like Frank is a…" Person? He was more than that, he was *Frank*. His connection to Tiber was impossibly close, and Tiber was on the edge, and I would give anything to be able to find him and hand him back.

"It's important to Tiber, so it's important to you."

He tugged his non-department-issued woolen hat down over his head, wound a scarf around his entire face, and pulled on gloves, turning into a snowman in the blink of an eye. I copied him because it was freezing out there. Then, armed with flashlights, we headed to the remains of the burned school; the structure an ominous reminder of how close kids had been to being hurt. We started our hunt in methodical circles, but I knew it would take a miracle to find him. Whoever had taken him from Tiber's car wouldn't have just abandoned him. Would they? What would be the point of that? It occurred to me that there might be a market for selling endangered species. I scrolled my phone and found my contact at Fish and Wildlife from the Billy Odette case—Dr. Susan Mason— and sent her a quick message with brief details. It was too late for her to see it now, but in the morning, maybe she'd be able to shed light on potential smuggling routes.

It was two a.m. when we gave up, both of us frozen, and headed home.

The lights were blazing, drapes closed, and the front door securely locked, and when I let myself in, every single head turned to me—dogs, cats, Renfield—and in the middle of them, Tiber had slumped on the sofa, asleep. There were shadows under his eyes as if he'd been fighting it, and even in sleep, he seemed tense. I stripped off my coat and everything that had been keeping me warm, then made sure the house was locked up again, turned out many of the lights, and sat down next to him. Duke shifted over as if he sensed that Tiber needed me right now.

I gathered him into my arms and held him.

"Anything?" he asked me, half asleep.

"Not yet," I murmured, and he held me tight and buried his face in my neck. He was crying again, feeling the loss of Frank from his pack as keenly as losing a child. He was scared and worried, and I was overwhelmed with arson and murder, but somehow, despite everything, wrapped in each other's arms on the sofa, we slept.

When I woke, Tiber was in the kitchen making coffee. I padded over to him, feeling rumpled and tired, and hugged him from behind. He didn't stiffen, he wasn't surprised, instead, he turned in my arms and hugged me.

"I'm so stupid to be jumping at shadows," he blurted.

"No, you're not—"

"And Frank will turn up today. No worries."

"Yep." I lied, because who the fuck knew if Frank would turn up, and lying was about all I had right now.

Then Tiber sniffed. "Get a shower, then get yourself out here for coffee and breakfast. I have waffles."

I did as I was told. I should be asking him if he was okay, actually, I should be telling him it was okay to be honest about how he was feeling, but I was selfish, and I needed him to pretend he was absolutely fine, because over here, I was crumbling.

DEVIN KNOCKED ON THE DOOR, "SIR?"

"Devin."

He looked tired. He'd been up as late as I had last night, but he wore a determined expression. "You will have seen my notes, but I'd like to go through the interview with Mr. and Mrs. Thompson with you." Sam and Lori. "I spoke to them when you were in Forks, and then with the fire…"

"I've seen the report."

"I know, but… this is too important for me not to officially give my opinion." He opened his notebook, and I could see him trying to remain objective as he cleared his throat. "Both Mr. and Mrs. Thompson claimed not to know anything about the body on their property." he began and met my gaze. "I believe them."

"Because it's my family?" I challenged him. After all, he was a rookie, and the power dynamic we had meant he might say what he thought I wanted to hear.

He tilted his chin. "No, sir!" he exclaimed. "My gut instinct."

I nodded and waved for him to continue.

"Mrs. Thompson was at home from three p.m. the day before until when the body was discovered. Her twins, Sarah and Aaron, were with her; and a friend, a Mrs. Rachel Lewis, confirmed that she visited with her children between four and five. I've spoken to Mrs. Lewis, who has a time stamped photo of her children, plus Sarah and Aaron. Mrs. Thompson spoke to several people on site, including two guests in cabin three, which would put her at home at eight-thirty, give or take a few minutes. I confirmed that time with the guests in question because I wanted to cross all the Ts and dot all the Is."

"Good call."

"Mr. Thompson claims to have been in Forks picking up a part for his truck, and then, arrived home at nine p.m. Mr. and Mrs. Thompson are, then, each other's alibi from that point on, until the deceased was found on their property the following morning."

He finished, closed his notebook, and sat on the visitor's chair.

"Can I ask you something, sir?" he said, and seemed nervous.

"Sure." I was still reeling that so much time was unspoken for, apart from Sam and Lori being each other's alibi. That was slim. Too fucking slim.

"What if I've missed something? What if I forgot to

ask them a question that could rule them out from being any part of this?"

I'd read his report, watched him summarize, and I knew in my gut, he'd covered all the bases. "You didn't miss anything. Your facts are solid, backed up by witnesses. You haven't glossed over a single thing."

"Okay, sir. Thank you."

He made to leave, but I called him to wait. "One thing I wanted to say to you, Devin?"

"Sir?" He was worried, frowning, probably thinking I was going to call him out on something.

"I couldn't ask for a better deputy. You ask the right questions; you have a keen eye. So, keep doing what you're doing."

His frown vanished, and I could see the twitch of a proud smile. "Thank you, sir. I'll um… coffee."

He came straight back with coffee and a muffin, and then, left me to my own devices. There was still no sign of Frank, nor forensics on the murder, nor anything on the fire. Half of a law officer's work was hanging around just waiting, and I was getting sick of it.

I was skimming through a stack of reports when the phone on my desk rang. The caller ID indicated it was the Portland PD, and I assumed they were calling with information on Jeff after I'd reached out to them earlier. That would at least be one thing on my list.

"Sheriff Thompson speaking," I answered, pencil still in hand.

"Hey, Sheriff, this is Officer Reynolds from Portland PD. Got some info on that guy, Jeff Strickland, you asked about."

I leaned forward, eager for any tidbit they might have dug up. "Thank you. Go on."

"We checked in with the hospital. From what we've gathered, Strickland has worked every day for the past seven days, hasn't missed a single shift. Several nurses and administrators vouched for his presence during the time in question. Given the distance and his work schedule, it'd be a stretch to think he had any hand in the incident you're investigating."

I drummed my fingers on the desk, processing the information. It was a loose end I was hoping to tie up, but this wasn't the outcome I'd expected. "Thanks for the update, Reynolds. I appreciate your team's swift response."

"Not a problem, Sheriff. If you need any more information, just give us a shout."

The buzz of my phone interrupted my thoughts, and I pulled it from my pocket to see Elisa's name flash on the screen.

"Sheriff Thompson," she began without prelude, her voice brisk and all business. "We traced the likely route John would have taken to that appointment he was supposed to have."

I could hear the faint rustle of leaves in the background, signaling she was at an outdoor scene. "And?" I prodded.

"We found his car," she said, a touch of gravity creeping into her voice. "Abandoned, trunk open, unlocked, down a heavily wooded lane, off the main road."

My pulse quickened. "Any signs of foul play?"

"No damage to the car, so it doesn't seem like he was

forced off the road. But get this, we found a tire iron on the grassy shoulder, not far from the car, and the tire iron is missing from John's car."

I frowned, trying to piece together the scenario in my mind. "You think he might've stopped to help someone with a flat?"

"It's a possibility," she mused. "And there's something else. We found a work diary inside the glove box, seems like it might be a backup, no calendar dates, he was using it more as a journal to remind himself of things. There's a list at the front—maybe a profile of clients he was actively working with. I've booked it into evidence, but I took a photo, and I'm sending it to you now. Also, can you send over the paperwork for me to take to the judge so we can get that warrant for the bank records?"

Fuck. What if I did that and Sam's name was right there, front and center? *Of course, his name will be there, idiot, warrant or not.* I couldn't avoid this, despite wanting to take Sam's name off everything, and all too soon, his name would be front and center to Forks PD.

After all, what if Sam did have something to do with John Melchet's murder?

He didn't!

My personal and professional lives were colliding, and it made my blood run cold.

"Will do," I said. "Keep me informed."

"Of course," she said, and ended the call.

A few seconds later, my phone pinged with a new message. I quickly opened the image attachment, scanning the names on the list. I wasn't surprised to see a listing for Sam and Lori Thompson, but it was the exclamation mark next to the name that shocked me. Only because I had no idea what it meant, but when people used that in a sentence, it implied dramatic.

"Okay, this is getting out of hand," I muttered to no one.

Devin had interviewed Lori and Sam and had reached the conclusion on his own—as much as that was possible —that they knew nothing about the murder of John Melchet. Of course, I believed my brother was innocent, but the evidence trickling in was not helping, and this was hitting home too hard. Add in Tiber, and his fears about a stalker, and I was losing my shit.

A myriad of thoughts raced through my mind. Who had taken Frank? Who'd set fire to the damn preschool? What was Sam's connection to John? How well did I know my own brother after all the years we hadn't spoken? The weight of unanswered questions bore down on me, adding another layer to an already complex investigation.

Chapter Ten

Tiber

I WENT BACK to sleep after Gabriel left that morning, and I didn't wake up until ten. It was Saturday, so I didn't have any client calls. The first thing I'd done was head outside with the dogs and look all over the backyard, and the front, hoping against hope that Frank would have magically reappeared. But he wasn't there.

I'd just arrived back at the house when the phone rang. Gabriel. "Hey!" I answered hurriedly. "Any news?"

"Yes. Jeff has been at work for the past seven days in a row. Yesterday, he was there all day. It's been confirmed with several eyewitnesses. He couldn't have been in Prophet."

"Oh." I blinked, staring off into space. If it hadn't been Jeff, then…?

"Look, I've got to go. But we're still looking for Frank, and we're going to investigate the fire too. You okay?"

"Yeah. I'm fine. Thanks for letting me know about Jeff."

"Of course. Talk soon."

He hung up without the usual *I love yous*. But I could hear the strain in his voice. What was going on with the murder case? Something that upset him. Only, he didn't want me involved.

Guilt jabbed at me. He had a lot on his plate with a murder on Sam and Lori's property and now, the fire. And here I was going off about Jeff, which it turned out was not a thing, and my missing tortoise. I knew Gabriel cared for Frank too, but still. Just because my boyfriend was the town's sheriff didn't mean I could, or should, monopolize his time. I vowed to be more mindful in the future. As soon as we found Frank, anyway.

I answered emails for another hour. After giving the pack their lunch, we took our usual hike down to the lakeshore. I kept the volume on my phone up, hoping to God someone would call about Frank.

It was cold and snow had lingered, frosting the woods, and dabbing the pebbles on the beach with ice. The sky was ominous, but quiet for the moment. Maybe there'd be more snow today.

I threw the ball for Duke, and he bounded around, glad for the exercise, while the other dogs sniffed along the shore and made low-energy feints at one another as if sort of wanting to play, but not really feeling it. They were aware of Frank's loss, too. Or maybe it was my heavy heart weighing them down. They were so sensitive to my every mood.

My mind drifted to all the craziness of the past few days.

If it hadn't been Jeff, then who had set the fire? Maybe it wasn't related to me at all. Maybe Samara had an evil ex of her own. Or maybe it had been an accident.

And whoever had taken Frank... maybe that had happened before the fire. My mind went again to the possibility some teenagers or pre-teens had walked by the car, or maybe ridden past on their bikes, and had seen Frank peeking up. If he'd gotten impatient, he might have raised himself to look out of the window. That rounded head and big claws would have been irresistible to a kid.

But would a kid break a car window? Seemed bold, but not impossible, especially if the kids egged each other on. Maybe Frank was, at this moment, sitting on some kid's couch munching on a carrot.

Please, God. Let that be the case.

I would put out fliers, I decided—at the mercantile, the vet's office, the cafe, and diner, and all over downtown. If some parent saw them, they'd know the huge tortoise their kid had brought home belonged to someone. People would be on the lookout for him.

And maybe the vet had had a call? Or maybe One-Eyed Jack had noticed someone buying an unusual amount of produce in the past twenty-four hours.

But what about the other strange things that had happened to me lately? The call from the stalkery guy? The person in my yard? Coincidence?

You're not paranoid if someone really is out to get you.

Things happened in threes, my Sicilian grandmother always said. Maybe I'd experienced a random chance series of oddities, the universe's vinyl record stuck in a grove called *punk Tiber*.

And then, I thought of the murder Gabriel was dealing with. A body found on Sam and Lori's property. It must have been upsetting for them too. Maybe I should go over there and talk to Lori, see if they were okay. Gabriel clearly didn't want me involved in the case, but an almost-brother-in-law could check in on family, couldn't he?

Armed with a long list of things to do, I whistled to the dogs and explained to them that we had to get home and work on finding Frank. They came without their usual reluctance to leave the beach, and we headed back up the hill.

I was putting the final touches on the *missing tortoise* flier when the dogs began to bark. It was the kind of bark that signaled a stranger's approach—usually a delivery vehicle.

I went to the door and peeked out of the narrow window next to it. I didn't see anyone. If it had been a delivery, the delivery person had come and gone in a hurry.

I stepped outside and closed the door behind me, not wanting the dogs to get out. On the cement front stoop, placed squarely in the middle, was an old, green thermos, the kind you took camping.

What the hell? I glanced around but didn't see a soul. I looked again at the thermos. It was just... a thermos. The dogs must have heard its arrival, hence the barking. But who left it there?

Not Gabriel. If he wanted to bring me a coffee, he'd do it in a to-go cup from Grounds for Joy, and he'd want a kiss for it. Hen? Libby? Maybe someone heard about Frank and was trying to be nice?

But I had a bad feeling all the same. As I stared at the thermos, it became a very bad feeling.

Maybe I was paranoid, but too much out of the ordinary had been going on lately. Something was up. I knew that as well as I knew my own name.

I couldn't stand there all day, though. I picked up the thermos gingerly. It was warm. I took off the plastic cup on top and tossed it down, then unscrewed the twist top lid. The thermos had a wide-mouth opening, so I got a good look at what was inside.

Soup. Green soup. Oh God. *Frank.*

I cried out and *threw* the thermos. Hot green liquid spilled out and splattered across the concrete step and the grass. Even while my head was telling me nasty, horrible things, another part of me registered that the smell and sight of the spilled soup was familiar.

I sniffed the air warily, stared. I squatted down and studied a small cube of cooked carrot. The thermos was lying on its side, open. I swiped a finger inside the lip and sniffed it. Cautiously took a taste.

It was split pea soup. It tasted exactly like the one they served at the diner in town.

Oh, thank God.

I closed my eyes in relief. Man, I'd thought… Clearly, I'd seen *Fatal Attraction* one too many times.

My cell phone buzzed in my pocket. I dug it out and glanced at the display, answered. "Gabriel?"

"Someone called in a report of a huge turtle spotted crawling alongside the highway. I'm heading there now."

I jumped to my feet. "Where exactly?"

"About a mile out of town from the mercantile."

"Meet you there." I shoved the phone in my pocket and raced inside to get my keys.

I SAW the sheriff's SUV parked off the side of the road and screeched to a stop behind it. I registered the sight of Gabriel walking toward me carrying a large sulcatas. He was smiling, and I saw one of the tortoise's legs move.

The relief was overwhelming. I was out of the door and hurrying to them in an instant. I crushed them both in a huge hug. "Oh, Frank!"

"He's okay," Gabriel said. "He looks okay, anyway."

"Is he?" I pulled back to take a better view, scanning his legs.

Gabriel shifted the tortoise in his arms to be more horizontal, and Frank saw me. Frank's emotions were subtle, but his legs worked faster when he recognized my face, and I could swear the look he gave me was *Finally! Where have you been?*

I cupped his head and gave him a kiss. "Oh, Frank. I was so scared. I'm sorry, buddy. I never should have left you in the car!"

He opened his beak in a silent cry. He'd been worried too. But, true to the accepting nature of animals, not nearly as worried as me.

"He look okay to you?" Gabriel asked.

I nodded and leaned over to give Gabe a quick kiss. "Yeah. I'll take him to the vet to be sure, but he looks okay. Thank you."

"I wish I could take credit, but Hen took the call. Just some good Samaritan who drove past him and thought he looked out of place."

"He was just walking along the road? He could have been hit!" I started to get angry again. "If whoever took him decided they didn't want him, why didn't they drop him somewhere safe in town?"

"Maybe they did, and he walked all the way here."

That was possible. Tortoises weren't the fastest creatures on the planet, but it was surprising how much ground they could cover if they were determined.

"Poor thing. He was probably trying to find his way home. He must be freezing. Come on. There are blankets in the car."

We opened the back of my car with its cardboard covered back window and wrapped Frank in the blankets. I hoped he'd be warm enough because the glass for this car would take a few days to get here. I stroked his head. I thought about mentioning the thermos to Gabriel, but it seemed so silly now. Turtle soup! My brain needed help.

"I'd better go," Gabriel said, as we shut the hatchback.

I *really* looked at him and saw the tension. And more. Something was truly disturbing him. He was afraid. Seeing the fear in him sent a wave of cold through my heart.

"Is something going on with that body you found?" I asked. "Is everything all right? Have you learned anything yet?"

He wiped his face with his palm and shook his head. "I can't talk about it, Tiber. I mean... I wouldn't even know where to start. And... I just can't. I'll tell you something when I can. But for now, I need to go."

He squeezed my shoulder—like he would anyone. Devin. Sam. Then, he walked away.

Whatever was happening, it wasn't over yet. And I got the first hint that, whatever it was, it might be more dangerous to my little world than I'd yet suspected.

Chapter Eleven

Gabriel

With Frank safe back at home, I had too much space in my head for the murder and the fire, and I'd even added to the murder board with a question mark over whether the fire and the murder were somehow connected.

If I stared long enough, I could probably create a feasible connection, but for now I had to consider them as separate. Lucas had nothing from arson, but expected news later today, and there was no point sitting here waiting for anything, and there was only one person I needed to talk to.

Sam.

I knocked at the house, but there was no one there, so I assumed that Sam was either out on a trail ride, or maybe I'd track him down somewhere on site. Thompson Cabins and Trail Rides had been my home once, and I knew it like the back of my hand, could see the work it took Sam to keep it going, felt a familiar surge of guilt that I'd left him to it, and allowed my dad to run me off. I'd chosen to be a city cop, searching for the absolute opposite of what I'd grown up in, but I might have stayed if Dad had been more accepting of me.

Or was I just a wanderer? I couldn't blame Dad for everything.

The familiar smell of hay and leather filled the air as I approached the stables, but the clinking of metal and hammering pulled me past them to what we'd always called Cabin 3, one of the ones right in the trees that always needed fixing due to rain damage even when we were kids. I peered around the corner and saw Sam up on a ladder, trying to fix a misaligned gutter, the ladder wobbling dangerously.

"Sam!" I called, rushing forward to steady it. The wooden rungs creaked under his weight from where he had one foot on a windowsill. "Are you trying to kill yourself?"

He stared down at me, a wry smile touching his lips. "Well, my life insurance would solve a lot of issues."

His words cut deeper than I had expected. "Don't fucking joke about that shit."

"I'm sorry," Sam added, his tone softening.

I shook my head, my grip on the ladder tight. "Are you done?"

He stretched a bit farther, pushed in the final clip and then, relaxed and climbed down the steps. "Yep." He pointed toward his house. "Coffee?"

I nodded, and we made our way inside.

"I assume you're here about the murder?" Was he asking, or making a statement?

"Some," I evaded, because I didn't want this conversation as we were walking; I wanted to see his eyes. Sam poured two mugs, while I mustered the courage to go all cop on him.

"On Tuesday the sixth, around eleven a.m., there was a confrontation at the bank in Forks, with John Melchet. One of the tellers said the guy John was arguing with was looked like me. Was that you?" My voice wavered, betraying my concern.

"Is it worth denying?" Sam chuckled.

"This isn't a fucking joke!" I snapped. "Did you go to Forks, see John, and confront him about what you owed? I'll find out soon enough when the warrants come in for the bank's records."

Sam blanched. "I wasn't joking; I was trying to lighten… shit…" He hesitated, stirring his coffee, his gaze fixed on the swirling liquid. "That did happen. I did get into a fight with the man, so if no one else did as well, then I guess it was me," he admitted, his voice low.

Fuck. Fuck.

"What happened?" I ground out.

"Are you asking as a cop, or my brother?"

I stared at him and, clearly, that was enough of an answer, that it was a combination of both.

"I went to the bank to ask for an extension, all up-front, thought I could find some equity somewhere, do anything not to have to ask anyone for help. I don't know why, but I got into my own head about where I was going wrong, and how it wasn't all on me, but that the bank had to take some blame. There was this guy, tattoos, somehow talking to him just pushed me over the edge. And then…"

He trailed off, taking a deep breath. "Then, I took it out on John, who was only doing his job." There was a deep sorrow in Sam's eyes as he met mine. "You know me, I don't do that."

He was right and wrong at the same time. The Sam I'd known growing up avoided confrontation, was the middleman between Dad and me, looking out for Ezra, until Dad found out I was gay and then, he'd backed out of being anything at all. Then, there'd been the time I wasn't here—could Sam have changed that much? "I know," I half lied, but it seemed to center Sam.

"I felt guilty straight away," he confessed. "But now that John's gone… it feels so much worse."

"What happened next?"

"I sat outside the coffee shop across the street, and I think I was waiting to calm down, to go back in and apologize, but then Lori called about Sarah falling over in the yard, and she was crying, and I left."

"And you haven't seen the vic—the loans officer—since that day."

He shot me a glance at the slip and pressed his lips thin. "I said I hadn't." I knew him well enough that I could see him bristling, but it was a clarifying question I would ask anyone in this situation.

"I had to ask."

I waited for him to argue, but when his gaze dropped to my uniform, he deflated and shook his head.

"It's not like you to lose your temper," I said softly, as a brother to a brother.

He glanced up at my face and sighed. "Is that a sheriff question?"

"No, it's a big brother observation."

"I lost my temper with you plenty."

I shrugged. "That's what brothers do, and I ran away, I deserved it."

The hard expression he had slipped away. "No one deserves the kind of temper Dad had, or the stuff I thought about you when you'd gone. But that day, at the bank, I was already on the defensive, scared of losing our home, scared… just scared… and I wasn't the only one. This guy, like I said, he was ranting about what he was owed, what I was owed, how the world had let us down, and it sparked something in me, a fire I guess, and that just fueled my outburst at the poor loans guy."

That was interesting. "Someone else was there about a default?"

Sam shook his head. "I don't think so. He was just one of these guys who was angry at the world, tattoos up his arms. Only, he said all the right things that wound me up, because yeah, I did feel I was about to lose everything." He sighed again, this one pulled up from so deep he shuddered. "I thought I was done being angry, but the thought of losing my home…"

"I get it," I said.

We sat in silence for a few moments, lost in our thoughts, then, he picked up the coffee cups and took them to the sink. I tracked his movements.

"I need to get on," he murmured, and then, ran the tap to rinse them.

My eyes caught a glint of silver, the old knife block that sat way back on the counter, and I frowned as something connected in my head. I crossed to them immediately, six spaces for everything from a tiny paring knife to a cleaver.

There were only five shiny handles.

Handles so familiar I felt nauseous. One was missing, and it was a match for the knife found near John's body.

"You okay?" Sam asked. "You look like you've seen a ghost."

"You're missing a knife," I pointed.

Sam blinked at me, then glanced at the block. "Maybe it's in the dishwasher or something."

I yanked open the dishwasher door, but it was empty apart from a couple of breakfast bowls.

"Where's the missing knife, Sam?" I near shouted.

He froze. "I don't know. What's wrong?"

"Has anyone been inside the house? Visitors? Break-ins?"

"What? No. I mean, Lori might have had a friend over, but what do you mean, break-ins?"

I stumbled back to the table, and took a seat, my head full of fear, my hands clenched in fists. The missing knife was a match for the murder weapon in appearance, and the coincidence was too big to ignore.

Why hadn't I seen this before?

"Gabe? Gabriel? What's wrong?" Sam's voice seemed distant, and I shook my head to clear the thoughts. *Look at this rationally. Look at the evidence. Watch Sam's body language.*

I met Sam's concerned gaze. "Tell me you had nothing to do with the death of John Melchet."

He frowned, and leaned back on the counter, his eyes never leaving me for a second.

"I'm your brother—"

"Sam. Just tell me." He couldn't know how much I needed him to speak the words so I could watch him.

"Jesus, Gabe." He pushed a hand through his dark hair, so like my own, and then, settled his hands at his sides. "I had *nothing* to do with the murder of John Melchet."

I watched his expression, searched his eyes for the lie, and even though he was my brother, and therefore, it was a given I would trust his innocence in my heart, I knew he was telling me the truth.

Sam hadn't murdered John.

He crossed his arms over his chest and stared at me, and I got up and hugged him, and not a backslapping quick thing, but a proper brother to brother hug, with feeling. He relaxed in my hold and unknotted his arms and hugged me back.

"Okay then," he murmured. "Okay then."

I needed to report this—it was my duty to report this—and I felt like a traitor who would put the job over believing their own family. Of course, I believed Sam, and even if I did mention the knife, there would soon be a reason behind it, and Sam wouldn't be connected.

Only, I'd seen cases before where circumstantial evidence had put the innocent on trial. He could lose everything. Fuck! As soon as I'd driven far enough from the cabins, I parked and, for the longest time, sat immobile in the car. *Fuck!*

I picked up my cell, thumbing to Devin's details, not even knowing what I was going to say, a huge wall stopping me from pressing his name. Once I did this, it wouldn't just be a connection between Sam and John through the loan, it would be through the murder weapon. It was as if I had the nails in my hand and was on the verge of slamming Sam's coffin shut.

I scrolled up to another name, Lincoln McGinnis. My old boss in LA had seen way more than me, and maybe I needed to reach out to someone else, get some advice. I hesitated for a moment, wondering if I should make the call. Finally, with a deep breath, I dialed the number. It rang three times before a familiar gruff voice answered.

"Lincoln."

"Hey, it's Gabriel," I began, my voice betraying the uncertainty I felt.

"Gabe! How's life as a small-town sheriff?"

"Challenging, in ways I didn't expect," I admitted, rubbing my forehead. "Can I get your advice on something?"

"For what it's worth," Lincoln chuckled.

"I've got a situation here, a possible conflict of interest. Back in LA, I'd just hand it off to another cop. But here, it's not that simple. It's a small town. I have one deputy, and I don't have the luxury of sharing things."

"Tell me more."

I paused. What should I tell my retired boss about an active case? Great, more lines to cross.

"I have a murder scene and way too much circumstantial evidence that connects it to my brother."

Silence, and then Lincoln hummed on the other end. I could imagine his expression, and that cautious way he had of approaching any situation. It had been him who'd seen something in the rookie cop and pulled me into his team, and it had been him who hugged me when it was time for me to leave. He knew more about what I'd seen and done in LA than anyone, and through all of it, he'd been a steady rock.

"Small towns have their intricacies," he began. "I can't say as I have much experience with small-town crime from your perspective, but remember, the principles are the same no matter where you go. The scale and execution might differ, but integrity remains paramount."

I nodded, even though he couldn't see it. "I get that. I just… I don't know how to handle the case, when I know my brother is innocent, without appearing biased."

"Okay," Lincoln began, the tone of a mentor returning to his voice. "First, transparency is key. Document everything, and I mean *everything*. Even if you can't hand it off, make sure there's a clear paper trail showing that you've made every effort to be impartial."

"Okay," I said. That was what I'd been doing, and I was relieved my instincts had been right.

"Secondly, consider bringing in an outsider if the situation demands. Someone from a neighboring town or county. They'll bring a fresh perspective, and it'll show the community that you're serious about ensuring justice."

"That's a good point," I murmured.

"And lastly, Gabe," he added with emphasis, "always trust your gut. If something doesn't feel right in all this evidence, circumstantial or otherwise, then it probably isn't. Trust your instincts, even if it means taking a hit now for the sake of maintaining trust in the long run."

I let out a sigh, feeling the weight lifting a little. "Thanks, Lincoln."

"No worries, it's nice to feel needed," he added with an edge of grumpiness.

"Retirement's treating you well then?" I deadpanned.

He chuckled. "Fishing, reading, the occasional consultancy. Not too bad, kid, but hella boring."

Something else poked at me, the question I asked him every time we spoke. I didn't even want to think about Cyrus Vine right now, but he was still there in my past.

"Anything on Cyrus?"

Lincoln sighed. "I was kind of hoping you weren't going to ask. He's going to appeal his conviction, some shit about mishandling of evidence."

"That's bullshit," I snapped. And it was, because we crossed every T and dotted every I in my last case with the team.

"*You* know that. *I* know that. But there's this hotshot new defense lawyer wanting to go up against the outgoing DA; don't know who hired him, but wants to make a name for himself, blah, blah, you know the score. It won't come to anything, but just giving you a heads-up."

"Thanks." I think.

"On a more positive note for us, not so much for Cyrus, he's not well, but I'm waiting on intel on his condition."

I considered the murder, the fire, and the secrets I was keeping from Tiber that was somehow the worst of this, and sighed. I was so done with what happened in the past.

"Can I ask you something else?"

"A twofer," Lincoln deadpanned.

"Kind of. I'm seeing this guy, well more than seeing, he's my partner. His name is Tiber. I… look, I haven't told him much about what happened in LA. Do you... what about your wife? What does she know?"

Lincoln sighed, and this time it was stronger and filled with regrets. "I told her enough so that she can sleep at night."

"I have nightmares," I blurted, then wished I hadn't said a thing at all. "But I'm talking to a therapist. I'm okay."

He went quiet again. "The nightmares are the worst part, and what you saw, what you had to do..."

"Yeah."

"You couldn't have saved Joe, even if you tried, he could still been on-site that morning even without you there, in the meth lab, and he would still have been killed, whether you were undercover as his boyfriend or not."

"I know."

"Don't carry guilt, and you want my advice?"

"Always."

"When you can, when it's right, tell your Tiber what you did, what you saw; don't let him find out from the nightmares you try to contain."

It was good advice, but I was already holding back everything with Sam, on top of not telling Tiber about Cyrus, the warehouse fire, and worst of all, about Joe.

"I will—"

"Do it sooner rather than later," Lincoln interrupted. "Don't let things fester, and maybe explain about the case? If you love this man, and you trust him, then let him in. Okay?"

"Thanks," I said. "I will. Stay well, okay?"

The call ended with shared assurances of calling more,

and then, I called Tiber because he was the one person who could yank back the shadows from my thoughts.

"Gabriel, hey!"

He sounded so upbeat, none of the darkness from the last few days in his tone.

"Just checking in on Frank." *And I needed to hear your voice.*

"He's good, happy to be home, eating like there's no tomorrow, and the vet said he's no worse for the wear, so thank God for that."

"I can't wait to come home and feed him some lettuce." At first, Frank had been this weird creature I felt I'd never connect with, but through Tiber, I'd kind of fallen for the scaly menace. "Tiber?"

"Hmm?" He sounded distracted, and I could imagine him on the floor, with Frank right next to him, and the image filled me with warmth and affection and regrets I wasn't right there with them.

"I love you."

"I love you, too." Tiber paused. "Are you okay?"

"Yeah, I just… had things on my mind, but I'm okay. Can't wait to come home."

"Five hours barring incidents?" he joked, and I glanced at the clock. Yeah, that sounded about right. "My last appointment is at four, I'll make dinner."

That sounded so normal, so right, and I grinned, even though he couldn't see me. I was so gone for Tiber, so in love with him, so certain we were meant to be together, and it made me warm from the inside out.

"See you later, baby."

"Hey, you know what?" Tiber dropped his tone, and I

waited for him to add some sexy suggestions to me getting home. I'm sure whatever list he came up with, I could add a hundred things to it. "I like it when you call me that."

"Bye, *baby.*"

"Oh, now I'm all hot, go and work, asshole."

I ended the call then headed back to the office, focused back on work, interrupted by a knock on the door, and Lucas poking his head around it.

"Lucas, hey, come in."

"Yeah. Look, I can't stay, got a feed delivery soon, but you should have an email about the fire from the fire investigators. It was arson."

My happy vibes slipped. "Thank you," I murmured, already opening my email, and clicking for the report, and not even seeing Lucas leave.

My fingers drummed a restless rhythm, my mind racing as I tried to process the implications of what I was reading. The origin of the fire was pinpointed to the rear door, which led out to the closed play area, and there were multiple ignition points with trace evidence of an accelerant. Someone had deliberately poured gasoline on the back door, and on the two windows into the small kitchen. There were no surveillance cameras, the security was on the front door, which was locked when the kids were there. No one took the safety of children in schools for granted. There were images attached, blackened walls, charred toys, and the melted remnants of what must have been dozens of art projects. It was a sickening sight. There were two smoke alarms in the building, and the building's owner—Samara—stated that both were functioning, but no batteries were found in either one. What the hell?

There'd been children in that room.

My niece and nephew included.

And Tiber.

The only evidence they'd bagged were pieces of cloth with traces of gasoline found near the ignition point, and the empty canister itself, with no fingerprints.

Whoever did that had no thought to discard the canister, so was this some random thing? Or an attempt on the life of the teacher, Samara, or to hurt the kids? Eight kids in all, and I knew their parents. Five families affected, and like Sam and Lori, all the kids came from homes I knew, the kids were happy, cared for, so it had to be the teacher who was the target—if indeed there was a target at all, and it wasn't a random domestic terrorist act, designed to inflict maximum mayhem and damage to the community.

What? Like Frank was just randomly taken by a passer-by?

Whoever it was—they were still out there.

My mind circled back to Jeff, but he was nowhere near here, and unless he'd gone into the hiring-bad-guys business, I couldn't see a link. After all, how would he have known Tiber was even going to be there that day? I sat back, my eyes drifting from the report to the photos of the burned preschool.

Chapter Twelve

Tiber

GABRIEL CAME HOME IN A MOOD. In *that* mood. It wasn't exactly a hardship as he pulled me into a deep kiss, still smelling of rain and the outdoors. The kiss heated me all the way through, and I wanted more.

"You're all wet!" I laughed, pulling away. "Let's get this off."

We both got him out of his puffy sheriff's department parka and boots, and then, we were on the floor in front of the woodstove, making out.

Gabriel tilted my chin with a finger, then he kissed me with an edge of desperation, but I was too gone to worry about that. If he didn't haul me off to the bedroom in the next minute, I was going to push him. I wanted more than just a kiss, and he must have gotten the message, because he tugged me to my feet, avoiding the sofa, hitting the wall, stumbling as we kissed and reached the bedroom. We paused for a moment to ensure there was no sign of animals in the room, then I shut the door and went straight back in for more kisses.

We stripped fast, the clothes went everywhere, but none of that mattered when the only thing holding me upright was the wall where he'd pressed me.

"I love you," he muttered into the next kiss.

I laced my hands around his neck, going on tiptoes to align my hard cock with his, then his hand was on my ass, and he half lifted, half carried me to our bed. We fell back onto the mattress. He wrapped his fingers around my cock, rolling us so I was laid over him. I loved it when he went all caveman on me, but recently, he'd asked for me to push him, somehow needing me to be more demanding. It wasn't something I'd ever done—Jeff had never let go of control—but it made me so hard and needy, and freaking excited, that I rocked against him and had to pinch myself not to come there and then.

I grasped his hands in one of mine, held them above his head, attempted to get words to form.

"Don't move," I tried to growl, but it sounded more like a plea, as his eyes darkened and he thrust up against me. I leaned over, rummaging in the drawer on his side of the bed, coming back with lube. We were a month past needing condoms, results negative, and the need to feel each other, to know the trust was absolute, meant so much.

"I love you," he repeated, wriggling, as I kissed him, and not shifting his hands an inch.

"I love you," I said back to him, flipping the lid to the lube, and turning to straddle with my back to him, letting out a groan as cold lube touched my skin. The noises he made in return were beautiful breathy moans of need, and his hips juddered as he wanted to move, his cock hard and ready.

"I want to touch."

I wanted to tell him no, that he had to lie there and let me work him over, but I wanted his fingers inside me.

"Touch me," I ordered, and he groaned as his fingers joined mine, tracing my hole as I added more lube.

"So beautiful," he whispered, pressing inside, his other hand caressing my balls, then sliding between us to press his fingers to my cock. He couldn't circle and grip me from this angle, but I didn't need him to, I wanted him inside me more than I wanted my next breath. "Gorgeous," he murmured, working me open, and crooking his finger, finding the sweet spot, pressing, and smoothing and whispering filthy words about how tight I was, and how he wished his mouth was there.

How much he needed me.

"Please," I begged, ceding some control, until I was facing him, stealing a heady kiss, straddling his lap, his cock sliding against my slippery-lubed ass. "My turn," I said, brooking no discussion. "Hands."

He knew what I meant, clasping his hands above his head, then gripping the pillow, as I slid down onto him.

"Fuck…" I whimpered, as he filled me, "you're so…"

So big? So much? So good? I didn't know what I was going to say as he pushed up to meet me dropping down, but finally, my body let him in, and balls-deep, he cursed at me, and I saw his hands flex. He wanted to be the one to take over, but that wasn't what he needed. He'd demanded I take control because he was desperate not to have to be in charge.

I reached for his nipples, tweaked them, pinched them, watched his eyes widen, his mouth fall open, and then, I began to ride him, and I whimpered at the sensation that was part pain and part ecstasy. I felt so full of him; I wanted him so badly; and I stilled, watching his eyes as he begged me for more.

I set a rhythm, stretching out what was happening for a minute, then another, sliding, slippery and slow, until he begged me.

Only then did I change, speeding up, leaning over, kissing him, and I was so close, but I needed him there first.

"Fuck," he exclaimed, thrusting up to meet me pushing.

"Stay still," I ordered, feeling empowered by the fact that this strong sexy man was doing what I told him to do. This was everything, this was him ceding control, and I loved every freaking second of it.

I thrusted faster; he closed his eyes, then opened them as if I'd demanded he do so.

"Close," he warned me, as I took him deep.

Now was the time… now… I needed…

"Touch me," I demanded.

And I swear he whimpered as he circled my cock, letting me fuck up into his fist and, then, down onto him.

"Fuck, I love you," he cried, and then stilled, went so quiet before moaning his release.

I tried words, but I had nothing as my orgasm crashed over me, hot and wet on his belly, and I collapsed onto his chest, snuggling into him, and holding him tight, and he hugged me back.

"Tiber…" he murmured, and I chuckled when that was all he had to say. "Tiber…" he repeated.

And I held him, and loved him, and it seemed I didn't have any brain cells left either.

"Gabriel," I whispered against his neck. "I love you."

I got up to make us both a cup of cocoa and pull a blanket out of the linen cupboard. Renfield hopped out and followed me, and soon after Gabriel joined us. He and the entire pack snuggled in when Gabriel and I cuddled under the blanket, backs against the sofa. With his arm around my shoulders, and all the kids home safe, I felt warm for the first time in days.

We'd needed that, needed to reconnect that deeply, and I was grateful.

Gabriel stroked my arm. But I sensed when his thoughts strayed. His whole energy darkened.

"Did you learn anything about the fire?" I asked tentatively. I didn't want to spoil the golden mood, but it felt like he'd already left it anyway.

He cleared his throat. "It was arson. They made the official ruling."

"Shit. Any idea who did it?"

"Not a clue." He sounded so downbeat.

"I'm sure you'll find them."

"Just… don't tell anyone. The report's in, but it's not exactly been announced."

"Of course not. What about the body at Thompson Cabins? How's that investigation going? Is there anything I can do?"

"I can't talk about it yet," Gabriel said. Then, he turned and nuzzled my cheek. "I want to, but I just have to put things in place to protect you and me, so I can't right now. I just need this. A few minutes *not* to think about it."

"Okay."

He kissed me, his tongue light and, then, surging into my mouth. He was distracting me with sex, maybe himself too. There was a desperate edge to him that worried me. But if he needed this, I'd happily give it. Again.

THE NEXT MORNING, Gabriel was gone by the time I got up. Poor man. He was burning the candle at both ends. But as I made myself coffee, it bothered me he was being so closed-mouthed about the new case. I'd helped him a lot on the murders of Mike Bressett and Billy Odette. Did he not remember? He'd praised my ability to read people then. Duke and I had found Billy's body, for Christ's sake. And Duke had identified Mike Bressett's killer. But now, he didn't want my input at all.

It upset me. Probably more than it should.

It was the weekend, so I took my time getting dressed. I was tying back my long hair when the barking started. Then, the doorbell. Someone was here.

It was not without trepidation that I went to answer it. Too much bad mojo was flying around these days, and I thought about the figure I'd seen in the yard. The mysterious thermos of soup. But when I peeked out of the window, I saw Libby Smith tapping her toe.

I opened the door with a smile. "Hey!"

"Hey, yourself. Come on." She motioned impatiently.

"Come on where?"

"I'm taking you out for coffee. Grab your coat. Let's

go. I passed by Grounds for Joy in a split-second decision to come drag your hermit ass out, and now my brain is wondering where the caffeine jolt went. Andale!"

Libby was not an easy person to argue with, and I didn't try. It had been a while since we'd touched base, and she was one of the few friends I had in Prophet. I grabbed my coat, promised the pack I'd be back soon, and let her shepherd me into her car.

Grounds for Joy was on Main Street in Prophet in an old brick building. The interior showcased the bare red brick walls with twinkle lights and a glass case of fresh baked goods.

"What do you want? My treat," Libby said when we reached the counter.

I ordered a latte and a croissant, and we settled down at a little table in the back, as far away from the two other occupied tables as possible. Libby had something she wanted to talk about, then.

But first, she asked about the animals, and I asked about her paintings. Libby was the one true celebrity in town. She was a renowned wildlife painter, and her art had been featured in national galleries, in the White House, and on postage stamps. She was in her sixties, wore no make-up, and was thin and granite-tough. She spent long days out in the woods taking photographs to incorporate into her art, including some of the local wolf pack, which had been featured in a series of paintings.

I'd never forgotten the time she'd taken me and a woman from the Washington Department of Fish and Wildlife out to observe the wolf pack. On that case,

Gabriel had included me from the start as *the local animal expert.*

He'd valued my input, then.

"So, how's the hunk?" Libby asked, studying my face.

"Fine. Good." I gave her a stoic shrug.

She grinned. "Uh-huh. Nice hickey, by the way."

I slammed my hand over my neck. "Really?"

She chortled. "No. But obviously there could be one. I'm glad one of us is getting some loving."

I laughed and felt my face heat. "A bit."

I thought about last night. It had been more than a bit. It had been... Phew. A change of subject was in order before my mind wandered too far in that direction. "So, um, what did you want to talk to me about?"

She raised an eyebrow. "Can't I just want to take you out for coffee? You're a cynical man, Tiber Russo."

"You can, but that's not why you picked me up today. What's going on?"

She looked around, then lowered her voice. "You're right. I needed to talk to you. I've been hearing town gossip. A lot of gossip."

"Gossip about what?"

"Shhh." She glowered. "I'd rather not add to it, thank you."

I glanced around. Besides Jade, who was behind the register and busy writing new specials on the whiteboard menu, an older couple at a table by the window, and two young teenagers playing video games on their phones at another table near the front, we were alone.

But I turned back to Libby and lowered my voice to a whisper. "All right. Out with it."

She sighed and fiddled nervously with her cup. Her reluctance worried me. If this was a friendly intervention, it was more serious than I'd assumed.

"Everyone's talking about the body they found at Thompson Cabins. Apparently, he was a banker. And apparently, he was Sam's banker. Rumors are swirling that Sam did it. Or maybe there was an argument, and it was an accident. But either way, people are concerned that our sheriff is going to cover it up. That's very much no bueno."

"What?!" I gasped.

"Shhh!" Libby leaned over the table. "Keep your voice down."

"What?" I said, softly. "The dead man is Sam's *banker*?! Are you sure? What do you even mean by *banker*? Who has a banker these days? I mean, people have *banks*, but—"

"Fine, he worked at Sam's bank, okay? And people think the Thompsons are in trouble, financially. Some people say gambling debts, and some say it was covid and a couple of years of empty cabins, but the rumor is Sam's got big money troubles. And a dead banker found stabbed to death on your own property is not a good look."

"Stabbed?" My mind reeled. Jesus, how did Libby know so much more about this than I did? I realized how little Gabriel had told me.

All this was really going on with Sam? Holy shit. And Gabriel hadn't said a word.

"People honestly think Sam is capable of murder?" I whispered. That pissed me off.

She shrugged and gave me a what-are-you-gonna-do look. "Desperate people do desperate things."

"No. No way."

"Hey, I'm on your side. And Sam's. And Gabriel's. I don't believe any of it. I just thought someone should give your honey a heads-up about it."

"He's damn good at his job!" I insisted hotly, and not quietly. Let the town hear.

"I know," Libby said in a soothing tone.

"He's way better than this town deserves."

"Agreed."

I harrumphed. I sipped my latte and thought about it. If the town considered Gabriel was covering up a murder to spare his brother… The thought made me ill as the ramifications grew like a snowball rolling down a hill. How involved was Sam? What would happen to Lori and the twins? Were they already being treated differently by people in town? Were they in trouble financially? What if they did lose the cabins?

And what if other law enforcement saw the conflict the same way the townspeople did and stepped in to remove Gabe from the case? And being sheriff—that was an elected position.

The elections were up this coming November, in fact. What if Gabriel lost his job? What then?

"I'm sorry, Tiber." Libby, very much a non-hugging type, patted my hand. "Sorry to be the bearer of bad news. But it's better to know, right?"

I nodded. "Obviously Gabriel was never going to tell me." It came out bitter.

Libby raised an eyebrow, but said nothing.

Libby dropped me off at the end of my driveway. I was lost in thought, and we hadn't lingered at Grounds for Joy long. I waved goodbye and walked toward my house, thinking.

I hadn't realized how bad things were with the murder case. I had to find a way to help, to support Sam and Lori. And Gabriel, of course. And I needed to get my head out of my own little dramas. My family, my love, had *real* problems. And I needed to be there for them, somehow.

I almost stepped on it. It registered at the last second that there was something on the cement stoop in front of my door.

I stumbled back, confused. For a moment, I just saw dark fur and thought it was Patch or Fudge.

It wasn't. It was a dead raccoon.

A dead raccoon lying on my doorstep.

I covered my nose with my hand. The smell was ripe even from a few feet away. I leaned in to peer at it. What the fuck, man? Had one of the pack put it there?

The dogs didn't have access to the front of the house since the backyard was fenced. Patch, the calico, had left me *gifts* before, but always small things—crickets, birds, bits of a mouse. I hated those, hated to see any animal killed, but there was no getting around the fact that cats were carnivores.

But this... Patch or Fudge wouldn't have gone after a raccoon, and couldn't have dragged it here if they did.

And it was in the same spot where the thermos had been.

Someone had deliberately placed this here. A chill ran through me as the fact sank in. I looked around, checked for footprints. The front lawn was hard and unyielding from the cold, and I didn't see any mud or wet spots on the sidewalk. Then again, it hadn't rained lately. I hadn't left prints either.

I stood, listening. There was nothing except the caw of a bird. My gaze hunted until I found it. A large crow sat on a branch in the big tree in my yard. It stared at me.

"What's going on?" I asked it.

It flew away. "Thanks for the help," I muttered.

I turned back to the raccoon. I pulled up the edge of my fleece jacket to cover my nose and mouth and leaned in to see if I could determine what had killed the poor thing. Its back was toward the driveway, and when I checked the other side of its body, I saw its guts. It looked like something you'd see on the side of the road, hit by a car.

And then I saw the words, written on the stoop in the poor creature's blood.

They read: *Diagnose this.*

Chapter Thirteen

Gabriel

TRACKING down a fellow law enforcement officer to work alongside me was an almost impossible thing to do. I wanted to avoid Forks PD, given its connection to the victim and his bank, so I tried three different sheriffs within a hundred-mile radius, and that was before ten a.m. All three were overstretched and couldn't spare the man hours away from their departments, all were as small as mine. I had to widen the net and struck gold with Richard Peterson over in Kitsap County. I'd gone for him because he had a department of eight, being in Silverdale, and I hoped he'd be able to spare someone—anyone—who could audit the work I was doing on this case.

He jumped at the chance, said he'd be here by one, and that was it. As promised, he was in Prophet by early afternoon, and he was already out there making Hen laugh over something to do with sourdough. I didn't want to ask what the story was, but it seemed the two of them knew each other. He was younger than Hen, in his late fifties, with short dark hair, strands of gray at the temple, and given he'd been with the Kitsap County Sheriff's Office for fifteen years, I could imagine what had put that there. About my height, he was solidly built, clean-shaven with a sharp jawline, and had a gaze that missed nothing. His uniform was only a little tight over his belly, but he didn't strike me as the kind of man who sat at a desk all day.

"Thank you for driving up here, Sheriff Peterson," I said as we shook hands.

"Call me Rick."

"Gabriel," I replied, and with the introductions done, I was itching for him to get started.

"Coffee?" Hen asked, but it wasn't a real question because she was already crossing to the coffee pot. "Rick?" she asked, and Sheriff Peterson—Rick—nodded and smiled. Yep, they definitely knew each other.

"We go way back," Rick offered, probably seeing my glance between them. "My brother used to apprentice with Jim when he first started out." Jim? Wait, Hen's husband Jim. Electrician. Okay then. "Cream and two," Rick added, and I swear Hen, happily married for thirty years, with grandchildren, blushed. He thanked her, all kinds of old-fashioned, and then, we took our coffee and the muffins into my office, and he sat in the chair facing my desk.

It occurred to me that I should have taken him directly to the incident room, but how in god's name I'd fit us *and* Devin in, I didn't know. Not that Devin was there, he was out with Lucas working the arson investigation, which was about as dead in the water as the murder of John Melchet.

We shot the breeze for a little while as we sipped

coffee and ate muffins, and then, he brushed crumbs from his shirt and leaned forward in his seat.

"This will be what, your third murder this year?" he asked as if he didn't already know, but I was happy to play the game of who had the worst county for murder, if it meant I could separate myself from the case where Sam was concerned.

"Yep." That was all I was going to give him.

"So how can I help?"

"As I explained, I have a conflict of interest in this case, and so I'm calling you in to monitor, and run the case alongside me. But you *can* say no."

"I came all this way," he said, picking another random crumb from his pants. "Where do we start?"

Refilling our coffees, we then headed into the tiny incident room, and I closed the door behind us, cracking the tiny head height window just to circulate some air, for what it was worth. An icy breeze gusted in, but then, it settled.

"Okay then." Rick stood right in front of the board, and he was so close I swear he'd be cross-eyed, but he seemed to be taking it all in. "Talk me through it."

So I did.

He didn't ask questions as I went through all the details, with some extra notes about the arson case, which, while unrelated, could be interesting for him.

When I was done, he sat in the seat Devin usually used and frowned at the board.

"So we have a body on your brother Sam Thompson's property. An argument between Sam and the victim that Sam has admitted happened. Sam is about to lose his property." He held up a hand as I began to correct him because I'd said that family had stepped in to fund the shortfall. "Which he isn't now, I get that. So, body on Sam's property. Sam's missing knife. Sam's argument with the victim. Sam's alibi shaky with a visit to a non-existent garage in Forks after an email was sent from a burner account."

I sat down then, the weight of all of that was too much.

"Forensics on the knife?" he prompted.

I shook my head to indicate we hadn't gotten them, but opened my phone to check my email. As if the universe was conspiring against me, there was a report from forensics, fingerprints on the knife, matched those of a suspect arrested in Port Angeles for assault, and the name? Samuel Thompson.

What assault? What the fuck?

"Sam's fingerprints are on the knife," I said.

"Any other prints?"

I re-read the file. "Another set of prints not in a database."

"Who else lives in the house with your brother?"

"Wife, Lori, two kids."

"Likely to be the wife's prints then," Rick suggested, and any flare of hope I might have felt died in an instant. "You'll need to get her prints also," he reminded me.

"Of course." I re-read the information in the file. "Some of the prints are smudged."

"Suggesting someone handled it with gloves or a towel?" Rick pressed his lips together in thought.

I wished it was that easy. "Or it could have been done during evidence collection?"

Rick leaned forward in his chair, his hands dangling between his knees. "Still, there's an awful lot of Sams in there. Let's get him. I want to talk to him, and his wife."

My heart sank. He was going to come to the conclusion this was all on Sam, and what did I do? I'd leave. Resign my position, and stand next to Sam and fight this all the way. This wasn't Sam's doing. He was innocent.

I picked up the phone to call my brother, but Rick stopped me with a raised hand.

"Don't call Mr. and Mrs. Thompson here. We should do this up at your brother's place. Take a kit to get Mrs. Thompson's prints."

The moment Rick suggested we head to the freaking murder site, a knot of anxiety tightened in my stomach. I'd assumed he'd want to interview Sam and Lori at the station, a neutral ground, a controlled environment. But this? It felt like a chess move, one I hadn't anticipated, something he'd maybe seen that I'd missed.

"Are you sure that's necessary? My... I mean, the kids will be up there," I found myself asking, my voice betraying a hint of concern. Rick's gaze was steady, unyielding.

"We'll be discreet," he reassured me. "I think it's best we talk there," he said, his tone leaving no room for argument. What could I say? How could I argue against this when Rick needed to see the site anyway, and in his shoes, I would want to take the soft approach, talk to suspects on their home turf, make it casual.

Shit.

"Give me the number," Rick said, and when I passed it

over, it was Rick who organized us heading up there in the next few minutes. When we got there, a friend of Lori's arrived at the same time, exchanging smiles, and assuring Lori they'd be in the barn, and *everything was okay.* I loved the way Sarah and Aaron ran to me for a hug, and I held them for so long, chattering about snowmen and snow angels, and how the barn cat, Fluffy, was getting fat.

Then, it was time for the main event, and I hated that Sam wouldn't look at me.

Hated it.

Rick's demeanor was professional, yet approachable, a balance that seemed to put Sam at a slight ease, despite the circumstances. He turned to Sam, his eyes steady and serious.

"Sam, are you okay with Sheriff Thompson being in the room with us?"

Sam blinked at me. "He's my brother. We don't have secrets."

"Okay, then, I'm going to be asking you some detailed questions about John's murder," Rick began, his voice firm, but not unkind. "I need you to be as open and honest as possible. This is an informal interview, but it's crucial to the investigation."

I could see Sam stiffen, the weight of the situation pressing on him. I wanted to reach out, to offer some form of support, but that wouldn't go down well.

The way Rick laid out the process made it sound so clinical, so matter-of-fact, but the reality was anything but. This was a dance around delicate truths and hidden secrets, a probing into the dark corners of the past.

"If at any point you need a break, just let me know,"

Rick added, his tone softening slightly. "I understand this can be difficult, but your cooperation is essential."

"I'm okay. I haven't done anything wrong, neither has my wife, so ask me anything."

"We'll start with your whereabouts on the night of the murder, Wednesday, February fourteen. Valentine's Day," Rick clarified, pulling out a small notebook and pen. "I'll need to know who you were with, what you were doing, and any interactions you may have had with John or anyone else connected to him."

"I already said all of this to Devin," Sam defended.

"How about you tell me from the start."

I listened as Sam detailed the call from the garage, understood the desperation of him wanting to keep the truck going on as little money as possible, knew he'd gone to Forks, and that there'd been nothing when he got there. It had been easy enough for me to check back on the email —or rather, it had been easy for Devin—a burner email, no such account, a fraud on Sam.

"And after?"

"It was Valentine's Day, I was with my wife," Sam said.

"Okay," Rick murmured. "And next, how about you start by telling me why your fingerprints are on file?" Sheriff Rick's gaze was fixed on Sam.

"Surely you know all that, it's on record," Sam said, and flicked a look at me, then dropped his gaze.

I felt like complete shit. "I'll wait outside." Sam didn't deserve for me to be there watching him, but he shook his head.

"Why? Haven't you looked it up already? Jesus, Gabriel... Sheriff... it can't be a secret to you."

What did I say? I had checked it out, but that was my job. I had no answer, but I knew it would be okay once he confirmed the details to Rick—although it might speak to a temper.

Fuck. My head hurt.

"How about you tell me in your own words," Rick asked.

Sam shifted under the scrutiny, pressing his fingers to his temples, but then, he straightened and pulled his shoulders back.

"I was a different person back when I was arrested," he began, his voice tinged with regret. "I was mad at the world. Everything seemed to be falling apart." He paused, glancing down at his hands before continuing. "Gabriel had left, Ezra was always in and out of scrapes—trouble— and Dad and I couldn't see eye to eye on anything, and then Lori... told me she was pregnant, and she threatened me that if I didn't get my head out of my ass, we were done. That day, I'd gotten into a fight with Dad, got in the truck and just drove, ended up in Port Angeles, just to... I don't know, forget, I guess. I got drunk," Sam admitted, the words filled with years of regret. "Someone accused me of starting a fight in a bar. It was all a blur, but next thing I knew, I was in handcuffs, being shoved into a squad car."

My heart stopped; if I'd still been here, I could have helped Sam, stopped him from fighting with Dad, gotten him to talk to Lori. *I could have helped.* Rick's expression softened slightly, but his eyes remained vigilant, as though he was trying to read between the lines of Sam's story.

"They threw me in jail for the night," Sam continued. "I was sure my life was over. Fuck, I was so damn desperate that I *nearly* called the number I had for Gabriel." He huffed, then shrugged at that, and guilt consumed me. Even if he had called me, four years ago, I was deep undercover, and Lincoln would have had to say I wasn't there. What kind of brother did that make me? Sam looked up, meeting Rick's gaze with newfound strength. "I couldn't even defend myself because I didn't recall a damn thing, but then, they checked the CCTV footage. Showed I wasn't the guy they were looking for. I was released the next morning."

"Okay." Rick nodded and there was a silence, a brief moment where Sam glanced at me and held my gaze. "I came home after that," he said. "And I decided it was time to turn my life around. I couldn't be that angry messed-up person anymore, and I wanted to win Lori back, and prove I could be a good dad."

"You are," I blurted, "You're the best dad and husband." He shot me a smile. Rick frowned. I backed down with an apology. "Sorry."

"Maybe you should wait in the other room," Rick suggested, or rather ordered.

Fuck. "Sorry, of course."

I let myself out, finding Lori pacing in the front room. She immediately crossed to where I stood. "And?"

"I know Sam didn't do it," I said. I'd spoken to a lot of guilty men, and Sam wasn't one of those. The only shame he carried was that he'd run out on his pregnant wife, and he hated himself for it.

The door opened and Sam came out, then it was Lori's turn, and she worried at the ink on her fingers from where Rick had taken her prints then interviewed her—at least I'd been invited back in for that.

She had very little to add: yes she recalled Sam being arrested, yes, it was a bad time, no he wasn't a violent or angry man, yes, he was under a lot of pressure, but no, Sam wasn't responsible.

"And neither am I," she added at the end of the impassioned defense.

Rick finished the interviews, his expression set, not giving anything away, but he thanked Sam and Lori warmly, and even visited with the horses, and spoke to Aaron and Sarah, who were out in the barn with a friend of Lori's, playing with the cat.

Then, it was time for us to leave, and after hugging Lori, I pulled Sam into an embrace.

"I believe you. I'll fix this," I promised him.

And as he nodded and eased away, he patted my shoulder. "I know."

I headed back into town, stopping at my house, which wasn't my home at all now. I only went back a few times here and there, checking if it was okay, grabbing my mail, and I nearly tripped over the pile of junk mail that had accumulated since last time, which was probably…

Jeez… two weeks?

I wandered around the place, checking windows; the furniture had come with the place, nothing was mine, and all my stuff was at Tiber's. I picked up the mail, put the crap in recycling, then thumbed through the rest, which was two utility bills and a bank statement.

I wasn't sure why I was even keeping this place.

Because it's so new with Tiber? No, I loved Tiber, and it was a forever thing, not something I was putting an end date on. *Because I'm scared that, one day, he'll have enough of my nightmares and tell me to move out of his place?*

I really needed to talk that one over with Tiber, but given all the rest of the shit in my head, everything seemed impossible right now.

Soon, though, I promised myself. Once this thing with Sam was fixed, there would be time.

Chapter Fourteen

Tiber

I BAGGED the poor raccoon and put her in the trash bin in the garage. I couldn't stomach a thorough examination of the carcass, but it reminded me of ones I'd seen at the side of the road. Had she been roadkill someone'd picked up? It was less painful than the idea that someone had captured and killed a raccoon in order to put it on my doorstep.

I went into the house, washed my hands, and got out my phone to call Gabriel. I stood there, hands shaking, and hesitated.

What had Libby told me? Gabriel had his hands and his worried mind, full with the body they'd found at Thompson Cabins and its possible connections to Sam. He needed to focus on that, and I needed to let him. I stood there for a long while, thinking while the dogs milled around me.

They were anxious, and it wasn't just because they

sensed my mood. Duke stood with his paws on the windowsill next to the door, staring out intently.

I took a deep breath, another.

Screw it. I wasn't going to be a victim. I could handle this on my own. Gabriel might not want me to help with the murder case, but this, at least, I could do.

I straightened my spine and called on my inner warrior. Called up fire.

Whoever was doing this was going to rue the day they'd messed with Tiber Russo and his pack. I vowed it.

But how could I catch whoever was doing this? I could set up a camera, maybe a Ring camera at the front door. But it would be visible. I had the feeling the culprit would spot it a mile away and approach the house from a different direction. Or sabotage my car. Not to mention the fact that it would take anything I ordered a few days to get here and set up.

Besides, I had a better security system already.

"Okay, guys. We need to talk. Come here." I walked into the living room, Leo, Gracie, and Ferdinand at my heels. I sat on the couch. "Duke! Come."

Reluctantly, Duke left the front window and padded over, too.

"Okay, listen up. This is very important." I looked each one of them in the eye for several long seconds, making sure they understood the gravity.

Ferdinand licked his lips.

"No, this isn't treat time. This is talk time. Here's the deal. Someone is trying to mess with us, and I need your help."

Leo yipped.

"No, we can't just ask the big, hunky sheriff. Gabriel is busy with important family business."

Ferdinand sniffed the floor for crumbs, and Gracie appeared nervous, but Duke and Leo watched me fixedly.

"I need you guys to be extra alert. Leo, Duke—you take turns at the front window. Gracie and Ferdinand, you can watch the back from the couch. Keep your ears trained. If you hear or see anything, no barking. Got that? No bark. You come get me."

What I wanted was to get a look at this person. What I wanted was to catch him-her-them in the act.

I repeated the plan a few times, and I led the dogs to the front window, then the back one, pointing to them and repeating each dog's assignment, then I opened the front door, and we all went out.

"Find the stranger's scent," I told them.

Of course, they all went to where the raccoon had lain and smelled there. But after they'd gotten enough of that, Duke wandered around the front yard, sniffing at the walkway, the driveway, grass, and bushes.

Little Leo trotted about, sniffing here and there, and Ferdinand, who had a very good nose, being a basset hound, loped after Duke, sniffing everywhere Duke sniffed, offering a second opinion.

Ferdinand and Duke seemed to agree on a section of leaves on a bush next to the driveway. I walked over there and Gracie and Leo followed. They all sniffed it.

"Is that the stranger? The one who put the raccoon on the porch?"

Duke barked, then issued a low growl.

"Perfect. Good job, guys. Good job!" I gave them all

treats. "If you smell that again, you let me know. Okay? Such good doggos."

I squatted down so I could give them lots of pets and get kisses. Secret weapon engaged. Together, we'd nail this bastard.

I GRABBED a notebook and made a list. The weird incidents in the past week included:

- *stalkery phone call with "Jim Smith" (might not be related)*

- *thought I saw someone in the front yard*

- *the fire at the preschool*

- *Frank's abduction and the damn soup in the thermos.*

- *Dead raccoon with creepy message*

Everything on the list could be written off as unrelated, but was that deliberate? Was someone trying to make me feel paranoid? That sounded like something my ex, Jeff, would do. But Gabriel said Jeff had been at work this whole time.

Who else disliked me enough to torment me? I hardly knew anyone because I'd hardly left the house since moving to Prophet three years ago.

Except it was public knowledge I'd been involved with two murder cases. That of the park ranger, Mike Bressett, and that of a local Makah man, Billy Odette. The people guilty for those crimes had been arrested. What if someone in their orbit blamed me for that? A sibling? Spouse? Friend? Whoever was doing this seemed to hate me, specifically. I couldn't think of another reason why anyone would.

Maybe it was naive to think I could help put serious criminals away and not face pushback. Unlike Gabriel and Devin, I didn't have the protection of a uniform, badge, and gun. I probably seemed like an easy target.

Fuck. I needed to dig up some town gossip of my own.

I knew exactly two people in town well enough to go to them for help—well, besides Gabriel and his family. Since I'd just spoken to Libby, I drove over to the mercantile to see One-Eyed Jack.

It was early evening, around five, when I got there. I shopped, putting the usual necessities for the animals in my cart while there was a short line at the register. Finally, the check-out counter emptied out, and I saw my chance.

"Hey, bruh." One-Eyed Jack smiled when I walked up with my cart.

"Hey, how's it going?"

"Well, no one's tried to immolate me lately, so I guess it's going fine."

I winced. "Guess you heard about the preschool fire."

"Sure did. Heard you were there. Heard your turtle was taken too. Glad you got him back. Any idea who took 'im?"

One-Eyed Jack was a Makah man and owner of the mercantile, which he ran with his wife. He'd been friendly with me since the first day I'd walked into his store three years ago, probably because I looked native. I should be squicked out that he knew so much about my business. But since I was here to get gossip, I could hardly complain.

"Nope, no idea who took Frank. Hey, I wanted to ask you about that."

He raised his eyebrows and scanned a bag of carrots. "About your turtle?"

"Well, not that specifically." God, it was so hard for me to ask for anything from anyone. I centered myself and dug up the words. "The thing is, it's not just the tortoise abduction or even the fire. Other things have happened at my house."

One-Eyed Jack glowered. "Dude. Like what?" I appreciated his protectiveness.

"Just… lurker-y things. I thought it might be someone associated with the Bressett or Odette murders. Do you know if Dell Prosser or Brad Callan have any close friends or relatives in the area who might hold a grudge?"

I bagged groceries while One-Eyed Jack rang them up, expression thoughtful. "Don't know anything about that Callan guy. He wasn't a townie."

"No, he wasn't."

"But Dell… he had friends. Ned, John, and Troy come to mind. They all played poker together. Used to come in on Fridays to pick up beer and snacks for the game."

Right. I'd seen those guys with Dell when they'd gone out on an ill-advised mission to hunt down the local wolf pack. Ned was Ned Crumper, the local UPS delivery man. John Slater ran the gas and auto service station in Prophet.

"Is Troy younger? Kind of overweight?"

"That's him." One-Eyed Jack shook his head. "Troy Hughes. He's the type of dude who'd look around for an old dog all day long just to give it a kick. As big a coward as he is a bully."

That sure sounded like the type of person who'd write stupid messages on a front stoop. I thought back to the day

Gabriel and I had broken up Dell's *wolf posse*. Troy had been the one guy I hadn't recognized. He was younger than the others, maybe 30's—unattractive and puffy. He'd worn camo like someone playing at being a badass, but he'd caved as soon as Gabriel said boo.

"Does Troy work in town?"

"I believe he worked at the hardware store for a short time, but got fired for bein' lazy. Now he just lives with his mom and spends his time shooting tin cans at the quarry. Course, that's just my guess. For all I know, he's got some secret computer business in the garage or makes train models for Etsy or somethin'. His mom's a nice lady."

"Did you happen to hear if any of those guys were upset about Dell's arrest?"

One-Eyed Jack made a face. "Nah, bruh. Everyone in town was shocked, like. But more pissed at Dell for what he'd done, especially all that bull-hockey about the wolves. Trying to pass his own crimes off on them? That was seriously f'ed up."

"I know, right?" Even thinking about it made me angry again.

"So I doubt those guys are out for blood. Don't see it."

"Is there anyone else Dell was close to?"

"He mentioned a brother a few times. He wasn't from around here, though."

That didn't mean the brother couldn't have come to the area to take revenge.

"Cool. Thanks. Have you noticed anyone suspicious hanging around town lately?"

One-Eyed Jack slid the full grocery bag toward me and snorted. "Dude, this is the only grocery store for miles.

Half the people who come in here are just driving through. You'd be surprised how many strangers walk through this checkout line."

My heart sank. "I hear ya. This would be someone hanging out for a while, though. Maybe someone new to the area?"

He shrugged. "There are a few, I guess. Always are. But I couldn't tell you anything about them."

I must have looked disappointed because his face softened. "But, hey, for you, bruh? I'll start paying more attention. It's not cool if someone's messin' with you."

A stab of gratitude hit me. "Thanks. I'd appreciate that."

"There was one guy that stuck out to me at the time," he went on conversationally. "But this was a while back."

"Oh yeah? Who? What? I mean…" I swallowed. *Slow your roll.*

"It was at least a month ago. Some guy came in regularly for about a week. City type. Kinda smarmy. He always had a camera with him. One of those big, professional deals. And he asked questions."

"What kind of questions?"

"About the town… Struck me at the time as being more than casual curiosity. Know what I mean? I wondered what he was up to. Come to think about it, he was real interested in our sheriff."

Gabriel.

I wanted, needed, to grill him. But a middle-aged couple who were probably tourists came up behind me. One-Eyed Jack glanced at them, but didn't seem in a hurry for me to move on. I plowed ahead.

"This guy asked questions about Sheriff Thompson? What kind of questions?"

One-Eyed Jack rubbed his forehead, his brow furrowed. "Not sure I remember exactly. Maybe how long he'd been sheriff. Something about how he was a local boy. I think? Oh—and pretty sure he mentioned the gay thing. Yeah. Yeah, that. I thought it was rude."

"Did this guy mention me?"

"Not that I—wait. Maybe round about. I seem to recall something like: *heard the sheriff's gay and has a local boy toy working with him*. That kind of thing, like nosing around to see if I had an issue with it. It struck me as a bit off, like I said."

A *bit* off?

"You didn't tell Gabriel about it at the time?"

One-Eyed Jack made a face. "It didn't strike me as *that* off, bruh. More like the guy had a problem with... you know. The gay thing. And I don't need to go runnin' to the sheriff with that crap. Anyway, he didn't stick around long."

"Okay. Thanks. I'll, um, check in with you later."

I went out to my car and sat there, thinking.

Why would a stranger be that interested in the town sheriff? And he'd known that I'd worked with him.

Boy toy working with him.

I very much resented that description, but that wasn't the point. The only times I'd worked with Gabriel had been on the Mike Bressett and Billy Odette murder cases. If this stranger knew that, he'd been digging into the press on those cases. Why would anyone do that unless they had a personal stake in one of them?

And the *boy toy* was obviously the safer target if you were out for revenge.

Whoever this bastard was, I had to deal with him while making sure Gabriel could focus on his brother's predicament.

It was the least I could do.

Chapter Fifteen

Gabriel

I HEADED TO THE OFFICE—THERE'D be no days off for me while this case was open. And I wasn't the only one. I was grateful to see Hen sitting in her usual spot when I arrived, and Devin and Rick working away in the tiny incident room.

I left them to it and went into my own office to catch up on emails and read over every word of documentation we had, sure I had to be missing something. Something that would prove Sam was innocent.

I worked all morning. By the time my stomach reminded me that food was a thing, Rick and Devin and Hen had already gone to lunch and gotten back. I headed out on my own to grab a bite.

I was crossing the street when, from a distance on Main, I spotted Tiber, his figure unmistakable, with Duke, trotting by his side. I quickened my pace to catch him, desperate for some Tiber-time and as I approached, I called out a happy "Hey you!"

Startled, Tiber jumped, his eyes wide with surprise as he whirled to face me, white-knuckling Duke's lead. For a moment, he was flustered, his composure slipping, but as soon as he realized it was me, his tension eased.

"Gabriel!" he said with a smile, but I wasn't letting that initial reaction go without comment.

"What's wrong?" I asked, concern lacing my voice.

Tiber smiled, but hesitated, his gaze flickering away before returning to mine. I knew him well enough now to see he was choosing not to answer directly, which made no sense. Only, then, he leaned in and kissed me, changing the subject as I lost myself in the kiss.

Duke nudged me and interrupted us with a heartfelt whine. . I smiled as I went to a crouch and turned my attention to the passion-interrupter, if that was even a term, giving him some affectionate petting.

"Are you getting coffees?" he asked and thumbed at Grounds for Joy.

"No I was thinking of getting... look... are you hungry?" I asked. "Do you want to grab a bite at the diner? Can you spare half an hour?"

"Sure." He brightened and hugged me again. "Sounds good."

With a nod, I connected to Hen. "Dispatch, show me away for thirty—I'll be at the diner if anyone needs me." *Please don't anyone need me—just for thirty minutes.*

"Sure thing, Sheriff." Hen sounded surprised, but didn't call me on it. I refused to feel guilty for pulling myself away from all the shit happening around me. Anyway, I didn't often take time for lunch, eating at my desk, hell, come to think of it, I *never* took a proper lunch break.

And this was Tiber.

And I missed him, even though we'd seen each other at breakfast.

He gripped my hand and leaned into me, then, with our fingers laced together, we walked into the diner chatting about Patch, who'd learned how to open the top cupboard in the kitchen.

"He was tossing down treats, which Ferd gobbled up. I had to sit Patch down and have a talk with him about Ferd's health. He didn't exactly promise to stop—you know how cats are. But I think I got through to him."

I chuckled. Tiber's deep communication with the pack never ceased to amaze and amuse me.

"Maybe you could put some broccoli florets on the shelf for Patch to knock down."

Tiber laughed. "Brilliant idea."

Inside the diner, amidst the clinking of cutlery and the murmur of a few other customers, all locals who glanced up and smiled, we found a cozy spot to one side, Duke curling up under the table. As we talked, our hands found each other, and I never wanted to let go, clinging a little desperately to the one person who made everything right.

"Are you okay?" Tiber asked, and it must have been the hundredth time he'd asked me that in the last few days, or at least it seemed that way.

"Yeah, sorry, it's just that everything is a mess." Then it was my turn to ask Tiber because he seemed a little distant, and the guilt inside me at not telling him the full details of Sam's case made me think he was pissed at me, and I hated it when Tiber wasn't happy with me.

I loved him, and I wanted every day to be skipping among the damn roses because both of us freaking deserved that. "Are you okay? You seem a little umm…"

"A little what?" he asked with a smile.

"Nervous. I mean you jumped a mile when I said hello."

He blinked at me, and I thought I saw worry in his expression, but then, he rolled his eyes and huffed. "I was thinking about things, and you called my name in your best cop voice, and you were right there behind me. Of course I jumped."

"My bad," I said.

His smile widened. "You're forgiven."

We were interrupted by the waitress laying down two plates, Tiber's a BLT, and chips, mine with a grilled cheese and a bowl of their homemade soup. I fell on the food as if I were starving, which earned me a chuckle from Tiber. Somewhere between a coffee refill and eating, I brought up the one topic that had been on my mind that wasn't my brother, or any other case on my desk.

"I checked on my house," I started.

"Yeah? Everything okay?"

"It's all good, but it got me thinking about why I even have the place now." I watched Tiber's reaction, saw the hint of concern there, but nothing that screamed give-up-your-potential-bolt-hole-and-live-with-me-right-now.

Maybe he thought we weren't committed enough and that I needed to have a backup place to stay? Was I overstepping? I hoped we were on the same page.

It was everything to me that I had a place to be me with the man I loved.

"It made me think," I continued, "about us, about the future." I took a deep breath, feeling the weight of the moment. "You asked me to move in, and I never actually said yes, I just left more and more of my stuff at your place, and I wanted to tell you that it's a yes, to moving in, but formally. I want to put my place up to rent—and if there's no takers, then maybe sell it?"

"Really?"

Was that hope in his voice?

"I want to make us *officially* official if that makes sense. Something more permanent. I'm with you, for the long haul."

Tiber's mouth dropped open, and he blinked at me, and I thought maybe I'd overstepped.

"Of course, if you don't—"

"Yes."

"Yes?"

"One hundred percent, yes. I love you. Completely."

"And I love you right back. But I want it done right though, paying my way at your place, rent, utilities or—"

"Whatever. Just yes." He leaned over the table, I copied him, and we sealed the deal with a kiss. I might have secrets I needed to keep from him for now, but that didn't matter in the grand scheme of things when we were in love and together.

Right?

Chapter Sixteen

Tiber

AFTER LUNCH, I kissed Gabriel goodbye, and Duke and I continued our walk up and down Main Street. Before Gabriel had arrived, I'd been taking Duke on a find-the-scent tour. But putting that off for a meal with Gabe had been more than worth it.

Moving in officially. I liked the sound of that. I liked it so much it was a little frightening. It had taken me a while to let Gabriel in. My past history with men—cough, Jeff—had been traumatic, and I hadn't been interested in meeting anyone.

But Gabriel's combination of tortured-soul-in-a-gorgeous-body had wiggled right past my defenses. I'd always been a nurturer, and the dark places inside him called out to me. Called out for light.

I had no regrets. He was a good man. A truly good man. My only fear now was losing him.

Which was all too possible with another murderer

running loose and someone from one of the past two cases out for revenge. God.

A tug on the leash got my attention. I looked at Duke, who'd sat down on the sidewalk to stare at me.

"Okay, okay. I'm present."

Duke barked.

"I *am*. We're looking for the scent from our front yard. I'm all in. Let's go."

We took our time. Duke sniffed everything and everyone. He was on leash, but *he* led *me* as I silently followed him. He didn't give anyone on the street a second glance, sniffing the air to catch their scent, then ignoring them. He nosed around every door, the curb, trash cans.

I figured even if my stalker wasn't a townie—Dell's brother, for instance—he'd been close by for a few days at least. He had to have come into town for something.

He being metaphorical, of course. I had no idea of the gender of my tormentor, or even if there was more than one.

At the entrance of Grounds for Joy, Duke's energy went into hyperdrive. He tensed, shaking, sniffed more enthusiastically in big woofs, and pawed at the door.

"Good boy, Duke. Good boy!" I rewarded him with a treat from my pocket.

I peered through the front window. Jade was at the register making a drink for an older, gray-haired lady. Two of the tables were occupied—one by a teenaged couple, and the other, by a single man, maybe forties, in a red-and-black plaid lumberjack-style coat. I'd never seen him before.

I swallowed. Should I go inside? Or call Gabriel?

No, I could do this. Gabriel was busy. I'd see if Duke responded to the guy in the coffee shop. If he did, I'd act my fanny off and apologize and not show any suspicion or recognition whatsoever. But I'd have ID'd him, and that was the point.

I pasted a neutral expression on my face and opened the door. Duke hurried in ahead of me, still vibrating with excitement and focused only on the scent. I waved a hello to Jade and didn't even glance at the guy in the lumberjack coat as Duke sniffed the floor and followed the scent... right past the man. It was probably just as well it wasn't him because he didn't seem friendly. Duke led me to a small table near a cold case of drinks and huffed around one of the chairs there, the floor, the seat. Then he sat and looked up at me proudly.

"Good boy. You're so smart," I murmured. I squatted down to give him a hug, scratches, and a treat as a reward.

Jade came over. "Hey, Tiber. What's up?"

Jade had worked at Grounds for Joy since I'd arrived in Prophet three years ago. She was a friendly, people-loving sort, in her thirties, with wildly colored hair—today it was purple—and piercings. It was the people-loving part that made her alien to me. But I did trust her.

I rose to my feet and kept my voice low. "Do you remember who was sitting at this table recently?"

She gave me an amused smile as if I was pulling her leg. When I didn't react, her expression changed to a puzzled one. "Why? What's the deal?"

"I'm looking for someone. Duke has his scent. He says this person used this chair recently. At least in the past two days, I'd say."

"That's so Nancy Drew. Awesome! Only lots of people sit here. I mean, we're not exactly Grand Central Station, but we're not *that* slow."

"Anyone you can remember. Everyone you can remember. Please, Jade. It's important."

She shook her head a little, confused, then she sighed. "All right. I can try. Want me to make a list? Like, write it down?"

"That would be so helpful. Thanks."

She started to walk away, paused. "Want a drink while you wait? Soy latte, right?"

"Yeah. Good idea." I didn't need more coffee today, but buying something was the least I could do.

I paid for a latte, a puppuccino, and a couple of sugar cookies, and went to a table—not the table where the stalker had been. I gave Duke the puppuccino and fed him a sugar cookie in nibbles. I didn't normally give my dogs sugar, but he'd done a big job today. I saw Jade writing things on a notepad, pausing to serve two customers who came in.

Fifteen minutes later, she came over to my table and handed me a note. She flopped down in the other chair at the table and petted Duke. "That's all I can remember. But I can't be sure it's everyone. I wasn't paying that much attention, you know?"

"No reason you would. This is perfect. Thank you."

I checked the list. She'd understood the assignment.

Billy and Dylan Stanchard – Brothers, locals, teens. Always order iced coffees.

Harriet Wilson – older lady, local, always sits at that

table and gets a "treat" at the start of the month after her social security check.

A tourist couple, 60's, never saw them before. Had soup and rolls.

Business suit guy, 40's, never saw him before. Americano black, muffin. Bit rude.

Troy ? – Local, regular. He's talkative. Hot chocolate and a couple of cookies.

Tall, tattooed guy. Never saw him before. Croissant and black coffee.

Martin and Marge. Co-workers at the accountant's office a few doors down. Regulars. Not sure of their last names. They eat lunch here a few times a week.

"This is amazing," I said, impressed.

She shrugged. "You probably don't care about the food, but it's how I remember people, so I just wrote it down."

"No, it's great. You never know, right? This, um, this Troy—is that Troy Hughes? Thirties? Big guy? He was friends with Dell Prosser?"

Jade's eyebrows went up. "Oh yeah, that's his last name. I forgot."

"Cool. And did you notice if any of them had a professional camera?"

She shook her head. "I don't remember anything like that. The business guy had a briefcase. I really can't say that's everyone who sat at that table. And Martin and Marge might have been over there." She pointed to a spot near the table with the scent.

"It doesn't matter. This is a start."

"It helps that you just wanted people who sat down. Most people get stuff to go. Like your honey." Her eyes twinkled. "He comes in a lot, but never stays. Unless he's with you."

I tried my hardest not to blush. "Yeah. That table is definitely the point of interest."

"If you give me your number, I can text you if I remember anything else."

We exchanged numbers, and I thanked her again. As Duke and I left the coffee shop, I thought about how there were advantages to living in the small town. A big city barista would never have done something like that for an occasional customer, or even been able to. But in a small town like Prophet, people were either locals or strangers, and the strangers stood out.

I paused on the sidewalk and zipped up my gray parka. It was cold and getting colder. The sidewalks were slippery. It hadn't warmed up enough to melt the dusting of snow that had fallen a few days ago. I liked the mountain-y feeling it gave downtown. It was not even midday, but the day was overcast and dim and the street lamps glowed in their best effort to spread cheer.

But cheer was not what I was feeling. I leaned against the brick wall at the side of the coffee shop window and studied the list. At least three of the groups could be ruled out—Harriet Wilson, who had to be in her eighties, the older tourist couple, and the accountants. I also didn't see why teens would be involved, but it wasn't impossible, I supposed. If someone had put them up to it. The two lone strange men were possibilities. And then there was the big one—Troy Hughes.

One-Eyed Jack claimed Dell's friends had been

appalled when they'd learned the truth of what he'd been up to. But what if that was true for John and Ned, but not Troy? Or maybe he acted appalled, but wasn't. Hell, maybe he'd even been secretly part of the whole wolf lie, and we didn't know it? He was unemployed and friends with Dell. He might've been paid to do something or other.

Most importantly, he was the only person on Jade's list I knew for certain was connected to one of the murder cases.

He's as much a coward as he is a bully.

I wasn't afraid of Troy. If he thought he could get away with trying to intimidate me with sneak attacks executed in the dark, he had a shock coming.

If he had a problem with me, he could damn well say it to my face.

"WHAT CAN I HELP YOU WITH?" Mr. Oberton was short and wiry with skin as tanned and aged by the sun as the old leather pouch my Navajo grandmother used to carry. "Got a project?"

I looked around the hardware store, trying to think of something I could use. "I need a picture hanging kit."

"Got a couple of those you can choose from."

Mr. Oberton came around from the register and led me to the rear of the hardware store. He stopped at a section with various brackets and nails.

"This is a good one." He took a clear-cased package with a banner that promised *Endless uses*! "Has ten of the wire-type hangers, ten sawtooth brackets, D-rings, wall anchors, and hooks in silver and gold."

"Sounds good." I reached for the package.

He held it away. "Course, this'll last you a lifetime. If you're looking for something cheaper, this package of hooks is only five dollars. What are you trying to hang? Know the weight?"

"Oh, I have a lot of different types of things to hang, so this is perfect." I grabbed the bigger package from his hand. "Thanks for helping me find it."

"No problem. Anything else? We have a sale on hand warmers. Two for a buck."

"Um, sure."

I grabbed a dozen of the hand warmers. I knew the dogs would love them for curling up with.

At the checkout counter, I aimed for a casual air. "Say, do you know Troy Hughes? I heard he used to work here."

Mr. Oberton grimaced. "Briefly."

"Do you happen to know where he lives? I need to talk to him."

"Want a bag?"

"No thanks. I'll just carry them."

Mr. Oberton handed me the package and hand warmers and wriggled his nose, considering. "You know that little stone bridge on Route 10? Just outside of town."

"Sure."

"The Hughes family live about a mile past that, I'd say. On the right. There's an old blue barn."

"Thanks. I appreciate it."

I'd left Duke outside, and I took his leash as I exited, walking him to my car. We got inside, and I considered it.

Though Gabriel wouldn't admit it, I knew one of the reasons why he didn't want to tell me much about this case was because I'd gotten myself into hot water on the wolf case. Gabe seemed to think I was foolhardy. And I didn't want to prove him right, yet again. But someone leaving nasty-grams and stalking around my place was a different thing than a killer. And I just wanted to confirm Troy was the one harassing me.

Honestly, I'd feel better if I could do that. Like turning on a light and seeing that the scary noise was made by a banging window. Troy didn't frighten me. The unknown did.

I'd drive out there and see.

I found the house with the blue barn where Mr. Oberton said it would be, though the blue paint was peeling off the sides. Whoever had once painted it a lively peacock blue had apparently lost their artistic streak. Not only was it rundown, but the two-story farmhouse that had once been white with green trim was badly in need of updating, as well.

I paused at the end of the driveway. But I wouldn't get any answers by sitting there. So I pulled in.

I made up an excuse in my head—an inquiry about poker games—parked, and put on a brave face. I let Duke out and kept hold of his leash.

I let him sniff around. He sniffed the lawn and the porch steps. He didn't seem very interested.

In for a penny...

I knocked on the door. After a few moments, a woman answered. She appeared to be in her sixties, with thin graying hair plastered to her skull and a worn, plain face.

But her eyes were kind, and she smiled. "Hello, there. And who are you?"

I smiled back and meant it. "Hi. You must be Mrs. Hughes. I'm Tiber. I was wondering if Troy was around?"

She twisted her mouth and gave a little head bobble. "No. No, he isn't, young man. I believe he's out with the Jackson boys. I expect him home for dinner, though."

"Oh."

"And who's this?" She leaned down to pat Duke's head. She did it like someone unused to dogs, like you might pat your stomach after a full meal.

"This is Duke."

"Nice doggie. I have a cookie around here someplace."

I was going to tell her not to bother, but I figured it was between her and Duke, and I shouldn't interfere. She vanished and came back with what looked like a Nutter Butter cookie, which wouldn't hurt him.

She held it up, unsure. "Will he just take it, or…?"

"You can ask him to sit," I suggested. "And if you hold it out to him, he'll take it gently."

"Okay. Can the doggie sit?"

Duke sat, focused on the cookie. She held it out warily, and he took it extra slowly and delicately. He was such a damn good dog.

"You like that?" Mrs. Hughes cooed, as delighted as if she'd never given a dog a treat in her life.

"He loves it," I said. "And he likes you."

She beamed. "He does?"

"Definitely. See the way he looks at you? Well, thank you for the treat, Mrs. Hughes. I'll catch Troy later."

I gave Duke's leash a little tug and started to leave.

"Who should I say came by?" she asked, raising her voice.

"Um… tell him it was an old friend. He'll know."

Driving back to town, I snorted at myself. *He'll know.* Yeah, probably not. If his mom told him it was an Indian dude, Troy would probably try to think of some Makah guy he knew.

But now what? I paused at a stop sign. The rural intersection was deserted. Where else could I look?

Should I even look?

Shooting tin cans at the quarry.

I turned left.

One of the trails I'd hiked with Gabriel—off the maps, but known to a local boy like him—was called the bus trail due to an old, abandoned yellow school bus that had, somehow, ended up parked in the woods, all the windows broken out, and half-covered in vines. The parking for that trail was next to an old quarry, and the narrow ribbon of a path winding up into the hills began on those mined stone faces.

When the quarry had been abandoned, or even what they had been mining for, I had no idea. All Gabriel had said was that it was before his time.

Apparently, it was also a place people went for target practice. I heard the guns as soon as I drove up. I parked next to an old blue Ford pickup truck. An even older white one, a vehicle that looked odd with a small frame perched on top of huge tires, was parked next to it. Did one of those belong to Troy?

Duke perked up, excited. Damn, he recognized the trailhead. He'd been with me when I'd hiked it with

Gabriel. "Not today, buddy." I gave his neck a consolatory squeeze. "Next time."

He whined.

"I know. But we're still working. I'll be right back."

I left the truck and walked to the trail, climbed it until I could peer down into the quarry. Three guys were there. And, yes, they all had rifles. I recognized Troy Hughes. Hell, he was dressed pretty much as I'd seen him the first time—in olive green camouflage cargo pants and matching long-sleeved shirt. Only he wasn't wearing a hunting vest today. He had on a sleeveless gray fleece zip-up and sheepskin-lined hat with ear flaps. He was drinking a beer from a brown glass bottle.

I'd never seen the other two. What had Troy's mother called them? The Jackson boys? They were Makah, or at least native, one with straight black hair down to his butt and the other with thick, wavy black hair to his shoulders and a heavy face. They were around my age.

They were having a good time, with the long-haired one joking and egging on the other Jackson, who was shooting. I saw two cans go flying into the air. Hoots and laughter followed.

I felt a prickle of unease. I could walk Duke over there. See if he reacted to Troy.

But—hey, look at me being all responsible and shit—I wasn't going to. I had no idea what the two guys were capable of. Or Troy for that matter. And they had guns. As Libby would say, no bueno.

They hadn't seen me. I turned around and went back to my car.

I studied the two trucks in the parking lot. I might not

want to take Duke to see Troy. But that didn't mean I couldn't accomplish the next best thing. The white truck with the monster tires had a dreamcatcher hanging from the rearview mirror, so I assumed that one belonged to the Jacksons.

I could easily see into the bed of the blue truck. There were a couple of bags of lawn fertilizer that looked as if they'd been there awhile. A fishing tackle box. An orange hunting vest—filthy. A shovel.

The shovel caught my eye. It was an old one, but the blade was shiny and textured, like it had been whetted lately. There was a bit of dirt on it.

I picked it up and sniffed at the blade, then took the dirt between my fingers, and smelled it.

Something in the bed of the truck flapped. It was a black plastic garbage bag. It was empty, but it had been used. I checked to make sure no one was coming, put down the shovel, and grabbed the bag. I opened it looking for any trace of fur or blood. There was a little dirt on the black plastic, but its color made it hard to see much. I brought it to my nose and smelled it.

The shovel and bag would be just what a person would need to transport roadkill from the side of the highway to my front stoop. I didn't smell death on the bag. But maybe the raccoon had been frozen and had left little trace behind.

I sighed and put the bag and shovel back. There was no way to tell.

I got Duke out of the car. I squatted down next to him so I could peer into his eyes.

"The scent from our yard, Duke. And from the coffee shop. Find the scent, bud."

I kept him on leash, half afraid he'd scent Troy on the air and go running after him. I led him to the blue truck.

He sniffed all around it. He didn't react to anything.

"Duke, are you sure? Try again."

He sniffed half-heartedly at the blue truck's driver door again. Yawned.

Crap! I was so close!

I sighed, frustrated. Duke blinked benignly.

"Okay, let's try the other one."

I led him all around the white truck, but he didn't seem interested in it either. Surely, if he'd gotten excited smelling a person's scent on a chair in a public building, he'd smell it on the person's vehicle too, if it were there. Wouldn't he?

But it wasn't as if Troy sat on the *outside* of his truck.

I glanced toward the quarry. I heard another gunshot. They were still at it.

I checked the driver's door of the blue truck. It wasn't locked. I pulled the door open. Inside, the brown leather of the driver's seat had been patched with duct tape.

I patted the running board. "Up, Duke. Find the scent, buddy."

He put his paws up and stuck his head inside, scented the air. With an expression of distaste, he dropped back down again. The smell of cigarette smoke was thick and cloying in the truck cab, and he didn't care for it.

I sighed. Would smoke conceal the human scent? I didn't know. I thought scent dogs had finer control than that, but Duke wasn't a trained scent dog, so who knew.

Fuck Troy Hughes for being a smoker.

I was about to shut the door when I saw it. Stuck to the dash to the left of the radio was a photograph. I leaned in, but it was hard to see it from where I stood. I gave the quarry another glance, then pulled myself up into the seat, looked.

The photograph was of Troy and another man. They both wore neon orange hunting vests, and they stood in front of a buck strung up on a branch, both smiling proudly, guns on their shoulders.

The other man was Dell Prosser.

Chapter Seventeen

Gabriel

"HE'S BEING SET UP," Rick announced as soon as I got back to the office, then fixed his gaze on me. I was still in defense mode after watching him interrogate Sam yesterday, so I barely recognized what he'd said.

"He didn't do it—wait, what?"

Rick shrugged. "No killer would be that careless to leave the dead body in plain sight on his property, use his own kitchen knife, and leave the knife in a spot sure to be found. Too many coincidences, too much that just makes your brother the target. So, what happens next, Gabriel, is we find out who wants to frame him, or mess with your family, and then, we arrest them. But before that, we have no choice, we're close to arresting Sam based on the evidence we have, and you know that."

I nodded, despite the relief that flooded me, the knowledge that I had been doing my job right, and that my love and trust in Sam wasn't going to be questioned, was enough to render me silent on the arrest part.

Arrest didn't mean conviction if I proved Sam was innocent.

Which I would.

A knock interrupted my flood of relief, and the door opened with Devin poking his head in. He shuffled sideways, then closed the door behind him, and after the usual greetings, the three of us stared at the board.

"How does the arson fit into this?" Rick pondered.

"I'm not sure it does, unless you see something we don't."

Rick stood up and tapped the photo of the school and the list of the kids and the teacher. "Family?" he asked and tapped on Sarah and Aaron's names.

"Sure, but that has to be a..." coincidence? My blood turned to ice.

Sarah and Aaron had been in that place when it burned to the ground.

Sam and Lori were being raked over the coals, with Sam being framed for a murder he didn't commit.

"Maybe the connection isn't Sam, or the kids." Rick turned his speculative gaze on me. "Maybe it's you."

I returned the look, not sure what he wanted me to say. Nothing about what happened in LA could visit me here, and I hadn't caused ripples since I returned home, not to the extent someone would try to get to me through my family.

Of the people connected to what I'd done in the city, the main person was in prison, ill; and he might well find out where I was, but he was one man without connections now, a lesser being than he used to be. His son was dead, his right-hand man dead, but the hangers-on, the ones who did his dirty work? I had a list of them, and of the six, only one was still alive, and he, too, was in prison on a lengthy set of charges. It wasn't on me that he'd ended up in prison —that had been down to his own stupidity in dealing drugs to kids in a school and being caught in a sting.

No. It couldn't be *anything* to do with me.

We broke for air, the small room too cramped, and instead, headed into my office, where the three of us went through everything again.

"So, the fire?" Rick prompted Devin, who pulled his shoulders back and nodded.

"Yes, sir," he began, and detailed all the information we had to date, going through the crime scene photos as he did, so Rick got an idea of layout.

"Okay, so the kids got out, with the teacher."

"Thank god."

"Did the kids see anything?"

Devin shook his head. "They're real tiny, and they just remember it was half exciting and half terrifying."

"And the teacher, Samara? What do we know about her? Could this be an insurance job?"

"She's devastated, has lost way more than she could ever hope to get back if that was the case. She'd converted part of her house to form the preschool, but digging into her background has given us nothing but a picture of a person grieving for the loss of her home, and the danger to her kids."

"She used that term, 'her kids'?"

"Yeah, they meant a lot to her."

Rick nodded, then passed out photos to me and Devin. "Go over these pixel by pixel, then pass to the left."

I stared at each photo. Nothing about any of them stood out to me, nothing apart from the sadness of seeing melted toys and the half destroyed white board with the date still visible in the corner. How the thing had survived, I didn't know, but that along with a corner wall, was left standing.

I scanned the photo from left to right, then right to left, up and down, and peered at the board.

"Did Lucas have a theory about why that part survived?"

Rick ran a finger down a typed sheet. "The report says that the wall there is brick, part of an old chimney, and the alcove saved it from the accelerant used."

"And it's still standing now?" Rick asked.

"Cordoned off; it's safe."

I was restless, and staring at photos wasn't my thing. "I need a break." Rick nodded, Devin hovered, and I headed out, just to walk. Only my feet took me up the hill to Sam, and I found him in the kitchen filling a thermos with coffee.

"Can we talk?"

He jumped at my voice, seemed pale and agitated, but he sat down, the thermos on the table in front of him, and waited.

"All the evidence points to you," I said without preamble. The kitchen felt smaller than usual, the ticking of the clock on the wall unusually loud in the silence following my statement. I leaned back, rubbing my temple as I studied Sam. His expression was unreadable, a mask I knew all too well. "And as I said, I know it wasn't you."

He held my gaze. "So you said."

He needed to know that I believed it wasn't him who'd killed John. "And not just because you're my brother, but this is too many coincidences, so now we need to consider every possibility. Is there anyone who has a grudge against you? Disgruntled guests? Enemies in town?"

"No, nothing like that."

I searched for something else. "What about Lori's work? She's a nurse—have there been any recent incidents? Deaths? Families who've lost loved ones?"

Sam shifted in his chair, his expression was one of concern and reluctance. "Lori's dedicated, Gabriel. You know that. But in her line of work, not every story has a happy ending."

"But something that might have happened?"

"There was a case, a couple of months back. Lori doesn't share the confidential parts of it, but I know it didn't end well."

My heart sank. "An unhappy family?"

"Possibly. But it's a stretch to link that to what's happening now," Sam replied, his fingers tapping a slow rhythm on the table. "Should I be worried about the kids? I mean they've already had the fire and—" His eyes widened. "Was the fire connected?"

I shook my head. "Not that we can see."

"My kids, Gabe."

My niece and nephew. "We'll find who did this, just for now, keep everyone close."

He blanched, but nodded, and my thoughts drifted, trying to find something. *Anything*.

"What about Dad?" Sam asked.

"What about him?"

"In his final years, he wasn't himself. He offended people, but still… Those were tough times, and Dad was vocal, you know that, and he had feuds over land, over trails, misunderstandings."

"And anything that stands out?"

"No. Wait… maybe. A dispute over land, with the Harker family, I think. It got ugly, and even though the deeds the Harkers produced proved the land in dispute was theirs, Dad never did back down before he died."

"Could someone hold a grudge for so long?" I mused aloud.

"In this town? Grudges can last lifetimes," Sam said, a hint of bitterness in his voice.

"I'll pay them a visit." Then, I leaned forward, my resolve hardening. "We need to dig deeper into every possibility, Sam. Whoever is behind this knows you, and we can't take any chances."

Sam nodded, his gaze fixing on mine. "We have to figure this out, Gabriel. For Lori and the kids."

"And for you." As he spoke, I couldn't help but feel Sam and his family were facing an unseen enemy who might be closer than I imagined.

At least heading out to visit with the Harkers was a step in the right direction.

The Harker family owned a vast amount of land that

abutted the forest and spread down over the side of the mountain, almost reaching town, and going over as far as where the Thompson boundary sat. I couldn't imagine a feud from five years ago still causing issues today, given Dad was dead now, or that it could lead to murder, but that was what I was here to find out.

Inside the sprawling rustic ranch house, I settled into the chair across from Connor Harker, the patriarch of the Harker family, Devin choosing to perch on the edge of the sofa, casting his gaze around the room and making mental notes. It was steeped in history, each antique telling a story of the generations before, and Connor's eyes, though aged, held a sharpness that told me he was still keen and observant.

"Mr. Harker, thank you for agreeing to meet with me about the land dispute," I began.

He nodded, a gesture of acknowledgment, rather than warmth. "That's closed. The land is ours, so if young Sam thinks he can reopen something, then he'll just be throwing good money after bad."

"This isn't about Sam," I half lied.

Connor huffed. "Then let's get to the point, Sheriff. Why *are* you here, and what does it have to do with my land?"

I hesitated, then decided to rip off the Band-Aid. "I wanted to talk about the feud between our families. Specifically, the details surrounding the land dispute with my father."

Connor's jaw tightened, and his eyes darkened. "That land," he spat out the words, "cost me a fortune in legal fees. Your father was obstinate, clinging to false claims, coming over here, drunk off his head, spouting all kinds of nonsense about how I stole it from your grandpa."

"But you found the original plans that proved the land was yours," I pointed out.

"I did, but that doesn't erase the stress and the unnecessary tension it caused." His voice was laced with a residual resentment that seemed to have simmered for years. He paused, his gaze shifting to a photo on the wall —a younger version of himself standing among trees, which could have been taken on the land in question. "All I can say is that you two better not start up your daddy's shit again, or I'll have my lawyers on this in a flash. I don't have issue with you boys, but only if you keep out of my business. If you try to start things up again, you'll have a big problem."

"You're confirming that you still have an issue with the Thompson family, so one more question. Can you tell me where you were the day and evening of Wednesday, February fourteenth?"

He blustered, and went bright red. "Now hang on a damn minute, you're not going to pin that business on me to save your brother." He stared at me, then he met my gaze with a pleased expression. "I have nothing else to say. You need to leave." He stared at me, and I wished I could read his mind, but there was too much resentment in his expression.

"If you could just answer the question."

He came right up into my space and poked my chest. "Get out of my house."

"Sir, if—"

"Get out."

I met his gaze steadily. "We'll call you down to talk at the station."

He sneered at me. "You do that."

I COULDN'T STAY in the office all night because, not only was I driving myself mad, I was also missing Tiber. Maybe I should share more about Sam—after all what would it hurt? If gossip was working its way around Prophet, even Tiber, as solitary as he was, would hear about it sooner or later. I was home a little after ten, letting myself in and finding Tiber waiting for me in the hall. He grabbed me and held me tight, so much so I struggled to get the door shut and locked, but as soon as that was done, I kissed him, devoured him, held him close, and promised myself I'd never let him go.

He backed me up to the wall, pressed me there, and gripped my hair, holding me still for the deepest of kisses.

"Love you," he murmured between each one, every time we took a breath, and then, he slowed down, as if he'd stored up the kisses all evening and needed to get them done as soon as I walked in. Whatever the reason, it was exactly what I needed. I needed this—needed to reconnect with the good in my life, with my Tiber.

"Are you okay?" I asked, the hint of a laugh in my tone.

He took one last kiss, then tugged me out of the hall, passing the family, and straight into our bedroom.

"I will be," he said as he shut the door, but then, he stood there, seemingly lost over what to do next, as if all he'd thought about was getting here and being with me, and that was all he wanted.

After removing my uniform, I placed it with care over the chair he'd put there for me, and he watched me strip until I was naked, with him still dressed.

I stepped closer to him, closing the space with slow deliberation. Tiber's eyes held mine, a soft smile on his lips. My answer to the smile was in the gentle touch of my hand on his cheek, the slight tilt of my head as I leaned in for another kiss, and as we kissed, I helped him take off his clothes until he was just as naked, then I tumbled him back onto the bed and wriggled until he was sprawled over me.

"Missed you today," I murmured.

He kissed the words from my lips, sliding against me, and I groaned. I wrapped my arms around him, then couldn't settle on that, so carded my hands in his long hair and held him close.

"Missed you too," he whispered. "Missed you when I went out with... the dogs... missed you..." He was becoming less able to make sentences, and he kissed me hard, and we pressed and pushed, and then, he was coming between us, my orgasm hitting from nowhere.

I rolled him onto his back, stole more kisses, then padded off to find a washcloth, cleaning us up, before unspoken, we snuggled under the covers.

"I wanted to talk to you," I whispered into the dark.

He moved to his side, resting his cheek on my chest. "Yeah?"

"About the murder and... Sam. It's... it's not good."

He lifted his head, stared at me, then sat up, crossing

his legs. "Yeah, people in town are talking. Libby took me out for coffee to warn me."

"She did? They are?" The last thing I needed was for the town to turn against Sam. And then me.

"Tell me about it." His neutral tone put me on edge, but then, he softened it by smiling with encouragement. "I'm listening," he said, and the words were bright with emotion.

This was so hard to say. "The evidence we've found so far is pretty damning. Everything points to Sam. But I know he didn't do it."

Tiber frowned; his dark eyes clouded with worry. "Of course not."

"I've called in another sheriff to work with me because of the conflict of interest."

"That sounds wise."

"And he doesn't think it's Sam either. Thank God."

"Because Sam *didn't* do it." Tiber's words were simple, but they were spoken with such utter conviction a chill ran up my spine. Was that one of his intuitive insights? I wanted to believe it was. I already knew Sam was innocent, but having Tiber confirm it hit me deeper than I expected.

"Thank you," I said.

Tiber just looked at me like *of course*.

"It's already so knotted up with my family," I continued. "That's why I can't have you involved too. Not just for the optics but, fuck, for my sanity. I need to know you're apart from it. Safe. Can you understand that?"

"Yes," he said, though the brief hesitation in his voice

meant I didn't entirely believe him. "But what are you going to do, Gabe?"

"I'm going to find the person who actually murdered John Melchet." It came out with such force, it startled us both. "I have to. I have to save my brother. I let him down before. If I did again…" There was no use voicing the dark things that came to mind should that be the case. Bottom line: I wouldn't be able to live with myself.

"What can I do?" Tiber asked with so much sincerity it hurt my heart.

I wrapped a strand of his hair around my fingers. "Just knowing you're here, being able to have this, is everything."

He hugged me. "Thank you for telling me. You don't have to worry about me. We're fine. Just do what you need to do for Sam. I love you."

"Love you, too." I said.

After a long moment of holding each other, he got up to carry out late night chores with the pack. I joined him, feeling lighter for telling him about Sam, but wishing the prickle of unease that wouldn't leave me alone, would just fuck off.

Chapter Eighteen

Tiber

A COLD NOSE NUDGED ME. I pushed it away, but it came back, insistent, hard.

I opened my eyes, awake in an instant. That was not the usual nose nudge. I sat up.

The night light in the bathroom gave enough light through the open doorway for me to see Duke standing over me on the bed. He stared at me intently, then jumped down to the floor. He took a step toward the door to the hall and glanced over his shoulder at me expectantly.

I felt to my right to wake Gabriel, but the bed was empty. Oh, yeah. Last night, after he'd told me about Sam, he'd gone back to the office, too worried to rest. Poor man. He was getting very little sleep.

I couldn't blame him. Why did the evidence point to Sam? What the hell? I wanted to know more. I wanted to know everything. But I had to respect the boundaries he'd set. If that was all I could do to help him, then that was what I'd do. And I had faith that he'd find the real killer. I'd seen Gabriel work investigations before. He knew what he was doing.

But, damn, I itched to work through this puzzle with him. If only—

A soft growl from Duke brought me back to the moment. He was still at the door staring at me.

He'd woken me for a reason. Something was wrong. And I was alone.

A cramp of fear wracked my belly. But I couldn't wimp out now. I took a deep breath to will the fear away. I got up and pulled on sleep pants and a T-shirt, then padded after Duke.

He went straight to the front door. Silhouetted in the dim moonlight of the window was Leo, standing up with his paws on the windowsill by the door, staring out, his entire body rigid and shaking.

Wow. I knew the will it took Leo not to be barking his head off right now. I'd have to reward him later. For now, I cupped his head with my hand and, when he met my gaze, pointed toward the living room. He got down from the windowsill, but he didn't go far. Duke and Leo both stood behind me in the hall, practically doing a bird dog point at the door. Leo gave a tiny whine in his throat.

Sometimes, I wondered if my dogs actually understood me or if I was deluding myself. But then, something like this would happen. They understood me alright.

I peeked out the front window.

We had a half moon tonight, and not much cloud cover because I could see the white half-orb in the sky. It was still dark, though, my road not having any streetlights. I narrowed my eyes and tried to find anything among the shadows. I kept checking near the big tree, a looming black shape against the grayer background, because that was where I'd seen someone before. But there was nothing there. I scanned toward the driveway…

Something flashed, then vanished. I rubbed my eyes and looked again. Another flash. It was a barely there glimpse of a pale face under a dark hoodie.

Like the one worn by the figure I'd seen near the tree.

The same person was in my yard again. What were they doing this time? I couldn't make it out, but they were near the bushes lining the road. There was another flash to the left. They were walking across the yard. The person in the hoodie was outlined for a brief moment in a swatch of moonlight before they disappeared around the side of the house.

The backyard.

I hurried through the house, tiptoeing so as not to make noise. There was no gate through the fence on that side of the house. But they could climb over it, if agile.

If I saw them in the backyard… if they went for Frank, I'd have to stop them. No way were they taking Frank again. *No f'ing way.*

Was it Troy Hughes? Whoever it was had moved quickly, stealthily, and more gracefully than I'd expect from him, but maybe that was presuming too much. Just because he was a big guy, didn't mean he couldn't be graceful. I needed to get a good look at the figure's silhouette.

I didn't see the hooded figure in the backyard. Frank's pond was in the middle of patchy lawn and visible in the moonlight. One clawed foot stuck out of his little shelter. He hadn't been bothered yet.

I hunted around for a weapon and grabbed a poker from the set by the woodstove, then returned to the back door.

I still saw nothing.

Suddenly Leo and Duke, who'd come with me to the back windows, raced for the front of the house again. I followed.

The hooded figure crossed my front yard again. Had they figured out there was no gate on that side? Were they going to go around to the other side of the house?

But no. They jogged down the driveway and turned right onto the road.

They were getting away. I had to act fast.

"Stay here!" I hissed at the dogs, then slipped out of the door, and ran, still carrying the poker.

Maybe it was stupid not to bring the dogs. But I was hoping to stay in stealth mode. Get a license plate number, or maybe even see the blue truck belonging to Troy. If the dogs had been loose, they would have chased and jumped the person, necessitating a confrontation. And maybe they'd even be hurt. That couldn't happen.

I was barefoot, which helped me stay quiet, but the ground was frosty and cold. I crouched low, using my car as a shield, and then a bush. I heard a car engine start. Damn. No lingering then.

As I heard the car pull away, I forgot stealth and ran to the road. A car accelerated toward town. It was a sedan, dark in color. I tossed the poker and sprinted after it, needing a better look. But it picked up speed. There was no way I was catching up.

It drove out of sight, and I stopped, bent over, and breathing heavy. Damn it! I'd had the culprit. They'd been in my yard. The dogs had done their job in alerting me, but I'd failed to do my part.

Had the car been black? Dark blue? Dark gray? If I had to guess, I'd say black. It had been a four-door and the back sloped a bit. Maybe an Audi? Or maybe one of a dozen cars with a similar profile.

Not Troy Hughes then. But what if he was smart and, thinking he might be spotted, he'd borrowed his mother's car? Or a friend's.

I'd learned nothing.

I walked back home, ticked off at myself. My bare feet left marks on the road where they melted the frost. God, it was cold. I picked up the pace and let myself back in the house with relief.

Duke and Leo were waiting. Leo decided he could bark now, and he did, letting it all out, his little body shaking with fury.

"I know," I reassured him. "The nerve of that person!"

There was no point going back to bed, so I turned on the lights. I wondered if One-Eyed Jack would have any ideas about who owned a sedan like that. Everyone in town was in his parking lot once a week or more.

Leo continued to give the front window a talking to.

Ferdinand, Gracie, and Duke all stood watching me. Fudge wove in and around Duke's legs, but Patch was probably still asleep somewhere.

Ferdinand padded over to the sliding door to the backyard, looked at me.

"All right. I need to check on Frank anyway," I told him.

I opened the back door, and we all spilled onto the deck. The dogs scattered to sniff around for the stranger or take a leak. I went to the pond.

Frank's clawed foot was still sticking out of the shelter. It felt cool to the touch but very much alive. I was startled when Frank's head poked out of his carapace. It was so dark out; I'd thought he was the other way around.

"You okay?" I asked him.

He blinked at me as if I was crazy, then withdrew completely into his shell.

"It's fine. Go back to sleep."

Leo was still barking. He was barking at Ferdinand, the basset hound, who was scrounging something near the fence.

Gracie stood at the back door wanting to be let in. I walked up the steps to the deck and opened the door for her. But Leo's barking was insistent, high, as if he were still barking at the intruder. I turned to look, uneasy.

Had the stranger come back?

But Leo was barking at *Ferdinand*. Who was eating something.

Something near the fence.

"Drop it!" I screamed, and I ran. *Oh fuck. Oh no.*

Ferdinand didn't drop it, not until I'd yelled it a few more times and grabbed a corner of whatever he had in his mouth. It was a piece of plastic. A big piece of cellophane wrap. The butcher's department sticker was still on it. And a few small bits of meat.

Hamburger. It had been a package of hamburger.

I was a goddamn idiot. The stranger didn't need to *climb* the fence to do harm. He only had to *drop something over it.*

"Oh, baby," I sobbed, grabbing ahold of Ferdinand. "Everyone in the house! Now!"

I didn't know if there was more hamburger in the yard or if any of the other dogs had gotten into it. All I knew for certain was that Ferdinand, who would eat anything, *had* ingested it. Maybe the whole package.

"Go! Go!" I got them all inside, away from anything else that might be in the backyard. Ferdinand was startled by my anxiety as I hurried him along holding his collar.

Once inside, I tugged Ferdinand to the laundry room and shut us both inside. I knelt down beside him.

He was ten, which was a senior for a basset, and the dark brown patches around his droopy eyes were speckled with gray. His gaze shied away from mine, and his head hung. But he looked more guilty than sick so far.

"I'm not mad at you," I said, trying to sound calm. No, I was mad at *me*. "But you ate something bad, Ferd. I'm so sorry. It's going to be okay; I promise."

God, I hoped so. I kissed his head and stood, breathing hard. It was two a.m. The vet's office in town was closed, and the twenty-four-hour emergency clinic in Forks was too far away.

My instinct was to get Ferdinand to throw up—fast. But that could be dangerous. It depended on what he'd eaten. If there'd been tacks, nails, or broken glass in the hamburger, vomiting could make things worse.

I left him in the laundry room, ignored the anxious milling of the rest of the pack, grabbed a flashlight from the hall closet, and ran outside again—still barefoot, still without a coat.

If the stranger had left one package, maybe he'd left more. I searched by the fence where Ferdinand had been eating, but I didn't find anything else. I ran over to the other side of the house, checked by that fence, and found nothing. I let myself out into the front yard.

I found it by the bushes where I'd first spotted the intruder. There was a large, round ball of raw hamburger meat partially wrapped in plastic. I grabbed it and ran back inside. In the kitchen sink, and under the glaring overhead light, I smooshed through the hamburger, looking for dangerous objects. But all I found was a clump of white powder in the center of the ball.

Poison then. Maybe rat poison. But nothing sharp. So there was hope.

I put the tainted hamburger into a Tupperware container to take to the vet and stuck it in the fridge to make sure the other animals couldn't get it. Then, I grabbed the hydrogen peroxide solution from the bathroom, and went in to make Ferdinand vomit. A lot.

I was up with the poor guy for the rest of the night. We were lucky, I'd caught it right away. The hamburger meat he yakked up was undigested, and it seemed about as much volume as was in the ball I'd found out front. But it was possible some of the poison had gotten into Ferd's system. The vet could give him IV fluids and monitor his organs for damage.

By the time dawn came, he lay sleeping uneasily on the linoleum floor, but he wasn't in the clear. I left him resting and took a quick shower. The vet clinic opened at eight, and I planned to be there with him when it did.

I went outside again, this time with Duke on a leash. I led him around the front and the back, looking for anything else the intruder could have left behind, and trusting Duke's nose to find anything I missed. But there was nothing else.

So my hooded friend had left two poisoned balls of hamburger about the size of a baseball, one in the front, and one in the back. Did he not know how many animals I had? Or what part of the property they had access to? Or maybe he did. Maybe, the goal had not been to kill them all, but just one or two. He was escalating, but he was taking his time about it. The thought made me sick.

I led Duke back to the front door, but instead of letting us in, I squatted down on the stoop and put my hands on his shoulders. "You and Leo did fantastic last night. You're such a good boy."

Duke whined.

"It's not your fault Ferdinand was hurt, and he's going to be okay."

Duke panted and glanced away.

"I promise he will. But we need to nail this person."

This time, Duke's bark was enthusiastic.

"When I get back from the vet, you and me will go into town again, and we'll walk around until we find the stranger's scent. Are you with me, Duke?"

Duke pawed my knee. He was definitely onboard.

I knew I should tell Gabriel about this. Letting him focus on the murder case was one thing, but now my pack was being threatened at home, and that was damn serious. Yet, the memory of the anguish he felt over Sam, the worry he'd confessed to me last night, was still fresh in my mind, my heart.

I would decide later, I told myself. I wouldn't see Gabriel until tonight, anyway. Until then, Duke and I had some work to do.

Chapter Nineteen

Gabriel

HEN GLANCED up at me from the front desk as I stepped back into the office, my hands filled with to-go cups from Grounds of Joy.

"Oh, you're in," I said.

"I heard you were here all night." She gave me a dirty look, shaking her head.

"Not *all* night," I hedged.

"Uh-huh. Rick left a message; he's out at the Harker place following up on your interview."

"Okay."

"And I have an Officer Jennings on line one for you, something about ANPR?"

I gestured toward my office, stole a fresh muffin, and headed inside, pressing the one as I lifted the receiver.

"Sheriff Thompson speaking."

"Good morning, Sheriff. I wanted to give you a heads-up on the email I'm sending regarding your ANPR request, which I'm copying to your deputy, Devin Randall."

"Thank you for getting back to us so fast."

"Not a problem. The plate number you gave us was caught by a fixed ANPR on the 101 just outside Forks. It was also caught by a mobile unit in the Timber Museum area. I'm sorry I can't be of any more help than that."

"Are there photos?"

"It was dark, but you can see the car and number plate, yes; the driver not so clearly, sorry."

I already had the feeling that would be the case—because that was just the way the luck was running. I thanked her and opened the email, checking both captures. The mobile unit one was inconclusive, however the one by the Timber Museum picked up the shape of the driver, albeit blurred. Still. I *knew* my brother, and it *was* him in the car. Sam had been in Forks at the time John Melchet was murdered, which backed up his alibi, given that forensics confirmed the victim had met his end right where we'd found him. It was the first real break we'd had, and I felt a wave of relief. But now what?

Devin strode in. "Security footage from the bank is here. Check your email." I found the email and let Devin poke at my keyboard until my screen filled with a black and white feed from the bank. The image was made of five filled squares and one blank one, and each was labeled: *front entrance*, *back entrance*, *parking*, *lobby*, *tellers*, and *manager*.

"Just the five? What happened to the one labeled manager?"

"Alarm company found a fault—ongoing, since fixed

—but the camera was offline for that day. I got suspicious, but when I saw the logs, it didn't appear deliberate, and the crossover from the lobby and tellers catches most of that area anyway."

We'd received the feed for the entire day of Tuesday, February 6th. Checking my notes, I saw that Sam had been there for an eleven a.m. appointment. I scrolled back to nine and checked from there.

"I have Sam in the parking, arriving ten-seventeen," Devin announced. "Sam moves to go inside, but then, sits at the bench outside near his truck. Ten-eighteen."

I made a note of the times, kept scrolling and reached ten twenty-three, when I hit on another man walking up to the bank. He paused at the door, then took a seat next to Sam on the bench.

Tall and thin, hair color indistinguishable under a black baseball cap, wearing a black suit. I paused it. "Ten twenty-three. Who is this guy? Wait, Sam mentioned something about talking to a guy at the bank who was angry at the world. Said he had tattoos, although we don't have records on what those tattoos were."

"That tracks. No good visuals on his face though."

To be honest both men were blurry and grainy, and I only recognized Sam because I knew him. I hated the way he was sitting so dejected on the bench. That was on me. If I'd never left town, if I hadn't become a cop, if I hadn't taken on the undercover responsibility, I could have been at home helping him.

Maybe this never would have happened.

Devin let out a thoughtful hum. "Is this guy important?"

"I don't know. Keep going."

The feed advanced. Ten thirty-six, the stranger put away his phone and said something to Sam. He pointed at the sky, probably talking about the weather. I caught a blurry glimpse of a dark pattern on his hand, so that was *the guy with tattoos* Sam had mentioned. I just wished the man would stare up at the camera so I could get a full look at his features, but the bill of his cap shadowed his face. It was kind of odd wearing a ball cap and a suit. Was he deliberately hiding from the camera? But he wouldn't do that unless he was there to cause trouble. And why would he be?

"Conversation getting heated," Devin murmured. "Ten fifty-three, Sam strides into the bank, visibly upset."

"Stay on tall guy, I'll track Sam."

"On it."

I switched to the lobby cam, watched my brother's expression as he passed through, determined, fixed on his purpose. I knew that stance—he was angry, wound up, sick of everyone's shit, and very different from the hunched dejection I'd seen when he'd first sat on that bench. I switched to the teller's point of view, but Sam wasn't in frame for long, and then, cameras caught him storming back out and getting into his truck. There was nothing that caught the argument he was alleged to have had with the victim. The parking cam caught him leaving, and I scrolled back on that cam to spot the tall guy leaving, catching the glimpse of the trunk of a car.

"Eleven-oh-three, you recognize the make of that car?" I asked Devin.

He shook his head after he stared. "Maybe a smaller SUV, they all look the same these days."

No number plates visible, no evidence either way to accuse or exonerate. Just a whole load of Sam getting pissed and storming into a bank, then coming out and leaving. And even if the tall man had egged Sam on, what of it? Talking wasn't illegal.

I felt sick, a cold iciness flooding me, something about that tall man made my hackles rise, in the way he sat maybe? Or maybe the way he pointed at the sky? Or how he walked? I couldn't see what made me feel so weird. Was he familiar? Maybe local?

"Okay, let's get some data down on this, can you do me a time-stamped report, let's say between nine and twelve. Attach the report from the security company about the camera that was broken. Cover all of our bases with screen prints. Okay?"

"Yes, sir."

After an hour more of staring, and unable to shake the weird vibes, I needed air, so I pushed my chair away from my desk. "I'm going to head out to pick up lunch. Do you want anything?"

"The usual, sir," Devin muttered, distracted, nose already deep in papers and scowling at the printer, and poking it because it wasn't printing a damn thing.

Rick caught me on my way out. "Heading out to get some lunch, you want anything?" I asked.

"Not for me, thanks."

"What did you get from Connor Harker?"

"All polite and aww shucks, no sign of the anger he showed you, has an alibi, says his wife threw a surprise birthday for a great grandson, and in his words, *everyone* was there. I'll write it up, and I've requested he send over photos so young Devin can confirm details."

"Okay."

I headed out, lining up at the coffee shop, waiting for my turn, checking my messages, seeing a couple from Tiber with attached photos and opening them up because I needed a smile. I sent back love, I added kisses, but he wasn't there to reply straight away, so I pocketed my cell.

"Morning Sheriff," someone said from behind, nudging my arm to get my attention. I glanced back and bit back a groan. Daisy Simmonds. Incurable gossip, owner of the Lake Prophet Hotel, a two-star B&B I'd once had the misfortune of staying in before I bought my little house off Main. Now, of course, I was living with Tiber. In Tiber's house. It struck me that I needed to shift the rest of my stuff out of my place. As if I'd ever have the time for that.

"Sheriff?"

I'd zoned out. "Ms. Simmonds, hello." I pasted on my best smile, because I needed to shove aside all the weirdness happening in my town, and focus on being the nice guy people expected me to be. Daisy was wearing her fake sympathy expression, and I waited for her to launch into a whole list of questions.

"Daisy," she corrected and touched my arm, getting a little too close. "You know after what we went through, you can call me Daisy."

What *I'd* gone through was a victim of a murder having stayed in her hotel, and of course, suspects and perpetrators staying there. There wasn't a *we* in there at all.

"Daisy," I acknowledged and widened the space between us.

"Terrible trouble at Sam's place," she offered.

I stiffened, although I tried hard to keep my smile in place. I glanced back at the line, two people in front of me now, and for a wild moment, I considered calling for a law enforcement favor and jumping the line, only that wasn't me, so I was left sandwiched between a tourist, evidenced by her fist full of Bigfoot merchandise, and Daisy.

"Hmmm," I offered, thanking the heavens that the person at the front of the line finished, passing me with a tray of coffees. It was John Slater from the garage. He inclined his head, and I nodded back. Now that was the kind of interaction I liked.

"Always the good ones. I liked Sam, a lot."

I bit my tongue to stop from spewing out a ton of defense for my brother. Daisy was acting as if there was guilt there, and I knew in my heart Sam was innocent. She pursed her lips when I didn't answer, her expression sly. "Heard that you have a new sheriff checking it out, given that the suspect in a horrible murder is your brother. I guess." She eyed me with speculation gleaming in her eyes, and I returned the look with a steady gaze.

Please let this line move.

In front of me, the tourist dropped eight keyrings, I counted them, plus two mugs, and when she began to ask questions about the different color options, I had to pull rank. A little, anyway.

"Excuse me," I said to Mrs. Tourist, leaning past her. "Jade, can I order the usual for us all, plus a coffee, cream and two sugars, and some sandwiches?"

Jade blinked at me, then smiled. "Of course."

"I'll send Devin in for them."

"It's okay, Sheriff, I'll drop it all with Hen."

"Thank you."

I sidestepped Daisy without even the courtesy of an imaginary tip of my hat, and then, hurried back to the office before she got it in mind to talk some more.

And I walked into chaos.

Rick was on the phone, shouting at someone about the fact they should ignore budget cuts and try, Hen was tapping away at her keyboard, and there was Devin in the middle of it, pale and looking confused.

"What?" I asked him.

"I don't know," he answered, "I think I found…" He headed back into the incident room. Rick ended his call with added drama and went in, gesturing for me to follow.

All three of us bundled in, but both of them gave me space.

"It's the bank surveillance. I almost missed it," Devin murmured. "But I went right past midday ten past, and the car came back, with the tall tattooed guy."

"He came back, the same day?"

"Yep. Show him," Rick prompted.

Devin pressed play, and yes, the car was back, and the tall man, baseball cap still pulled down to conceal his face, stood right where the security camera could capture him. He pushed back his sleeves, lifting a coffee cup and saluting, as if he was playing for the camera, and then, paused a moment before heading out of frame.

"The fuck?" I asked, and Rick nodded.

"That look deliberate to you?? Rick asked.

"Yeah."

"So Devin paused it. Show him Devin."

Devin rewound, paused at a particular moment, fussing to get it right, and I almost snapped at him to get it done already given how tense the room was. Then, he stepped back, an image frozen on the screen. No face, still hidden, but there was a view of tattoos, too blurred for accuracy, but that seemed like it could be a cross, then some curved leaf design, wrapped around the man's arm, ending at his hand.

"Is that a cross? And flowers?" I murmured, and then, the wind left me, cutting me off at my knees, and I slumped into the chair. "Shit." No. It couldn't be.

"This means something to you?" Rick asked, his hand on my arm, trying to jolt me out of whatever I'd slunk into.

"It could be a coincidence. It could be nothing." Who was I kidding?

"What does it mean?" Rick pressed. "You know this tattoo?"

"Something like it, maybe. Possibly. I don't know."

That urgent push of fear and worry was right back, poking at me, and I felt sick. The cross and the vine had been what Cyrus Vine had tattooed on his arm, and some of the guys who worked for him had the same design off their own backs—wannabe gangsters. He'd never asked anyone to do that, said he found it distasteful they were appropriating his own past pains, and was horrified when his son decided to have the same thing inked on his arm.

It had to be a coincidence.

But why would this man have stood so obvious, in front of the camera with that coffee?

Why show us the tattoo?

What the fuck?

Hen knocked on the door, calling to say that coffee and lunch was here, and I yanked open the door, striding into my office, turning at the last moment. "I need time," I explained, almost snapping the words. Then, I shut my office door in everyone's faces, and pulled out my cell. Lincoln answered on the third ring.

"Hey, Gabriel," he began with a smile in his voice as if I was calling to shoot the breeze. What I was about to say would rock everything, drag me back to what had happened in LA.

"The cross and the vine, Linc. The fucking cross and the vine."

Lincoln was silent. Then, he cursed, and I could hear him moving about, and waited for him to react. "Okay. Start from the beginning."

I explained about the security footage, my voice shaky, screen-grabbed it, and sent it to Lincoln who acknowledged receipt, then listened without interrupting.

"This could be a coincidence," he echoed my thought.

"But it's not, is it," I said. "I need you to check in with Cyrus Vine. If this is him, then I want whatever is happening here to stop, because they're pulling my brother into this, framing him for something he didn't do. What the fuck, Linc?"

"I'll call in some favors, but don't jump to conclusions just yet, okay?"

"I have a freaking sheriff here taking over the case. What happened in LA wasn't supposed to get shared. I was done. It was finished."

"I'm on it, Gabe, okay?"

We ended the call when there was nothing else to say. Lincoln calmed me down enough that I was okay to go back out and lie about what I'd seen. He reassured me that Cyrus Vine had no power, that he was an old man, sick, dying of liver disease, lost in his own head, and remained incarcerated.

"And?" Rick asked as soon as I stepped out.

I pasted on my game face. "I thought I recognized the tattoo, not from seeing one before, but the intent. I was wrong. My sources tell me I'm wrong."

"Do you want to share your sources?" Rick pushed, and Devin looked curious.

"I thought it might be connected to an undercover case I worked, my old handler says I'm wrong to jump at that particular shadow is all."

"Okay." Rick stared at me for a moment, and I knew he wanted to ask more, but the code of undercover work was that it remained that way for as long as possible. Devin printed off the frozen screen, cursing at the printer again.

And I drank my coffee.

Choked down some sandwich.

And forced back the fear that was stuck in my chest.

Chapter Twenty

Gabriel

I'M CAUGHT IN A NIGHTMARE.

I know it's not real, I know if I just reached out for Duke I could stop this, but there's nothing rational about what is happening. I'm on a bench, and it's so cold that it chills my bones, and I'm shivering. There's a man sitting with me, a silhouette against the wooden siding of the bank. It's odd, but all the people walking past don't seem to notice him. I do. I can't help but stare. He's staring back, not at me, but at a security camera above a doorway. His face... It's a blank canvas, devoid of features, yet covered with tattoos that slither and writhe like living things over his skin. There's a silence in the air, and I try to talk to him, but I can't get the words out.

"Gabriel!"

The world flips.

Suddenly, I'm not on the bench anymore. The cold is replaced by heat—an intense, scorching, suffocating heat.

Smoke curls around me, stinging my eyes, clawing at my throat. Fire. Everywhere, fire. It's licking at the edges of my vision, crackling, and consuming everything in its path. I'm terrified and my feet can't move. I can hear someone screaming—a desperate, haunting sound clawing at my insides. "Help him! Help him!"

"Gabriel! Wake up! Duke, help me!"

The voice is familiar, a voice that means home, means safety. But I can't see them. I can't find them. I'm running, but I don't know where to. My lungs are burning, and I have to get away. I have to find the voice. But Joe is there; he's crying and screaming for me to save him as he falls into the flames and vanishes, and the fire is burning hot and—

I woke up on the floor, the covers strewn around me, Duke barking in my face, pawing at my chest, and no sign of Tiber.

Shit!

The remnants of the nightmare clung to me, the heat of the fire still prickling my skin, the echo of the screams vibrating in my ears, and I needed Tiber. Where was he? Was he in the fire?

I scrambled to stand, and then, Tiber was there, helping me up, and I grabbed him and held him tight until he eased himself away and flicked on the bedside light. His eyes were wide with shock, and there was blood.

Why was there blood?

"What did I do?" I asked desperately, and he reached up to touch his lip, then pulled back his hand and stared down at the blood.

"I'm okay. I caught my chin on the wall."

"How? Did I push you?" Oh god, I hurt Tiber.

"I tripped."

All my breath left me in a rush, and I collapsed on the side of the bed, burying my face in my hands, Duke pushing at my leg. I stopped to scratch his ear, and he whined up at me.

"Sorry," I apologized, to Tiber and Duke. "I think I'm going to…" I couldn't find words. "I'll leave you to sleep." I kissed Tiber and hugged him. "Go back to bed."

I stumbled out into the kitchen, my limbs heavy and the shadows making me jump. I switched on the lamp in the front room, and both kitchen lights, all the animals waking up and letting me know they were there.

"Cocoa?" Tiber asked from behind me.

I whirled on him, realizing he'd followed me out. "I'll do it, go back to bed."

He moved past me to organize drinks, then pulled down a tin of cookies, shooing animals away from the sofa until I could sit down, then he covered my knees with a blanket, curled into the corner with his own blanket, facing me, his feet just a few inches from my leg, and cradled his cocoa. The pack all crowded around. All except one.

I blinked. "Where's Ferdinand?"

Tiber grimaced. "At the vet's. He, um, he got into something bad yesterday."

I felt a stab of alarm. "What? Why didn't you tell me?"

Tiber held up a hand. "Because you're busy. He's fine. Vet says we got it in time. Don't worry. He just kept Ferd there overnight to give him another batch of IV fluids."

I took a deep breath. "Good."

"Now talk to me," Tiber pressed. "What's going on?

You came in so late, we never got to check in. Did something happen yesterday?"

"Nothing that makes any sense." I thought of the man at the bank and found myself shaking my head in confusion.

"Okay," Tiber said. "You don't want to talk about the case. Then tell me about the nightmare."

"The fire at the preschool. The murder. It all gets inside my head and mixed up."

"You thrashed out, and you were calling for someone."

I stared at Tiber. "Who? What name?"

"Joe," he said, and my heart stopped. "You said you couldn't save him." He stopped, stared down at his drink, then glanced up, and his dark eyes were bright with emotion. "Who is Joe?"

I could sit here and pretend I had no idea, call it a figment of a nightmarish imagination, but I'd be lying. Tiber was looking at me with such compassion, and I knew, then, that I needed to explain about the horrors I kept inside, otherwise, his compassion might well turn into hate against for closing myself off.

"I had to leave him," I blurted, the pain of it ripped from inside me, then I repeated it so low it was barely noise at all. "I had to leave Joe."

Patch jumped onto my lap, circling, and curling into a tiny ball. I owed Tiber an explanation, and if it started with the bare bones of what happened, then that was how it had to be. What if he ended up hating me?

"I was undercover, part of a team that takes rookies, or the newer cops, and puts them out there in the world to…" No, that wasn't how to start it. I signed up for the undercover stuff, and the blame was mine. "See, when you're a rookie, no one on the streets knows you, add in that I was gay, and I fit with the Vine family from day one."

"Family? You mean Mafia?" Tiber's eyes were wide.

"No. Shit, no." I stopped to sip at the now cooling cocoa, then smoothed a hand down the mound of Patch's furry back and butt, the movement soothing. "But the dad, Cyrus Vine, was keen on his son following him into the family business, meth mostly, but guns as well, lots of bad stuff going down." I swallowed, hard, the rest of the story stuck in my throat. Tiber knocked my knee with his foot, and I glanced up at his encouraging smile. "Don't hate me."

"Nothing you could do would make me hate you, Gabriel. I know you. I love you."

We'll see. "So, we had this arranged meet. Cyrus' son, Joe, was gay, so he was the perfect in for me to infiltrate, and my backstory was a wannabe loser type who had ideas beyond his capability. Lots of swagger, bright clothes, kind of annoying."

"The opposite of you, then."

I shrugged. "Cyrus liked me, told me I was a good match, confident to his son's quiet side. I was undercover nearly two years, and it got to the point where..." I stopped, and Tiber nudged my knee again, and Duke pressed his cold nose on my hand. "I forgot my own name, y'know, like I was more my undercover name than I was Gabriel."

"What was your undercover name?"

"Zachary Owens. Zach is what they called me."

He regarded me with a gentle expression, tucking stray hair behind his ear. "You definitely don't look like a Zach."

"What do I look like?" I needed the breather to ask that.

"You look like a Gabriel. My angel."

I rolled my eyes at that one, but the humor in his eyes did lighten the mood a little. "Well, Joe fell in love with Zach, or at least Joe fell in love with the undercover me. He was actually a good kid…" I paused again. "Well, not a good kid, but not as fucked up as his dad. His dad hated that Joe wasn't interested in the business, so he had a bodyguard assigned, who clung to him like glue and was always trying to get him involved in something or other, and Joe would go out of his way to avoid him." I scrubbed at my face. "See that is what happened; my opinion of him was skewed, and I was looking for the good in him, even if he was running his own shit—porn, coke. He wasn't a saint, only somehow, I thought maybe I could save him."

"But you couldn't."

"There wasn't even the possibility of it. Joe wanted more without getting his hands dirty, but I could have stopped him…"

"Gabe? You can't control everything."

"No, I know," I admitted, and my belly hurt. "I couldn't have stopped Joe any more than I could have stopped his dad. I fed as much intel as I could, daily, back to my handler, and when I got word of a location for labs outside the city, and a huge shipment of raw materials, with Cyrus widening his net, it was the culmination of all that work. Word came down that we were closing it down; we were finishing it."

"Did you?"

"We tried. I left Joe at home, told him to stay. I wanted him safe, because Jesus, whatever his faults, he was still young, and I still had that hope he'd turn out different from his dad, you know? Shit, he was only twenty-three."

"And you were?"

"Not much older," I admitted. "That's not the point."

"So, tell me what the point is?"

I ignored that, intent on getting this out before I lost the will to do so. "It went down, but Joe turned up, there was a gunfight, an explosion, fire. We arrested Cyrus—he's behind bars—and my job was done."

"But what happened to Joe that it chases you in your nightmares?"

Jesus, this was the hard part. "Joe was caught in the fire, he fell through a floor, vanished right in front of me, and he screamed for my help, but he was trapped, and I couldn't reach him. SWAT made me move back, but Joe's bodyguard dragged me, put a gun to my head, he was going to kill me, and I told him he should never had let Joe come there. He shot at me, but the floor shifted, the shot went wild. There was another explosion. I was lucky I was far enough back. The bodyguard panicked; he was desperate to get to Joe—I don't know why. Maybe he felt guilty, maybe Cyrus' wrath would be worse than dying. Whatever it was, he ran into the fire."

"They both died?"

I nodded. "The fire burned for days. And then, it was

over. I was done, and I resigned, buried myself in alcohol, fucked up everything. And then, I came home."

Tiber's eyes were so full of sympathy it hurt my chest. "That's your recurring nightmare. About Joe and the fire."

I nodded. "The fire, Joe begging me for help, me not being able to reach him, the smell, the pain, the horror." I scrubbed at my eyes. "Fuck."

I fell silent, wrung out by the nightmare and the emotions of everything I'd told Tiber. I needed him to react so I could deal with whatever happened, but he poked me with his foot again, and when I glanced up, he was crying silent tears.

"I'm sorry. I didn't mean to make you cry? I can leave, I don't have to—"

He scrambled over to me, Patch went flying, Duke walked backward into a table, and then, Tiber was clinging to me, hard.

"It must hurt so much," he said over and over against my neck, and then, I heard the one thing that I would remember forever. "I love you, Gabriel Thompson. I couldn't love you more. And I'm here, okay. I'm always here."

IN THE OFFICE, the morning after the nightmare, in the cold light of day, the fear subsided a little. I felt better for telling Tiber, and he hadn't turned on me, or hated me. He understood, and that seemed to be what I needed.

I called Lincoln as soon as my butt hit the chair, and it was as if he was waiting for me to call.

"Gabriel, it's all clear on Cyrus. he's not got long now,

and he's not physically or mentally capable of being responsible for what is happening in your town. He's lost all his power, doesn't hold any sway in the prison, or out. I worked down the list, and with the people who worked for him dead, I can't see a single reason why it would be him messing with you."

"I wrote a list of people close to the Vine family, people who could have known about me, and it has six names," I said. "Then, adding on Cyrus, of course, that makes seven. I've accounted for them all, the only one who isn't dead is Harry Lawson."

"Yep. And he's serving twenty in Oregon State. He was a barely educated wannabe and a small cog in Vine's operation. It's a stretch that he would be able to reach you."

I ran my finger down the list I had. At the top and discounted for now was Cyrus Vine himself. After all, Lincoln had checked and removed him for me. Not only that, but I'd done my own research, and he was a shell of a man, physically, mentally, and yeah, he held no sway at the prison hospital he was dying in. So that left six—the ones that I wanted to account for, because fuck, ice trickled down my spine and my hackles were up.

One. *Tony Austin, arrested at the warehouse, dead in prison.*

Two. *Victor Arbor - shot and killed at warehouse.*

Three. *Jemma Melrose - shot and killed at warehouse.*

Four. *Harry Lawson - alive. Serving 20 in Oregon State for murder.*

Five. *Joe Vine - Cyrus' son - dead in warehouse fire.*

Six. *Mario Terrell - bodyguard to Joe, dead in warehouse fire.*

I only had one other idea. "What about the civilians we rescued, the ones forced to work on the product?"

"Jesus, Gabriel, now you're reaching. You freaking *rescued* them and got them back to their families, they're not going to come after you." He made it sound as if I was paranoid—and I was. The nightmare was so real, me watching the floor collapse under Joe, me trying to reach him, but stepping back, unwilling to die for him, and then, Mario trying to shoot me, and him running into the fire.

A horrific death in a blazing inferno that burned so hot it had taken down the entire block.

"Sorry to worry you with all this," I apologized.

Lincoln snorted. "What else am I gonna do in retirement? Learn flower arranging?"

The dichotomy of Lincoln flower arranging with his big beefy hands made me snort, and it helped to lighten some of the lingering fears from last night. We said our goodbyes, but I was barely off the phone, in the middle of texting Tiber about how much I loved him—because, yes, I was that man now—when Devin shoved open my door without knocking.

"You need to see this," he announced, then vanished, so I assumed I needed to follow him. I found him in front of our case boards, pinning up a photo time stamped with today's date.

"So the school site is open," Rick said and pointed at the board. This was about the fire? I needed to switch gears and focus on the familiar photo. "It's cordoned off, under covers, safe to the general public, but it's open, which means that whatever the fire guys put in place is not going to stop a determined someone from taking a pen and adding a name to the board that still remained intact. Right?"

"What?" I asked. "What name?"

Devin tacked up another shot, or rather a zoomed-in image from the larger photo, then stepped back, and pointing at them both. "I don't know who this name is, and it could just be kids writing on there, but it might be a lead?" He sounded so hopeful, and I peered at the photos, from the main view, to the focused section.

My blood ran cold.

My heart stopped.

My undercover name from LA was scrawled in bright red capitals at the bottom of the kid's roll call names.

Zachary Owens.

Rick had been right. There it was in black and white. Every suspicion I'd had was confirmed with horrifying clarity. This wasn't about Sam. Or old family feuds. This was about me, and they'd tried to kill my niece and nephew.

I stood up so fast my chair slammed into the wall. "My family. I need to… get to them…"

I'd never moved so fast.

Chapter Twenty-One

Tiber

IT WAS after lunch by the time I'd picked up Ferdinand from the vet, fielded two client calls, and took everyone out for a walk.

Gabriel's nightmare last night, and his revelations about his undercover work in LA, had left me feeling dark and anxious. Gabriel was a good man. It had to have been so difficult for him to deceive someone, maintain a pretend relationship, and then witness his lover's death. That would haunt anyone, much more so someone with a strong sense of duty and honor.

But it wasn't just my empathy for his past that weighed on me. Everything felt wrong. There were the murders that had occurred in Prophet, and the current threat to Sam. There was Ferd and Frank and poison and dead raccoons. Troy Hughes and his obvious loyalty to Dell Prosser, whom I'd helped put away for murder.

It was more than I could sort through, but all of it

weighed me down—weighed us all down—to the point of suffocation.

I had to talk to someone. I went for a drive.

When I pulled up at the little log cabin in the woods where Stone Whiteplume lived, I had a disquieting sense of stepping into a past life. The totems and figures decorating the shaman's driveway and front porch took my mind back to the summers I spent on the rez with my grandmother, to native lands, native magic. I sat in the car for a while, breathing deep and looking at everything. The raven's feathers and shells over a window. The lines of protection inscribed on the porch steps. The dreamcatcher on a post in the middle of the winter garden.

I was drawn to this place, especially with the turmoil inside me, but why? Stone didn't know me. We weren't friends, and he wasn't a counselor. He sold charms and spells, and I wasn't here to buy one, so what possible excuse did I have for bothering him?

Then again, maybe buying a protective charm wasn't a bad idea.

Wood smoke curled out of the cabin's chimney. Stone came out dressed in a buckskin coat with fringes, and black earmuffs. He sat on the steps of his porch holding one tin cup of coffee and placed another tin cup on the step next to him.

I got out of the car. I sat next to him, gratefully wrapping my hands around the warm cup.

"Cold," he said.

I bit back a smile at his laconic demeanor.

"Very cold. Snow's sticking."

"Three days now," Stone agreed with a hint of pride, as

if he was responsible for the snow staying around. Hell, for all I knew, he was.

"How's the garden?" I ask, nodding my chin toward it.

"Still got kale," he said, "but who wants to eat kale?"

I chuckled. "Why do you grow it then?"

"It's good for the winter time. Tough son-of-a-bitch. Like me."

"I see."

"People don't like the way I taste either," he deadpanned, but the smile that followed gave him away.

"That's probably a good thing."

"Yup. That's what I say."

We sat and sipped our coffee. He waited for me to come out with it. I thought of a half dozen approaches in my mind and dismissed them all. I finally got tired of my own hesitation.

"Can you tell if someone has been cursed? Or is under attack?" I asked, feeling a little silly.

"Someone? You, for instance?"

I grimaced. "Me. My boyfriend. His family. My pack. It's been... a lot. And I thought it was all unrelated. And maybe it is. But it just feels... heavy."

"Like you're under a dark cloud?" Stone suggested.

I nodded. "Yeah. Exactly like that. But it's weird. Usually if something's about to happen, I'll see crows. Like, they're a heads-up. And I haven't seen them lately."

Stone grunted. "When even your totem hightails it, that's a bad sign."

Great. That was helpful. I took a calming breath and waited for him to tell me more.

Stone drank his coffee for a while. He didn't say

anything, and he didn't look at me. But I could feel the air spark around him. He was definitely doing something.

He spoke. "There is a death energy around you. It doesn't stem from you, but from someone close to you. But it is serious, and it intends you harm. You and your entire household."

I'd known as much, but it ramped up my inner fear a few dozen notches. "Why? Why me?"

He gave me a curious glance. "Have you wronged so many people, so badly, that you don't know who this is?"

"So it's someone I wronged?"

Stone shrugged. "Must be. A woodpecker goes after a certain place on a certain tree because it knows there are worms or insects inside, not because it just feels like pecking at bark. People don't hate for no reason." He looked me up and down. "There's worms in there somewhere."

I considered this. "But you said it doesn't stem from me, but from someone close to me."

"Did I say that? Then it must be true."

I clenched my jaw in frustration. "You don't remember saying that?"

"Sometimes the spirits speak things I do not know. You are a go-between. You should understand this."

A go-between. The last time I'd visited Stone, that was what he'd called me. A messenger. In my case, I was a messenger between the animal and human worlds. Not a bad gig, if you asked me.

"All right. So someone intends us harm. What can I do to stop them?" I asked.

"Three options. Right the wrong you did them, protect

yourself, or run away. I have a special on right now for protection medicine pouches. Or for a grand, I can cast you in a circle of light."

I had to smile. I appreciated his marketing savvy. "I'll look at the pouches."

He grunted. "Up to you. But if you decide you need the circle, come back. I only hope it's not too late."

His tone was so regretful. Yeah, he had marketing savvy all right. Or, on the other hand, he might legit have a premonition of my imminent demise. But I still went for the pouches.

I bought two. I'd never get Gabriel to wear one, and I wasn't sure I believed in it myself, but I still put it around my neck.

At this point, I'd take anything I could get.

I DROVE BACK HOME and picked up Duke. I parked at the first business on Main Street, and Duke and I headed toward the center of town with him on leash. We were on another sniffing mission. I didn't know what else to do. I was hoping we'd run into Troy Hughes so Duke could give him the once over. But at this point, I was open to anything. Anything at all.

Halfway there, I heard the distant sounds of a crowd and glanced down a side street. The town park was two blocks over, and there were a lot of cars parked there. It sounded like a game was in progress.

Really? In February? Then, I remembered Prophet had something called winter games, which was a mix of different sports. It sounded like, today, the kids were playing baseball.

I shook my head. They were braver souls than me. I started to walk on with Duke, my normal introvert behavior. I didn't want to run into people I actually had to say hello to.

But I stopped. Wasn't that the point of today's excursion? To see if Duke could find the stalker's scent? A local gathering was prime opportunity. Maybe Troy would even be there. And, if not him, others from town.

I wrapped Duke's leash once again around my hand, crossed the street, and headed for the park.

As I approached, I saw the bleachers held a few dozen people. The team in the field looked like Little League— kids of around ten wore coats and hats or ear muffs over Little League uniforms. One of them, taller and lankier than the others, was on the pitch. He drew back the ball and raised his knee, a clear study of pro on TV. He let the ball fly.

The crowd in the stands was even more bundled up than the kids. I'd scanned the faces I could see, searching for Troy. If he was here, Duke could confirm or eliminate him immediately, and right now, I needed that. Needed to make some progress.

I thought of Ferdinand and a spark of anger gave me courage.

You do *not* fuck with my animals. Period.

Duke was sniffing at the dirt next to the stands with interest. Then, he snatched a bit of food. It was a potato chip.

I clicked my tongue. "Come on, Duke. Let's find this

asshole." I led him to the front of the bleachers and started up, leash pulled tight, Duke on my right.

Duke looked at the people we passed with interest because he was a friendly dog. But there was no recognition. A few people said hello to me, or wanted to pet Duke, but I didn't know that many people in town and most ignored us. I kept climbing, on a mission.

We reached the top of the bleachers and started down the aisle behind the last row. A little girl in a red fuzzy hat, red mittens, and white coat twisted around and saw me.

"Tiber! And Duke!"

Sarah and Aaron and Lori were here. A smile stretched my face, and Duke and I hurried over to them. "Hey, Thompsons."

"Hey, you!" Lori was enthusiastic, standing and turning in her seat to give me a big hug. "I've been wanting to call you."

"Me too," I said, holding her longer than usual. "But I wasn't sure if I should. Gabriel."

"Gabriel," Lori agreed, pulling back to meet my gaze. Her eyes were damp. "God, it's been a shit show," she murmured, too low for anyone to hear.

"I know." The pain in her eyes gutted me. "But he's going to take care of it," I promised, knowing in my soul that it was true.

"Right?" Lori wiped her eyes with a mittened hand. "I have to believe that, or I'd melt down."

"Tiber!" Aaron tugged on my coat. "We're the blue team, and we're ahead by two! I'm gonna be in Little League when I'm nine, but Dad says maybe there'll be a

Tee-ball team next year, and I'm big enough for that right now!"

"Tee-ball? Whoa, that's the big time," I told him.

"I know! I'm gonna be a pitcher, 'cause I'm really good at throwing things." He mocked a pitch, then sat back down to watch the game.

"I just wanted to get them out of the house today," Lori said in a low voice, ruffling Aaron's hair fondly. "And Aaron adores baseball. But it's colder than snot out here."

"Mom, can I take Duke for a walk?" Sarah asked, stroking Duke's head.

Lori's upbeat expression fell, and she looked around at the crowd. "No, honey. I need you to stick close to Mommy, okay?"

Sarah pouted.

I was about to tell her that Duke could hang out with her for a bit when Duke rushed between me and Lori, almost knocking me over. "Hey!" I blurted. I barely managed to hang on to his leash as he dived for the stairs.

The leash held, Duke was yanked back, and he twisted wildly in midair. He landed on a bench seat, his whole body straining away from me, hackles raised, barking and snarling. His frenzy was such a surprise it took my brain a moment to catch up. Oh. *Oh.*

I tried to figure out who he was reacting to. I followed his gaze to the ground near the bleachers where a few people stood watching the game.

Just beyond them, near the trees, stood a tall figure in a dark olive rain slicker, hood raised, the features of a masculine nose and chin just visible.

I saw the man at the same instant as he saw me. He

stared up at me, and I felt the malevolence rolling off him. The pure hate. My heart pounded and heat trickled through me—a chemical cocktail of fear, anger, and confusion.

Who the fuck are you?

"Hey! I'm tryin' to hear the game," complained an older man, turning in his seat to glare at Duke.

"Yeah. Take your dog elsewhere," snarked a young guy in a purple parka.

"Tiber?" Lori asked, concerned.

"I need to go," I said. "Stay here with the kids. Don't move." I let Duke pull me down the bleacher aisle.

I had to watch my steps or risk tripping headlong. By the time we reached the ground, the hooded figure was no longer by the trees. I looked around, but didn't see him anywhere.

Duke had his scent, though, and he was still straining against the leash, freaking out. My hands were trembling as I took out my phone to call Gabriel. But Duke was still yanking so hard, I couldn't dial.

"Hey. Hey!" I squatted down and pulled him close to me.

Priority one: calm the dog.

"Duke, it's okay," I said to him. "Shhh. Quiet. I got the message. I saw him. It's okay now. You did great."

Duke barked a few more times, then whined and abruptly sat. He panted anxiously.

"I know. He hurt Ferd. And he was in your yard, and that's so unacceptable. I'll take care of it. I promise. It's okay."

Duke barked once, a more commanding bark than

anything I'd ever heard him utter. Then he stared, fixated on a point across the street.

Okay then. We were going after him. Fine. I let Duke lead the way.

He pulled hard, his paws digging into the ground and, then, the cement, as if he could fly. We left the park, jogged across the street, then started back uphill on the side street, heading for Main.

We hadn't gone a block before I realized my mistake. The February streets were deserted. There were businesses here—shoe repair, dry cleaners, and the like—but they had drawn into themselves in the cold, curtains closed, doors locked. There was no one around. *No one can hear you scream.*

Crap. This felt bad. I had to make it to Main Street where there'd be more people.

"Duke, go!" I said, starting to run.

But it was too late. As we passed an alley, someone grabbed the back of my parka and hauled me in. Hands spun me, and I dropped the leash. Then, I was shoved, hard, and shoved again before I could get my balance. I stumbled back, barely keeping from landing on my ass. There was the blur of an angry face, then I was slammed against a brick wall.

The stranger pushed his forearm into my throat. And now I could not only see his features, I could *smell* him. I'd never seen the man before in my life. He wasn't old, early thirties at most, dark hair, ruddy face, breath sour and reeking of ashes.

"You ain't going anywhere," he snarled.

I lashed out, hitting him as hard as I could, but it was

as if my blows were nothing. Then, I heard the cock of a gun and froze.

The stranger pointed it to the side and I saw Duke, his leash dangling, standing at the end of the alley. He was barking his head off, but he didn't come closer.

"Tell him to shut up and get the fuck away, or I'll shoot him," the stranger said in a voice so cold, I knew he was serious.

I tried to swallow, but the arm on my throat pressed too hard to work my throat. I gave as much of a nod as I could and opened my mouth to show I was willing to speak if he'd let me. The pressure on my throat eased up.

"Duke," I croaked out. "Duke!"

His barked quieted. He looked at me, then at the stranger, panting. *Tell me what to do, Tiber. I'm scared.*

"Go find Gabe. Go find Gabe, Duke!" I called out.

Duke turned tail and vanished.

"Aw, so sweet," the stranger mocked. "Regular Lassie, ain't he?"

I didn't bother to answer. I studied his face. I saw disgust. I saw… not hatred exactly. More utter disregard, as if I, *my life*, meant nothing. As if he'd just as soon squash me under his boot like a bug that dared cross his path.

"Why?" I asked.

He put pressure on my throat again, arm hard as steel, crushing me.

"Why the fuck not, Dog Boy?"

Chapter Twenty-Two

Gabriel

THE SUV KICKED up dirt as I slammed the brakes on outside Thompson Cabins. I was on autopilot. Find Sam, Lori, the kids, get them somewhere, anywhere. I couldn't think about how this was connected to LA, or who was doing this, my family was in danger, and that was all that mattered.

I was out of the car and heading into the main house in an instant, Sam sitting at the kitchen table nursing a coffee, papers spread out around him.

"Gabe, hey, I managed to—what's wrong?" He stood so fast the chair fell over.

I must've looked like a mad man, my weapon out, fear in every inch of me.

"Are you alone?" I snapped.

"Yeah, the kids—"

"Where are Lori and the twins?"

"Watching baseball down in town, why?" He came right up to me, gripping the arm not holding my gun. "What happened? Are they okay?" He shook me. "Gabriel!"

I was freaking my brother out. I was shocked, and I had to…

… snap the fuck out of it.

"Nothing," I lied. "But let's go find Lori and the kids, yeah?"

I must have said enough to get Sam to move, but not enough to convince him his family was okay. He grabbed me and dragged me out, even as I was walking that way; and back in the SUV, we barreled down the hillside in silence, to town, dropping the car right by the entrance for the park, the ballgame still in progress despite the cold, people clapping, smiling, the scent of hotdogs wafting from two vans at either end. There was no chaos here, no tears, or shouting, or hell.

Sam darted past me, climbing the stands, and finding Lori, Sarah, and Aaron, and pulling them close before bundling the three of them down to me.

"What's going on?" Lori asked.

Everyone in the crowd was staring at us—I could feel the weight of every stare, and I looked right back, searching for a familiar face, or a stranger who stood out. Nothing. The game had stopped, and I raised a hand to indicate all okay, then bundled my family into the SUV and headed to the office.

"What's wrong?" Sam asked me, Sarah on his lap, wrapped under his seat belt, Aaron in the back with Lori. I glanced in the rearview mirror—Aaron was crying, hell, Sarah was crying next to me, and Lori was pale.

I'd done this to them, scared them, panicked, and dragged them into whatever this feeling I had going on was.

"Someone might be…" I glanced at Sam and shook my head. I wanted to tell them, but not in front of the kids. Not now.

"Is this 'cos of Duke?" Sarah hiccupped. "He was angry and barking."

"It's okay, sweetheart," Lori soothed from behind. "Uncle Gabriel is here now."

Only something caught my attention. "Duke?" What? Why was Duke at the ball game?

"Tiber was dragging him away, and people were angry. Is Duke in trouble?"

"Tiber?" I pulled the SUV to a stop. "Why was Tiber there?"

Sarah blinked at me, tears in her wide eyes. "I don't know," she whimpered, and Sam shot me a warning glance, and I backed off. Why was Tiber there? Why was Duke barking? That wasn't what he did. Not if he was with Tiber.

Shit.

Shit!

Rick headed over, hustled the kids, Sam, and Lori out.

"I need to get Tiber!" I connected to his cell, but it just rang and rang, and then went to voicemail. "Call me!" I nearly shouted. "Where are you?"

I heard barking, distant, and I was torn. The barking

was closer now, and I tensed. The dog sounded distressed. I should do something. *Tiber would do something.*

Where is Tiber?

"Gabriel? What's going on?" Sam asked from my side. Why was he even back out here? Then Rick was there, ushering him away. I blinked at my brother—he deserved the entire story, but the dog... the barking... Duke? If he was near here, then Tiber must be too, and I felt relief for a moment, but then, why was Duke barking so much?

"I have to find Tiber!" I said.

Rick nodded. "Go."

The world around me slowed down, every second stretching out, and a new kind of fear gripped me, helplessness, cold and unyielding, a vise around my heart. "Tiber!" I shouted, and ran in the direction of the barking, tangling in Duke's leash as he jumped out at me around a corner. His bark was loud, discordant, too much to process. I grabbed at his leash and went to my knees, smoothing his fur, staring into his eyes.

"Tiber?" I asked him—*shouted* at him—and he barked once, ending in a whine as he pawed at me. Come on, was he *really* telling me something? Was that even a thing?

Of course it was. I'd seen the way Tiber listened to his animals. I'd seen Duke react to danger, recognizing people. I wound the leash around my hand, then made a split decision and unhooked it—feeling as if I needed both hands free. He danced around me, barked again, then scampered back and away, turning at the last moment to stare at me. I took out my gun, safety on for now, dismissing the fear someone would capture an image of the crazy sheriff with his gun out following a dog.

Fuck them.

This was *Tiber*.

He trotted far enough ahead that I broke into a run, realizing he was taking me the back way to the ball field, and then, he stopped dead and sat. This was the middle of nowhere in my small town, a maze of old buildings that were being repurposed, neither in the main street, nor far enough away to escape being developed. There was some scaffolding, no people, and then, I heard shouting.

"No!" someone called, and my heart cracked… Tiber.

Weapon high, safety off, I approached the entrance to the alley, going low, hearing grunts, and shoves. What the fuck was happening? I took a deep breath, stepped into the alley. Tiber was shoved against a wall, a gun at his head, blood on his face. I couldn't see the perp's face, but his intention was clear.

"Sheriff's Department! Lower your weapon!" I shouted, and the person whirled to face me, grabbing Tiber, and holding him in front of him, half hiding his face.

"You first," the person demanded—a man, firm, controlled, ice in his tone, a cap low on his face, his head blocked by Tiber, who stared at me with wide eyes.

I'll save you.

"Sheriff's Department! Lower your weapon!" I repeated.

The man holding Tiber chuckled. "Well, hey there, *Owens*."

Owens? Zachary Owens.

This man was from my time in LA for sure, or he knew of me. We were at a standoff, I wouldn't put Tiber's life on the line by holding my weapon on the perp, but then, if I lowered it, Tiber could be dead, then me, and what would I have to show for any of this?

"Who are you?"

"No one that mattered to you," he growled, and a prickle of unease poked at the back of my neck. "So now what?" he added, and chuckled again, almost manic.

I had to lower my weapon. I stared at Tiber, met his steady gaze, and a soft smile curved his lips, as if he thought I could save him. As if this wasn't, maybe, the moment he died.

"Look after Duke," Tiber said, firm, clear. "Duke!"

"Tiber," I whispered, every ounce of love inside me poured into that single word.

The perp tightened his hold around Tiber's neck. I could see Tiber trying to dig his nails in so he could release himself, but the man didn't flinch.

In a blur of movement, Duke shot out from behind me, ducking low, winding around Tiber, and going for the perp's knees, jumping so hard the perp stumbled back, taking Tiber with him. In that instant, I saw what to do. I darted into the space, added my weight to the fall, twisting at the last moment to slam the perp into the ground face first, knocking his gun loose. Duke, with a mouthful of jacket, was snarling and growling. I sat on the man, yanked his hands, and handcuffed him, then glanced at Tiber who'd crawled back to the wall, his hand holding his throat, Duke at his side as soon as the perp was subdued.

I turned the perp, dragged, and heaved him onto his back, yanked off the ball cap and pulled down the scarf, ready to read him his rights.

Shocked and stunned at who I saw.

Mario? Mario Terrell.

Joe's bodyguard, the one who'd tried to shoot me at the warehouse, then followed Joe into the fire and, supposedly, burned to death.

Chapter Twenty-Three

Tiber

"Can you swallow? Here, take a sip of water." Lori fussed over me in the kitchen at the station. Her brow furrowed as she pressed a glass into my hands.

I took it and drank, gingerly. My hand went to my throat. "Hurts."

"Oh God. Is he okay?" Gabriel's voice quavered, and he gripped my other hand as if he never intended to let go.

"Fine," I rasped.

Lori gave Gabriel a worried glance, but addressed me. "Is there a sharp feeling when you swallow? Do you taste blood?"

I shook my head. "No. Just sore."

Her fingers probed oh-so gently at the area. "It'll be black-and-blue in a few hours. To be safe, you should go into Forks or Port Angeles and get a soft tissue scan."

"I can take you," Gabriel offered.

Yeah, I really didn't want to do that. Plus, I knew

Gabriel had a bad guy sitting in the next room, and I wanted to know who and what his deal was, probably as badly as Gabriel did. "I'll be okay. You need to work." Geez, my voice sounded rough.

"It can wait." Gabriel gave Lori a questioning look.

"It wouldn't hurt to have it checked," she repeated. "There doesn't seem to be any hardcore damage to your arteries, windpipe, or voice box, but there may be soft tissue damage."

"Which they'd treat with aspirin and bed rest," I rasped.

"True."

I put down the glass of water and turned to Gabriel. "How about I tell you if I feel any worse—"

"Or if the swelling increases," Lori put in.

I nodded. "If that happens, we can go. Meanwhile, go figure out why that guy is after us. Okay?"

Something dark passed through Gabriel's eyes. His throat bobbed with a swallow. "Lori, Sam has the kids. Can you stay with Tiber?"

"Of course."

"Come get me immediately if anything changes," he insisted. Then, he gave me a desperate hug. Whispered *I love you* in my ear, gave Duke a quick hug too, and left the kitchen.

I sighed and sank into a chair. We sat there in silence for a moment, but the fear and worry were all over Lori's face. And there'd been that darkness in Gabriel's eyes.

"You know who he is," I whispered.

Lori startled out of her thoughts. She blinked at me and took a deep breath. "Not exactly. But…"

"Tell me."

"Rick said he might be from Gabe's past in LA."

Oh. *Oh God.*

Gabriel's past had lingered in his nightmares, which were awful enough. But it had never occurred to me that those nightmares could be real. Could be *here.*

Lori went on. "And I think that's the asshole who's been trying to set up Sam. Frame him for murder."

"The body at the cabins," I said, dazed.

"And the preschool fire," Lori added bitterly. She shuddered. "He could have killed all those kids! If Gabriel doesn't murder that bastard, I will."

God. I opened my mouth to tell her about the stuff that had been done to me. To Frank and Ferdinand. But I hesitated. Lori was upset enough. And it was small beans compared to what Sam and Lori had been through. Anyway, it didn't matter now because the guy was in custody.

But wow. The idea that the cold-blooded creep who had nearly shot me in the alley had been around my house, around *my pack*—plus Sarah and Aaron, and Sam and Lori... It was terrifying. It was a miracle Gabriel had gotten him before he'd killed one of us.

Hen came in and insisted on making me a cup of hot tea and giving a few treats to Duke, who lay at my feet. I sipped the tea. It was a pleasure-pain thing. It still hurt to swallow, but the heat was soothing. Hen left, intent on giving us some space.

To my surprise, Lori took my hand. "Tiber, I'm scared."

"Me too."

And I was. Maybe it was a delayed reaction to the attack in the alley. It had been surreal, brutal, and shocking. The physical pain had been one thing. But the *violence* of it, the violation, the way my very life had been so disregarded… that had shaken something deep inside.

"I'm so scared for my kids and scared for Sam." Lori began to cry. "What if it's not over?"

"Gabriel has him. It's over," I said, with more confidence than I felt.

I put my arm around her, winced because apparently my shoulder was also banged up, and told her to let it out.

She cried, and I tried hard not to. Her tears had dried up when Devin walked in a few minutes later, his expression bashful. "Sorry to disturb you guys. But, Tiber, I need to get a statement from you about what happened. And I'll need photos of your throat and any other wounds or bruises. For the courts. Standard procedure."

"Yeah, Devin, no problem." I looked at Lori. "You okay?"

She sat up, sniffling, and put on a smile. "Yeah. I'm fine. Go ahead. I need to check on the kids anyway."

"Okay. See you soon. Come on, Duke."

I followed Devin, and Duke followed me, into what appeared to be Devin's office. He closed the door behind us.

"Pictures first, I guess. Maybe by the window?" He waved the camera.

Devin was so tentative, I felt obliged to help him out. I wasn't sure if I made him nervous because I was the boss's squeeze, or if he was that way with everyone.

If he was anything like me, it was everyone.

I stood by the window and offered him views of my throat, pulling down the neck of my T-shirt. I discovered marks on my ribs I hadn't yet felt, and he saw some on my back when he checked, so I ended up practically stripping in his office so he could get photos of everything. There was a deep scratch on my right forearm I had no memory of getting. It had bled onto my coat.

Focusing attention on every bruise and scrape reminded me of the attack. Bruises and cuts were one thing, but he'd held a *gun* to my head. If that had gone another way... I had to take deep breaths to keep from getting sick.

Devin winced like a little boy caught in the act. "I'm sorry. This probably isn't great for victim comfort, is it? But Gabriel said—"

"It's okay. Gotta be done."

"Almost there."

When he'd finished with the pictures, I pulled my T-shirt and coat back on. I had a feeling there was a nice scrape on my ass too, from when I'd fallen, but I'd be damned if I'd mention that.

"Have a seat, Tiber. I mean, Mr. Russo." Devin pulled out a little folding chair for me. "I need to record this. Is that okay?"

"Fine."

Devin seemed on firmer footing as he sat at his desk and turned on the tape recorder. "This is Devin Randall of the Prophet Sheriff's Office interviewing Tiber Russo, a resident of Prophet." We confirmed the date, time, and location. "Mr. Russo, can you tell me exactly what happened?"

I glanced at the door. "Sure. But... maybe we could wait for Gabriel?"

I had a lot to say, but I wanted him to hear it too.

Devin frowned. "Sorry. But Gabriel is busy with the suspect. He asked me to get a statement from you. So I'd like to do that. But if you insist—"

"No. It's fine." I sat back in the chair. I'd just have to repeat myself later. What I really wanted, I realized, was Gabriel himself. I was anxious to hear what he'd learned.

A hug wouldn't hurt either.

"Is it true that the guy who attacked me is someone from Los Angeles? From Gabe's past?" I blurted.

Devin blinked, and his cheeks went pink. "You should ask the Sheriff about that."

"Right. Right. Of course." I waved a hand. "It's fine."

"I understand," Devin said. "You love him, and you want him with you right now after such a traumatic event. Anyone would. And I'm sure he wants to be with you, too. But believe me, Gabriel is doing whatever he has to do to lock this perp up so he can't hurt you anymore. You and Sam and Lori and the kids."

"Right." I relaxed back. "You're right."

"We can wait to take the statement if you want," Devin offered.

I shook my head. "No. Let's do it while it's fresh."

"Okay then. Can I get you water or anything?"

"Um. I had some tea from Hen, but I left it in the hall."

"Let me get that for you."

He disappeared and returned moments later with a steaming cup. He put it down on the edge of his desk closest to me. "Here you go. I nuked it for a minute to warm it back up."

"Thanks." I picked it up. The warmth felt good on my hands. "Devin?"

Devin sat down. "Yup?"

"I think you've got the victim comfort thing down."

He gave a bashful smile. "I... thanks."

"I'm ready now."

"Okay. Take your time. But I want you to tell me everything."

He started the recorder, and I began with the figure I'd seen in my yard.

Chapter Twenty-Four

Gabriel

I SAT ACROSS FROM MARIO, his hands cuffed to the table, his gaze defiant, and hell, he was even smiling.

"Couldn't you find a *smaller* room?" He rolled his eyes, and the fluorescent light flickered above, casting an unsettling pallor on his face as he grinned up at me, ignoring Rick who stood beside me. Both of us had our body cams on, and Rick placed a recording device on the desk, then switched it on.

"Sheriff Rick Barnes, Kitsap County Sheriff's Office in attendance." He added the date and time, and then glanced at me to carry on.

"Sheriff Gabriel Thompson, Prophet, in attendance. The accused is—"

"That would be me," Mario said loudly, leaning toward the recorder. "Mario Terrell, deceased." He chuckled then, and my chest was tight. Mario had somehow orchestrated a subtle, yet vicious campaign against me, one that endangered everyone I loved, and he was sitting there laughing like it was a huge fucking joke.

"How did you get out of the fire?" I asked, scanning any visible skin for scars.

"Blah blah, luck, blah, collapsing doorway, whatever." He examined his nails, and I got the feeling he didn't want to hold my gaze as he glossed over what had to have been a traumatic event.

I glanced at Rick, who gestured for me to carry on.

"Why not just come to me if you knew where I was?" My voice was calm, but inside, I was anything but. "Why go through all this? The school fire, the dead bank officer on my brother's land, framing Sam… Why?"

"Who said I had anything to do with any of that?"

I schooled my features, gesturing at his wrist where the edge of the vines poked out of the sleeve. "You stood there and near enough told me."

"I did?" He sounded surprised, then smirked at me, the fucker. "Now, I'm sure I would recall doing that. So who says it was me?"

"Why did you kill John Melchet?"

"Melchet? I don't recall that name," he said, tapping his fingers on the table in a staccato beat. "Boom boom tish," he added at the end of a drum roll. Crazy had a name today, and it was Mario Terrell.

"Why did you place the body of John Melchet on my brother's land?"

"Again, not sure who you're talking about."

"Did you break into the residence of Sam and Lori

Thompson on or around the day of February thirteenth to steal a knife to then use in the murder of John Melchet?"

He shrugged. "No."

"We *will* ID you now, against that video, and pull out every single reference to your vehicle. It's just a matter of time before we link you to everything."

He smirked again. "You can try."

A small kernel of doubt sat inside me—he sounded so convinced we wouldn't find anything, but he was wrong. He *had* to be.

"Seems like you just have me on losing my shit with Dog Boy." He stared up at me. "And you really don't get it, do you, Gabriel?" His voice was laced with contempt. "That was all about making you suffer. You think you're some kind of hero, but you're not. You're a fraud and with a little push you'd break all the rules."

I took a seat then, and shuffled it a little closer, Rick leaned against the empty situation boards.

"I'm a fraud because I couldn't save Joe?"

He sneered. "Fuck you."

Why would he have jumped into the fire for Joe—the same as I would for Tiber?

Mario had gone into the fire to save Joe, he'd shadowed Joe so often, but that had been about Cyrus and his orders. I would have gone into a fire to save Tiber and knew it would have destroyed me to watch him die. Hell, just seeing the bruises on his neck was enough to knock me sideways. I had a lot to ask... but none of it made sense... I was lost in it all.

Then it hit me. "You loved Joe?"

Mario's eyes flashed with a twisted satisfaction. "Ding-

ding! Ten points for the small-town sheriff." Then, he leaned forward. "You see, Joe was everything to *me*, but somehow he thought you were everything to *him*. He trusted you, loved you, and you let him die just at the moment he saw you for the liar you were, Gabriel. You chose to save yourself." He sat back in his chair, his tone bitter. "You're no better than the criminals you chase."

His words cut deep, but I kept my composure. "You could have come after me directly, Mario. Why involve innocent people? My family? My partner? Why the preschool?"

He laughed, a hollow, bitter sound. "Because pain to a loved one is what hurts you the most, doesn't it? Seeing them in danger, knowing it's all because of you. You don't deserve peace, Gabriel. You don't deserve love after you tried to destroy mine."

"How did you—"

"And fuck you were slow, I had to write your name on a damn board to even get you to take notice." He dropped the gruffness in his voice, made it falsetto. "Look at me I'm Sheriff Thompson, and I'm shit at my job." He rolled his eyes, his normal voice back. "I fucking hate you," he spat.

Contempt dripped from every word. Mario's obsession with revenge, his need to make me suffer, it all stemmed from his grief and loss. He saw me as the embodiment of his pain, the target for his misplaced vengeance, and I could understand that. Hell, I still carried the guilt of what I'd done.

"Do you think this will bring Joe back?" I asked. "Or that this will ease your pain?"

Mario raised an eyebrow, and for a moment, I thought I saw something else in the broken man beneath. "The Joe I loved will never come back," he whispered. "And that's not fair."

Fairness. The word hung dark and heavy in the small room. Mario's actions, driven by a twisted sense of justice, were his way of balancing the scales, as perverse as it was, and I didn't have to be a psychologist to understand that. He couldn't accept the fact that Joe had died because of his father, because of the pain his family was inflicting on addicts, creating new addicts, and all he saw was the complete unfairness of his loss. So, he'd turned his grief into a vendetta, a way to exert control in a world that had robbed him of what he cherished most.

I sighed, feeling a weight in my chest. "Mario, I'm sorry for your loss. I truly am. But I told him to stay away, you were the one who brought him to the scene. Hell, I tried to get to Joe, I nearly had his hand, but he fell back when the floor gave way."

Mario's expression was odd, not a mix of anger, sorrow, and resignation, but something manic. A kind of glee that didn't sit right with me. I wondered how far over the edge he'd gone after seeing Joe die, Cyrus arrested, and friends killed in the fray. Probably too far for me to reach him, and after a pause, when I just stared at Mario, Rick jumped in.

"Forks PD will be here soon to transport him," was all he said.

Mario leaned forward again, rattling the cuffs on the leg of the table, lifting the weight of it a little, as if to show us he could flip it and be out of here in seconds.

The issue for him was that the room was so small there was no way he'd extricate himself from the iron fretwork.

We had him.

He was done.

THERE WASN'T MUCH ELSE to do.

With Mario delivered to the Forks PD who'd come for him, and with Sam, Lori, and the kids back home to deal with the fallout, it was Rick, Devin, Hen, and Tiber, plus a quiet Duke and myself who ended up in reception, all of us shaken for different reasons.

Hen slipped behind the reception desk, moving papers around as if that was what she'd always meant to do, Devin excused himself to clear the incident room, and then, it was Rick's turn to ask me what seemed like a million questions.

"Hope we can get him on the murder, don't think it will take much to get that. Still, even though your brother is looking less likely to be the culprit in the murder case, I'm staying until we're finished, until we find out for sure what happened."

"Agreed."

Rick went over to his temporary desk, already skimming his notes, as Tiber leaned into me.

"I'm going to get Duke home," he said. "And I need to check on the rest of the pack."

I wrapped an arm around him, leaned down and pressed a soft kiss to the reddened area on his throat. I didn't want to let him out of my sight. "Can you wait a while? I just have to write this up…"

"I'm okay. It's over. Just come home when you're ready. I'll put that frozen lasagna in the oven; we'll sit and eat and watch a movie, and forget this ever happened. Or, failing that, we could just sit on the sofa, and I could hold you close and never let you go."

I pressed a kiss to Tiber's head. "He was going to kill you. How can you ever get that out of your head?"

Tiber sighed. "You, the animals, we'll work it out, make things right." He didn't sound all that convinced, but we'd cover that later, when I was back home with him, and could wrap my head around everything. "Anyway, I need to get home and check on the kids. And Duke needs all the treats for being our hero." He kissed me.

I carded my hand through his hair, deepening the kiss, then parting to rest my forehead on his. "I love you. Just remember that."

"Of course," he said and kissed the tip of my nose. "And I love you. Always. See you soon. Text me, okay?"

"Do you need a ride?"

"No. I'm parked down the street."

I watched him leave the office, Duke trotting along at his side, and part of my heart went with him.

"What's next?" Rick asked.

I sighed. "Something doesn't feel right, something I've missed. The way Mario acted in the interview, as if he truly didn't care about being caught. Like it was part of his game plan."

"Really?"

I glanced up at Rick, but he didn't seem convinced, so

I stowed my fears, and moved on to the next thing on my list—I owed Lincoln a call.

I added as much to the report of what I knew had happened, kept it to the facts without giving too much away about any connection to Lincoln, his team, or what I'd done undercover.

And hoped to hell this was over.

Chapter Twenty-Five

Tiber

I FELT as though I weighed about a thousand pounds as I parked in my driveway and climbed painfully out of the driver's seat. I was sore everywhere and so tired I wanted to lie down right there on the asphalt. That seemed reasonable given it was already dark out on this winter night. Some of the aches were from the physical attack in the alley, but I had the feeling my body was also hungover from the overload of adrenaline and fear—nasty chemicals, those. And, maybe, some of it was the relief of knowing it was over. Like, I could finally rest. Safely rest. And I wanted to, for about twelve hours straight.

But I was a dog parent, so there was no stumbling right to bed for me. I had to feed the pack at least, and let them play in the back for a while, and then, maybe, I could take a nap while the lasagna was baking.

I opened the back of my Subaru to get Duke. He was exhausted too, and deeply asleep on the dog bed in the back. His paws twitched. I smiled down at him, reluctant to wake him up. Maybe, in his dreams, he was running once again to find Gabriel to save me. Such a good dog. He'd also been on high alert for a few days, and his doggy brain must be exhausted.

"Close it," said a voice, very low and right behind me. Something hard pressed into the back of my head.

I froze. I tried to speak, but nothing came out. For the second time that day, a gun was pushed against me, and a wave of icy terror washed through me.

"Close it," he repeated.

I closed the hatchback hard, and Duke sat up immediately.

At least he'd be safe in the car.

"Good. Now walk to your front door. Slowly."

I did as he asked without a word, my steps awkward and heavy. But the tired fog in my brain evaporated with the fresh rush of fear and the hard pumping of my heart.

Another one. There's another one.

An accomplice? Had to be. Someone else from LA? Probably. Didn't mob types have accomplices? Hell, wasn't that the definition of *mob*? As in: a group? Gabriel had said it wasn't a mob, but it had sure sounded like one to me. We should have known. I should have known. So much for my vaunted intuition.

We reached the front door. I stopped, waiting.

"Here's how it's gonna go," the man said. He had a grip on my upper arm now, as well as holding the gun to my head. My skin crawled at his touch. "We're going in, and you're going to keep those dogs off me. You'll go right to the back door and put them out. Your whole mangy pack. And if any of them go for me, I'll shoot it. And then, maybe, I'll do a lot more shooting, too. Understand?"

"Yes."

"Repeat it."

"We'll go in, and I'll immediately put them in the backyard."

"Then do it."

I dug the keys out of the front pocket of my jeans. My hands were shaking, and my fingers were numb. He said nothing as I fumbled, finally got the key in the lock, and turned it.

Bark, bark, bark, bark, bark!

As usual, the pack was waiting for me at the front door. They were happy and relieved to see me, as always when I'd been gone a while, as if they thought I might never come back. But their excitement turned to worry and warning when they realized I wasn't alone. Leo was aggressive, coming in close and eyeing a way to get to the man's leg. He wasn't a biter, but I could see he was seconds from taking a chunk of flesh.

"Get back!" I said firmly. "Go on. Leo! Back. Go on you guys." I shooed with my hands, using my angry voice. My heart tripped, and I felt a wave of nausea at the idea of any of them being shot. The thought helped me be as commanding as I needed to be as I ordered them all down the hall, through the living room, opened the sliding glass door to the deck, and got them outside.

Gracie and Ferd went willingly and fearfully, running out to the yard, happy to escape. But Leo paused in the doorway, looking back at me, and then, at whoever was behind me, panting. He whined.

"It's okay," I told him, softening my voice. "I'll be okay. Go on."

He took a step back onto the deck, and I closed the door on him. We stared at each other for a moment through the glass.

My little hero. He'd been with me for so long, comforted me during the Jeff years. I loved him so much.

"Good. Now turn around, slowly, and take a seat on the couch."

I blinked and turned away from Leo. I went to sit on the edge of the couch, that gun pressed to my head the whole time. I gripped my hands in my lap. They were freezing cold.

The barrel of the gun disappeared, and then, he came into view. He took a seat on the chair opposite me, gun resting on his thigh and pointing at me.

We stared at each other.

A sense of dread settled into my gut. It was him. The strange man from that client call—the one with the dog that wasn't his dog. The one who'd asked—

Do you scream in bed?

I shuddered. What did he call himself? Jim Smith.

I should have known. I *did* know, only I'd thought I was crazy. I swallowed hard.

He studied me like a scientist examining an alien parasite—with loathing, but also a hint of curiosity.

I studied him back and felt something new stir in my chest. It felt a lot like pity.

He wasn't old. My age. But at some point in time, he'd

been hurt, badly. His dark hair was cropped short and lay uneven and patchy on the right side. He wore a black turtleneck now too, under an expensive-looking gray parka. Maybe it was seeing him in person, or maybe he'd had some make-up covering it up on the Zoom call, but I could now make out red scarring coming up from under the turtleneck on that right side, angry red vines crawling onto his jaw. And his hands—not gloved now—were covered in burn scars. He was too thin, frail-looking. And he seemed strung out, like he'd been medicating. Painkillers, I thought. There'd been a lot in the past. Burns were excruciating. Maybe he still took them. Or maybe he did other drugs to keep the nightmares away.

I didn't miss that he had to steady the hand holding the gun by resting it on his thigh. It still shook a little.

"You're Joe," I said, and the pity in my heart grew.

He sneered. "Fuck you."

Well, that was eloquent. I pressed my lips tight.

"So, you're what he really likes?" Joe said, in a mocking tone. "Honestly, I don't see it."

I said nothing.

"Is it the long hair?" he mused. "The whole native squaw thing? Or maybe you have a big dick."

The pain in his voice was so raw it rubbed against me like sandpaper. Yes, I felt sorry for the guy. "You must have loved Gabriel a whole lot, if he's worth all this."

"I hate him!" Joe screamed, his face going red. "He ruined everything! And he lied to me—every word out of his mouth was a lie! And he left me to—" His voice hitched. He stopped talking and took a moment to regain his composure, breathing deep.

I waited.

When he spoke again, his voice was cold. "We spent months arranging this. We had such fun planned. But now Mario has been arrested, so." He raised the gun. "Guess we'll just have to cut to the chase."

A wave of calm and peace passed through me. Maybe my reserves of fear had run dry, I'd felt it so much this past week. But if he was going to shoot me, he was going to shoot me. There was nothing I could do. "You can kill me, Joe. But it won't change anything."

His lips trembled with rage. "No. But it'll hurt him, and you know what? That's good enough for me."

A dozen thoughts raced through my mind. Joe was weak. I could make a run for it. Maybe I'd get shot in the back, but maybe not. I could go for my phone in my pocket. Or I could dash for the kitchen, grab a knife. I could drop and roll.

I didn't do any of those things. "Can I get you something? Hot tea?" I asked.

"Shut up," he snapped. His jaw worked. The gun resting on his thigh pointed more determinedly at me. "I need to think."

"Okay. Want some tea while you think?"

"Do you think I'm stupid? You'll just try to get away!"

"I promise I won't."

"Shut UP!" he screamed.

I shut up.

He thought for a long time. The darkness that passed through his eyes was so awful, I had to look away.

"Okay," he finally said. "Guess this is the big finale. So, here's what you're gonna do. You're gonna get Zach—

I mean *Gabriel*—to come here. Alone. And if you try to warn him, or give away the game, you will be gut shot, and all your animals dead, long before he can show up. Do you understand me?"

"Yes." At the thought of my poor sweet animals being killed, my pity for the guy evaporated. A cold bullet of anger entered my heart.

"Good. So, what would you say to him over the phone to get that to happen? Tell me word for word."

I thought about it. I could see what Joe was thinking clear as day. By *finale*, he meant confronting Gabriel. And he wanted to hurt him. He'd kill me to do that, he'd already said as much. Maybe he'd make Gabriel watch. And then he'd kill Gabe too.

If I brought him home. If he walked in that door unsuspecting.

But if I didn't, Joe would kill me and the whole pack, then wait here until Gabriel came and found our bodies.

I shuddered at the thought.

"Surely, you can think of something," Joe insisted, his tone implying I was stupid. "Tell him you're naked and waiting."

Man, the pathos in his tone was scary. Equal parts hatred and jealousy.

I shook my head. "He'd never believe that. I wouldn't bother him at work for that. Especially not when he has a suspect in custody."

"What a boy scout," Joe sneered. "If not that, what?"

I wracked my brain. Apparently for too long.

"What would you *say*!" Joe shouted, waving the gun at me.

I swallowed. "I'd... I'd tell him that one of the dogs was sick. Very sick. He'd come home for that."

Joe narrowed his eyes as if he didn't believe me. But he considered it. "Why wouldn't he tell you to just take it to the vet?"

"The vet in town isn't very good, and their hours are random," I lied. "If one of the dogs was really sick, we'd drive him or her to Forks. But we'd only do that if it was an emergency. And Gabriel would come home to go with me."

Joe rubbed at his temple with his free hand. That hand shook too. He was in pain; I could see it. And it made him impatient. He appeared torn, but he said, "Fine. But you'd better be convincing, or you're dead. Do you understand?"

"Yes."

"Say it!"

I took a deep breath. "If I'm not convincing, you'll shoot me on the spot."

"Yeah, you get it. And all your little critters too."

"Yes."

"Okay. Give me a minute. Don't move. Remember, I have the gun."

Joe stood, pushing himself up using the arm of the chair and his free hand, moving stiffly. Yup, he was definitely in pain, but he kept the gun trained on me the whole time. Shaky or not, he was dangerous. When he was on his feet, he walked over to me and stood behind the couch, gun barrel pressed to the back of my head. "Okay. Now get out your phone. Slowly. And don't press anything. Just hold it."

I took my phone from my pocket, holding it in my open hand so he could see it.

"Turn it on."

I did. A selfie with me, Gabriel, Leo, and Duke filled the screen. We were on a hiking trail. We looked so happy it brought a lump to my throat.

Behind me, Joe cursed. "He's a fucking liar, you know. He'll do you dirty in the end, just like he did me. He doesn't care about you."

I said nothing.

I heard him take a deep breath. "Okay. Call him. Put it on speaker. And remember you're one twitch of my finger away from having your brains all over this living room. I will do it. I swear to God."

"I believe you, Joe. Stay calm. I'm going to do what you ask."

"Then do it!"

I brought up my favorites and dialed Gabriel. I put it on speaker. My mouth was bone-dry.

He answered on the second ring. "Tiber? Hey! Are you okay? How're you feeling?"

It took me a second to remember what he was talking about. Oh, yes. My throat. Geez, that conversation felt like a lifetime ago. "I'm okay. I'm… fine."

"Yeah? So, what's up?" A slight twinge of worry was in his tone, but he suspected nothing.

The gun pressed harder into the back of my head. I took a deep breath.

I was going to take a risk here. How much did Joe know about me? Clearly, he knew a lot. He said they'd been planning for months. Maybe it even tied into that stranger One-Eyed Jack had mentioned, the one with the camera that had been asking questions about Gabriel and me. Had they hired a private eye? Or had that been Mario?

It didn't matter now. But did Joe know the names of my pack? I didn't talk about them on my website. And it wasn't in the public record. Besides, most people didn't take animals seriously.

"Tiber?" Gabriel prompted, more worried now.

I took a breath and let it out. "Sorry to bother you, but I was wondering if you could possibly come home. There's something wrong with one of the dogs. With Rhonda. We might need to take her to the vet in Forks, but I want to get your opinion first. She's been throwing up a lot."

There was a pause on the other end of the phone. "Which dog?" Gabriel asked, confused.

I closed my eyes and prayed. "Rhonda. I know, I know, she was fine this morning. But she threw up all over the house while I was gone, and now, she's just lying there." I held my breath.

Please get it. Please.

There was silence for several beats. Then: "Okay. I'll come right home." He hung up.

I wanted to cry. I dropped my phone in my lap and composed my face. *Dear God, let him have gotten the message. Please.*

"That'll do," Joe said. "Hand me the phone."

I held it up and he snatched it from my hand. I heard the clatter as he threw it somewhere. Then, he moved out from around the couch to stand in front of me. "Now, we're gonna tie you up." With his free hand, he dug a handful of zip ties from his pocket and tossed them onto my lap. "One of the dining room chairs will do. Get up. Come on."

I gathered the zip ties in my hand and stood.

"Hands up and move!" Joe shouted, just to show who was in charge.

Once again, I thought of going for the gun, trying to grab it. I didn't know if I could overpower him, because he was super on edge and the gun would likely go off the moment I went for it. Too risky.

I raised my hands, still clutching the zip ties, and walked around the couch. The chairs in the dining area were wooden and had arms. Joe had me zip tie my own feet to the chair legs, and then, he zip tied my wrists to the chair's arms.

The dining area was closer to the sliding glass doors, and I could see all the animals huddled there, staring in at me. Gracie, Ferd, Leo, Patch, and Fudge. I conjured up a smile for them, gave them a little nod. *It's all right. I'm all right.*

I hoped they were spared, at least.

"There," Joe announced, sounding relieved. He put his gun down on the dining room table well out of my reach, despite the fact that my hands were zip tied. He was shaking badly now, as if it had been an effort to hold it together. He slumped against the table, dug a prescription bottle from a pocket, and swallowed two pills.

"There're drinks in the fridge," I said.

"Shut up! Save your breath. I don't want anything from you. I hate you!"

"Okay."

He closed his eyes and panted—against pain, probably.

After a moment, he opened his eyes. "Napkins? Dish towels?"

"Dish towels are in the drawer next to the sink."

He took the gun and moved away. A moment later he was back with a dish towel. "Open up."

I did. He shoved the dish towel in my mouth. It wasn't pleasant, but I could breathe. I stared at him.

"Tape?" he asked, then cursed when he realized I couldn't talk. Instead of removing the gag and asking me, he left, and I heard rummaging, drawers opening and closing. He returned with a roll of duct tape and taped over the dish towel and around my head. Damn, that would be a mess getting out of my hair. Assuming I survived.

Finally, he was satisfied. He studied me. "Cinderella is all dressed for the ball. This'll be fun," he said, attempting a grin.

But I wasn't fooled. He wasn't having fun. Revenge is always better in your head, I think. In real life, not so much.

He sneered at me, as if reading my mind. Then, he left me and went to the front of the house to wait for Gabriel.

Chapter Twenty-Six

Gabriel

"Who the hell is Rhonda?" I asked my empty office, already up and out of my seat ready to head home to help out. Maybe, we had a new member of our little family I didn't know, or this could be Sid's friend—after all I hadn't seen the damned spider yet.

"Heading home for a bit," I advised Hen, but she waved me to a stop.

"Lincoln is returning your call on line one. You want to take it?"

I was torn—I didn't like the tone of Tiber's voice. He'd sounded shaky, so whoever Rhonda was, I was getting there as soon as I could. Only, I'd tried Lincoln twice, and he'd been on a call, and this wouldn't take long, so I headed back to my office and took the call.

Lincoln didn't beat around the bush. "Gabe, hey, you have news on the case?"

He was silent as I explained what had happened in the

briefest of brushstrokes, how Mario had orchestrated everything, how he'd stalked and intimidated, and caused doubt and fear for me and my family, and Tiber.

"Well shit," he muttered, "but Mario is listed as dead... was dead... shit..." He went silent.

"Lincoln?" There was no answer. "Lincoln?"

"Hold on," Lincoln said, and I glanced at my watch. I'd give him a minute then I was gone. Staring out of the window, I began to hum, no idea why the Beach Boys were playing in my head, probably because of the name Rhonda... I hummed some more, then sang a line: "*Help me, Rhonda. Help, help me, Rhonda.*" My watch hand moved on, and Tiber was my priority. "Linc, I'm heading out now, I'll call you back."

"Fuck! Wait!" Lincoln snapped, and it shocked me into stopping. "Mario is alive?"

I really wanted to leave. "Very much alive, and in custody with Forks PD."

"He's marked as dead in the reports, but fuck, Gabe, the fire that pulled down the warehouse, meant there was no evidence, no coroner's report. We've worked under the assumption he was dead, but there's nothing to back that up, and it's worse."

"How can it be worse?"

"You saw Joe Vine fall through the floor right? You told me his clothes were on fire; that he fell right into the center of it all."

"Yeah."

"Well shit, Gabriel, there's no coroner's report on Joe's remains, either. They never found his body."

I froze. *Rhonda. Help me.*

Tiber was in trouble.

I dropped the call in an instant, dived out of my office and thrust open the incident room door where Rick and Devin were staring at a board for the loan officer's murder, still very much part of this whole investigation.

"Tiber's in trouble; let's go!"

I sprinted to the SUV, Devin right behind me, Rick huffing to keep up, but then, somehow, we were all in, and I was streaking away from town, heading for home, and my heart pounded with fear.

"What happened?" Rick asked, fighting to get his seat belt on as I tore around a corner. The world outside blurred. I heard the click of his buckle as we hit the main road.

"He said Rhonda," I tried to explain, but my heart pounded in my ears, and the back end of the car slid dangerously out of control. Panic flared in my chest, but gripping the steering wheel, I over-corrected in desperation, my breath held tight in my lungs. Thank the gods, the car steadied. A fleeting sense of relief washed over me, but there was no time to savor it. I could almost hear Tiber's voice in my head—*Rhonda,* added my own spin, *help me, Rhonda*—a distant whisper urging me to hurry. The town became the forest, the roads bumpy and uneven, Rick cursing next to me, Devin holding on for dear life.

"Stop the car, Gabriel!" Rick shouted over my fear. "We can't go in hot!"

"I will, closer!" Each mile was a blur, each turn and straight was a step closer to him, to whatever danger he was in, and adrenaline was like fire in my veins.

Joe? That was impossible right?

A quarter mile out, right before the last bend, I stopped the SUV and started to unbuckle to get out. Rick stopped me, a hand on my arm.

"Plan?" he asked, and he was right—I needed a plan that wasn't just running right into our home and putting Tiber in danger.

"You and Devin circle around to the back, stay in the trees. I'll take the front. Check in when we know what we're dealing with." I hoped to hell it was Tiber standing there with some kitten, or a mouse, he'd named Rhonda. Hell, I'd even be okay with a freaking snake, or worse, a spider. The night was our ally, cloaking us in darkness, and we separated, as I advanced with caution, my gun ready, using the trees as cover, all three of us connected by our radios. Each step I took was measured, my senses on high alert, and all my training kicking in to override the desperate fear for Tiber. I clambered over the small fence to the front of the property, catching my foot and nearly falling, steadying myself on the trunk, and then weapon high, I waited for a moment.

"In position, no visual on Tiber," I said.

Devin repeated the same, then Rick, who added he had a visual on animals clustered around the back doors staring inside.

"Stay where you are, radio silence until I say so. I'm moving in for a closer look."

Staying in the shadows, I took a brief glimpse through the side window, and my heart sank. Tiber, tied to a chair, chin tilted with stubborn determination, tape twisted around his mouth and into his hair. He glanced my way, but there was no way he could see me, and I couldn't see anyone else with him. Fear clenched my chest like a vise. I felt powerless, a feeling I hated. I had to do something, fast. Moving with care, I positioned myself to get a better view down the hallway, trying to assess the situation.

That was when I spotted the man near the front door, casually glancing out the window down the path, a gun in his hand.

Joe.

Joe Vine.

Very, very much alive and in my home.

I radioed Devin, and he confirmed they could see him too. "What should we do?" Devin's voice crackled through the radio.

I weighed our options. I had a clear shot at Joe from here, but taking that shot was risky. I was no expert marksman, and the thought of killing Joe didn't sit well with me. My past was already heavy with guilt, and I didn't need more blood on my hands.

I considered my next move. The situation was delicate, and one wrong decision could make everything worse. I needed a plan to save Tiber without unnecessary violence. My mind raced. The gun in my hand felt heavier with each passing second. I knew I had to make a decision soon, but it had to be the right one.

I flicked on my radio. "Stay back, radios off," I said to Devin and Rick, then I holstered my gun, switched off my radio, and with nothing more than the desperate need to keep Tiber alive, I stepped away from the shadows and into the light cast by the porch lamp, and directly into Joe's line of sight.

The moment he saw me, he grinned, but it wasn't a smile, there was no joy there, it was feral and more of a snarl. He opened the front door, headed back into the house, and I followed him inside, with caution. He stood slightly behind Tiber, pointing his gun at Tiber's head.

"Lose your gun," Joe ordered, his voice raspy. "Take it out, throw it over here."

I raised my hands, couldn't meet Tiber's steady gaze, not wanting to see even a second of fear in his beautiful dark eyes. Joe was shaky, his familiar blue eyes cloudy, and I could see scars tracing from his neck up his face, and his hands... shit... they were a knotted, twisted mess. What kind of pain must he have felt as he burned? I should have gone after him. Tried to save him. *I thought he was dead; he fell so far, into a fucking inferno.* "Let Tiber go, I'll stay, and we'll talk."

"Lose the fucking gun, Zach." He spat the name and imbued it with so much hate that I knew this scene was heading for an unhappy ending. There was insanity in his expression, and I was the person who'd done that to him.

"Joe—" I stopped when he pressed the barrel harder, forcing Tiber's head to tilt forward. The danger was real, and every instinct screamed at me to act, but I had to be careful.

With deliberate slowness, I unsnapped my holster and removed my weapon, making sure my actions were exaggerated enough for Joe to read them as non-threatening. Holding the gun with just two fingers, I tossed it over to him. He kicked it away, and it slid under the sofa —the same sofa where Tiber and I had spent countless evenings snuggled up together.

I knew I had to say something, anything to defuse the situation.

"Joe, I didn't know. I thought you were dead," I started, my voice steady despite the turmoil inside. "You have to believe me. I cared about what happened to you. I told you to stay away that night."

"Zach told me!" he snapped. "Not Gabriel the cop, not the real you."

"You weren't part of what your dad was doing, you shouldn't have gone—"

"Fuck you, Gabriel. You lied. You said you loved me, you fucked me, you… made love to me." His voice wavered again, his hand unsteady, and one wrong step, and Tiber would be dead.

"It was my job, to try and save people your father was killing, but that doesn't excuse it. I still have nightmares about it." The words were true; the guilt had been a constant shadow in my life, and still chased me in my nightmares. I'd gone so deep undercover I'd forgotten my own name, and my heart hurt with the memories. "I was going to get you out; I had a plan to get you away." He stared at me, but the sneer lessened, the pain in his eyes softening a little. "I cared about you, Joe, that wasn't a lie." It was a lie, but the person I really did love was in danger, and I would do anything—say anything—to keep Tiber alive.

"I loved you, and you let me die!" He tensed again.

"We could have started over somewhere else. If you'd just stayed away."

I could see a flicker of something in Joe's eyes, a momentary hesitation, and I pressed on. "I know I can't undo the past, but I'm truly sorry. Can you forgive me?" I asked, hoping we could resolve this without violence.

"Mario went into the fire for me," he murmured. "He loved me for real." His hand started to shake, and he had to use the other one to steady the gun. "He would have died for me."

"If I thought for one minute you weren't dead, I would have tried—"

"To do what!" he spat. "Dived into fire to rescue me?"

"Yes, Joe, I would have." That wasn't a lie—I wouldn't have let someone die, that wasn't me.

"Fucking Angel Gabriel," he muttered, his eyes glassy with emotion, and for a heartbeat, it seemed as though Joe might lower his gun, might accept my apology, might sit down and talk. But then, his expression hardened, and he raised his gun to aim at me. "You first? Or him? What do you want, huh? If I shoot you in the belly, you could take hours to die, you'd be in agony, and your lover could watch. Or how about the other way around. Huh?" My heart stopped, and time seemed to slow down. Joe took a step away from Tiber, held the gun unsteadily, then drew closer to me. "For what you did to me, for putting my dad in prison, for destroying my family, fuck, for the pain I feel every fucking day..." He paused. "You first, slow, and low, and then, each one of his fucking animals, and then, him. Seems fair."

Another step.

A shot pierced the air, shattering the silence. Instinctively, I braced for the pain of impact, but it never came. Instead, it was Joe who faltered, slumping first to one knee, and then, the other, as his gun clattered to the floor. It must have been Rick or Devin who found the opening and took the shot, striking Joe in the leg.

Joe scrambled toward his fallen weapon; his desperation clear. I couldn't let him reach it. I dove for the gun, my fingers closing around the cold metal just as Joe's hand brushed over it.

The struggle was brief, but intense. We grappled for control of the weapon; my strength pitted against his agonized movements. The gun kicked with a shot, and with a final push, I wrenched it from his grasp and pointed it at Joe, who had collapsed to the floor, his head buried in his hands. The fight left him, shaking, and he was silent, save for the labored breaths heaving through his body. I kept the gun trained on him, making sure my weapon under the couch was well out of reach, not taking any chances, even as he seemed broken, a shadow of the threat he'd been moments before.

Rick and Devin rushed in, guns at the ready, taking over the scene, as I crossed to Tiber, and unpicked tape from his face, not touching what was tangled in his hair. I grabbed a pair of scissors to cut the ties at his wrists and ankles, then fell to my knees in front of him. He embraced me, and we held each other tight, and all I could say, over and over, was one thing.

"I love you; I love you. I love you."

I don't know what Rick and Devin did, I couldn't move at first, even as Tiber cradled my head in his lap, but then, I sat back on my heels, watching as Tiber tried to pick the tape from his hair, tears streaming down his face —in pain, or fear, or because he hated me for what had happened, I don't know.

It was all a mess.

And that was when I noticed the stain on Tiber's shirt, and Tiber's hands red in his hair.

"Tiber?" I asked, yanking at his shirt, revealing a wound on his hip, not deep, but bleeding. "Tiber!"

He blinked at me. "I think a bullet... I think... it burned... Gabriel?"

I searched his body, looking for more wounds, a splash of scarlet on the wall behind could be his blood, but he was upright, the blood had stopped, he was okay. "It grazed you. Didn't penetrate. Thank God."

This must have been from Joe's gun when we were fighting over it, and fuck, it could have been so much worse. I pressed the towel that Joe had used in Tiber's mouth against the wound and didn't care what was happening behind me.

"Ambulance is fifteen out, but I called Lori," Devin said after his radio crackled with the news.

Getting Lori to attend was a good call. After all, she was the closest thing Prophet had to a paramedic, and when she arrived, she cast an assessing glance at Tiber's flesh wound, then dealt with Joe first. I didn't watch. I was too busy holding Tiber. I wished I could let the animals in, but this was a crime scene.

"Talk to him," Tiber demanded, and shoved me away. "Gabe? Look at me."

I glanced up, his features so dear to me. "I'm not leaving you."

"Talk to him," Tiber insisted. "Then, help me get out to check on our family, okay."

I left Tiber reluctantly, crossed to Joe, who stared up at me, confused.

"You were supposed to hurt, supposed to lose everything!" he yelled, then closed his eyes and was silent, his face a mask of pain.

"I'm sorry," I said from my heart. I was sorry about what happened in LA. I was sorry I'd been doing my job, and I was sorry he'd lost everything. I would always be sorry, but Tiber... he was my everything, and Joe had pointed a gun at his head.

And that was all I had to say, and all that Joe was able to hear as he slipped into unconsciousness. I backed away as Lori started checking vitals.

"Get Duke! He's in the car!"

I went out as quickly as I could, brought Duke back in, then walked in to see Tiber using blunt scissors to hack at his hair, his movements choppy.

"No," I said and stilled his hand.

But he gripped me hard. "Cut it out. All of it. The bits I can't see. Now."

His determined expression forced my hand. I carefully cut away the tape, and some of his beautiful hair, and each snip broke a little piece of my heart.

But then, we bundled up, Tiber shaky, sirens in the distance meaning Joe would be gone soon, we went into the yard, and let the love of the animals, all sitting respectfully and not crowding us, fill the broken bits.

And through it all, we held hands.

Chapter Twenty-Seven

Gabriel

AFTER THE CHAOS subsided and we had cleared the scene, the atmosphere in our home gradually shifted. Devin was staying close to Tiber, his presence reassuring. Lori, with her nurturing instinct, combed Tiber's hair, tidying it as best she could with the kitchen scissors, trying to bring some order to it. Somehow that was the worst of it, seeing locks of his long dark hair chopped off. He was quiet as Lori fussed over him.

Then Sam and the kids arrived, and I was on edge, worried their arrival might overwhelm Tiber. Only, as they entered, Tiber's face lit up with a weak, but sincere smile.

"Hey, guys, you're up late," Tiber said.

The kids, usually a bundle of energy, entered quietly, their eyes wide with a mix of curiosity and concern. They didn't seem tired, even though it was close to midnight, but maybe they'd crash here. They looked at Tiber unsure how to react to whatever was going on in the house.

"It's okay," Tiber said to them, noticing their hesitation. "The animals probably need some attention. Why don't you help me with that, go into the kitchen and make sure they're all doing fine?"

I watched them go through to the kitchen and caught a glimpse of Duke standing right behind the door staring out at where he knew Tiber and I were. The scene—the normality of it all—was a stark contrast to what had happened, and I felt nauseous. I wanted to ask Tiber if we were still okay, if our relationship could withstand the strain, but the question felt selfish at that moment, considering the danger my actions had put him in.

Before I could gather my thoughts, Tiber turned his gaze to me, his eyes searching. "Gabriel, are we... are *we* going to be okay?"

I couldn't make sense of what he was asking. "What?"

"I didn't mean to let him use me as bait." He was frustrated. "I should have fought back—"

"None of this is on you; he had a gun. Fuck." I hugged him close. "I'm sorry this followed me, I'm sorry... fuck... I love you, Tiber." We clung to each other again, and I buried my face in his short hair, already missing the silky length, and hating that he'd have a reminder of tonight every time he checked himself in the mirror.

I'll make things right. I'll keep him smiling.

"Sheriff?" Rick asked from behind me. "We need to head out to Forks."

I knew we did, but I didn't want to leave Tiber, and he must have read that in my expression.

"I'll be okay. I have the animals, and your family," Tiber reassured me. I gave him one last kiss, then crossed to where my brother was standing, slightly back from the rest. I wanted to ask him to keep an eye on Tiber, but also, to tell him that I loved him and Lori and the kids, and that I was so damn sorry they'd been dragged into this. He stopped me by hugging me tight.

"It's okay," he said, and his reassurance meant something. "We're okay. Go finish this thing."

"I love you, Sam," I said.

"Of course you do," he snarked, although the humor didn't quite reach his eyes. "I'm awesome."

Then, it was Devin, who was alert and staring around the house as though he expected bad guys to jump out of the walls.

"Deputy," I said with a nod. *Watch over them.*

"Sheriff." He returned the nod. *I will.*

Then, to everyone, but mostly to Tiber: "I'll be home as soon as I can."

With those words, I stepped out, leaving Tiber in the care of my family—his family. The promise I made hung in the air, and the image of Tiber, managing a small smile amid the love and support of family, stayed with me as I walked away.

IT TOOK ages to get in to see Joe. He'd suffered blood loss, but the bullet had passed through the fleshy part of his leg and missed major arteries, and he didn't need surgery. In fact, he'd gotten off lightly—a couple of stitches, and he'd been assessed as medically fit for us to question. He'd waived his rights to legal counsel, but the doctors were concerned, and it was a big mess. Doctor Makers was designated to come in with us to monitor Joe, and an assistant was asked to document everything. The hospital had rules about non-medical personnel interactions with patients, which we had to respect, but we weren't going in to coerce Joe into anything, we just wanted to talk.

In the end, it was a moot point, as Joe demanded we come in and frowned when the doctor insisted on attending.

He was sitting up in the hospital bed, any pain I'd seen in his expression smoothed out by what the doc summarized for us as a high dose of pain meds. Despite the drugs dulling his physical pain, there was a deep-seated hate in his eyes, an emotion the medication couldn't touch. Rick was by my side, plus Officer Elisa Dowden in from Forks PD, following up on the investigation into John Melchet's murder. For a moment, I even imagined we'd be able to interview Joe sensibly, but his expression twisted when I approached the bed.

"You!" Joe yelled. His words slurred, a side effect of the medication, but his tone was unmistakable. "You walked away, living your happy life, while I... I was left with nothing but pain."

I struggled to find the right words to defend myself, and instead, I slipped into law enforcement mode as Rick took point.

"Joe, tell us about John Melchet."

"Fuck you!" Joe shouted, but not at Rick—this was focused on me, his yell dripping with bitterness. "Enjoy visiting your brother in prison."

I took a deep breath, trying to steady my emotions. "Just tell us, Joe. What part did you play in the murder of John Melchet?"

"You know, Gabriel, I wanted you to pay," Joe said bitterly, ignoring the question, his voice low, but filled with resentment. "You never loved me back. And the irony? Mario actually loves me, scars and all, but I can't love him the way I should because of your lies."

His words stung, and I felt a wave of guilt wash over me. "Joe, I—"

He cut me off, his anger peaking. "I've been watching you all, and seeing you happy was like a knife twisting in me. Why couldn't I love Mario the way I loved a liar like you?" The room felt suffocating as Joe's pain and anger filled the air. "Get out! Make him leave!" he demanded, pointing at me. "Get! Him! Out!"

"I'll go," I said and backed out the door, leaving Rick and Elisa to carry on.

Joe's actions, driven by pain and a desire for revenge, had nearly cost Tiber his life. It was hard to reconcile the Joe I once knew with the man filled with hate in that hospital bed, and I couldn't help but take some of the responsibility and hold it inside. Joe's hatred, my guilt, and the stark realization of how close I had come to losing Tiber collided, and I bent at the waist, finding it hard to breathe.

How was I going to make sure Sam wasn't going to pay? How did I prove Sam was innocent?

I slumped to the nearest chair, a junior officer from Forks PD checked on me, thrusting a bottle of water into my hands, but I couldn't speak, not even to thank her, desperate to be in the room with Rick and Elisa.

When they came out at last, Rick ushered us into the visitor room we'd been given, then leaned against the wall, his expression serious.

"There's something you should know about Joe," Rick began, his voice low. "His ID shows his name as Jim Michaelson. He's been living under an assumed identity, probably since the fire."

I frowned, trying to process this information. "But changing his name would mean leaving all of his father's estate behind. Why wouldn't he have just said who he was?"

Rick nodded. "He wasn't exactly forthcoming, but I got the impression he and Mario were worried they'd be arrested if anyone found out who they were. They chose to disappear."

I could feel the weight of his words. "But his dad's crimes aren't his responsibility. Joe didn't have to hide. Mario maybe, but Joe… not."

"It's not just about responsibility, Gabriel," Rick said, glancing back toward the hospital room. "Fear makes people do irrational things.

"He should have…" Come to me? And what would I have done? I was a cop, and it would never have become anything more than me being undercover and pretending to be his lover. It was a lot to take in. Joe, living in the shadows, haunted by his past and his father's legacy. His actions had brought us all to this moment, a culmination of years of pain and misunderstanding. The complexity of

Joe's situation was overwhelming, and I couldn't help but feel a pang of sympathy for him, despite everything.

Rick must have seen the conflict on my face. "He was going to kill both you and Tiber," he reminded me.

I nodded. The idea of what might have happened to Tiber if things had gone differently was chilling.

"He's under arrest, charged with two counts of attempted first-degree murder—yours and Tiber's," Rick confirmed.

"But he refuses to talk about the murder of John Melchet," Elisa added. "So, we're going back to the office to continue interrogating Mario, and I'm sorry, Gabriel, but Sam is still in the frame right now. Who knows, maybe the man will change his tune when he knows we have Joe under arrest."

I could only hope.

Because I wanted Sam's name cleared.

I wanted this done.

BACK AT FORKS PD, next on our list was interviewing Mario now that we had Joe in custody, a fact I knew would shake Mario. When I walked into the interrogation room with Elisa, Mario's posture was relaxed, until he saw me, and his eyes narrowed.

"Well, hey there, Zach," he said and smirked. "Oops, my bad. *Gabriel*. And you brought in a cop friend. Nice. How many in the gallery?" He waved at the mirror, then winked. "How about someone out there gets me a coffee?"

Rick stayed outside, watching through the two-way mirror. Elisa took lead, started off by ignoring Mario, and informed him straightforward about Joe. "We have Joseph Vine in custody."

I watched his reaction; Mario's eyes widened a little and his body tensed.

"Is he okay?" he asked, his voice laced with concern. Gone was the laid-back man who pretended he didn't give a shit what happened, and in its place was a worried man.

Elisa kept her focus. "Mario, what part did you play in the decision to murder Gabriel Thompson and Tiber Russo?"

There was no flicker of reaction to that, and that told me everything I needed to know—he'd known what Joe intended to do. They would toy with us, hurt everyone I was close to, play psychological warfare with me and my family, but at the end of the day, Tiber and I were supposed to die.

Only Mario ignored the question and returned to his fixation on Joe. He asked again, "Is Joe okay?"

"He's in the hospital," was all that Elisa gave him. "Tell us what you planned after the murders."

"What did you do to Joe?" He yanked at his cuffs and surged toward me, but he was never going to reach me.

I didn't flinch. "What was the rest of your plan?" I asked without hesitation.

"No comment." He slid down in his seat, as far as the handcuffs would let him. "No. Fucking. Comment."

Frustrated, Elisa decided to push harder. "What about the murder of John Melchet? What do you know about that?" she asked.

But Mario had a defiant expression. "I'm done

answering questions." He ignored all further attempts at conversation.

We left him there, and the three of us huddled outside.

"The evidence in John Melchet's murder still points to Sam Thompson. If you guys really believe Mario and Joe are responsible, you're gonna need some proof."

She exchanged glances with Rick, and they both turned to me, and all I could do was nod. Only, we were halfway back to Prophet—Rick driving, both of us silent —when my cell rang, and Devin's name was on the screen.

"Devin?"

"Sheriff, techs tracked the GPS on the phone we took from Mario. It's not exact, but we may have found the general location where Mario and Joe were staying. Lake Sutherland, near Port Angeles. Forks PD will meet you there, and I'll drop a pin if we can narrow it down."

The pin dropped by a group of cabins just as we reached the turnoff to Lake Sutherland, seeing a cruiser blocking the road, ten minutes out from the Storm King Ranger Station, and a ranger standing by it with Elisa.

I pulled up on the side of the road, and Rick and I hurried over, but there was no time given to introductions; Elisa cut to the chase.

"We think we have the cabin, seven. It's the most remote, down the end of this road. Ready?"

We headed down the road about a couple hundred yards, then took a fork up an incline, and arrived at cabin seven, backing onto the trees beyond, with a wide patio facing the water. There was no sign of life from the outside, so we split up, walked the perimeter, and met at the front door, weapons drawn—although what we expected, I don't know.

It certainly wasn't the domesticity we saw inside.

Medication laid out on the counter, pain meds, one bed had been slept in, a condom box sat on the bedside table, food in the fridge, canned goods on the side, plates in the sink, and then, Elisa opened the door to a second bedroom.

"In here," she called. "Fuck, you gotta see this."

We went in with caution—the bed had been pushed to one side, bedside tables as well, and on the large wall there were photos.

A lot of photos. I holstered my gun and stood in front of the display.

Photos of me, dated from last summer and onward, including an article that appeared in the local paper about the wolves. Was this how they knew where I was? How was that even possible? And had they been here since then? Watching me—watching us. There were photos of Tiber and me, notes about routines, pictures of our home, of the animals, and maps, and then, as I moved down the line, photos of Sam, Lori, and the kids. Financial reports were under the photos, noting the loan, connected to the bank, and then, a line to the employees I recognized.

The manager—Bernice Lerner—with a question mark.

John Melchet, again with a question mark.

They'd decided John Melchet was an easier target, had even pulled together a detailed profile of his life, where he lived, his car… and a description of the place he'd been found with a list of pros and cons about Sam being blamed, and a checklist of poisons for animals.

It was meticulous.

It was enough to prove what the people who'd rented this place had planned.

"They've connected Mario to the cabin," Elisa announced, and handed over her phone. "It's enough to dig deeper, check plate recognition, track phones, but we know what we're going to find."

The relief that flooded me was overwhelming. We had them. Sam was off the hook for Melchet's murder.

Chapter Twenty-Eight

Tiber

It was a relief when the house cleared out. Not that I didn't appreciate all the concern and pampering, but I could only take so much of that before I craved quiet. I needed time to detox, and digest, and maybe curl into a fetal ball for a while. Still, it made my heart ache in a good way that Sam and Lori treated me like family. *We are* family.

Lori tried, once again before leaving to get me to go to the hospital. But Joe hadn't added anything new to the collection of aches and pains left by Mario, and the flesh wound from the bullet didn't require stitches, so that was a big no for me. I needed to be home.

I waved goodbye as they drove off, and went back into my little house, turned the door knob lock and the deadbolt behind me. I went around to all the windows and checked the latches and lowered the blinds. I locked the sliding glass door to the deck. Then, I let the troops out of the kitchen, where I'd shut them away from the hubbub, and collapsed onto the sofa.

Leo jumped up and nestled into my chest, Ferd wiggled his way up, as did Gracie and Patch. But Duke stood near the wood stove, panting, and not meeting my gaze.

"Duke." I snapped my fingers. He wouldn't look at me. He tucked his chin and stared at the floor.

"Aw, Duke." I shifted Leo, got up, and went over to hug the yellow lab. "It's not your fault. You did nothing wrong."

Duke tugged away from me; eyes averted. Despair rolled off him in a way I hadn't felt since his owner, Mike Bressett, died.

He felt guilty for not protecting me, for being asleep in the car and not on guard. And maybe, too, he'd been frightened that he'd lose me. He'd probably heard the angry stranger's voice inside the house while he was stuck in the car unable to help. I knew he carried PTSD from when his beloved Mike had been hurt, right in front of him.

I looked at the rest of the pack. Leo was still shaking and Gracie cowering. It wasn't just Duke. We were all in a bit of shock.

I made a fire in the wood stove, handed out extra treats, laid a blanket on the floor, and we all cuddled. I made Duke lie next to me. This little house was our haven. Our safe place. That violence could find us here was a wound to the psyche. But there was no point in thinking about that, worrying about it. I figured it would take time for me and the pack to feel secure here again.

Or not. An hour later, Leo and Ferd were romping around playing tug-of-war with a rope toy, Duke was sleeping peacefully at my side, and Patch was giving a tongue bath to a purring Fudge.

Animals, man. They have such an amazing ability to live in the now.

Me, not so much. I wanted to take a shower, but I honestly couldn't convince myself to leave the warmth of the fire or the security of the pack to go do it. I didn't want to be alone, vulnerable, and naked. Bathing would have to wait.

Gabriel texted three times to check on me. It was after eleven when I heard the key in the lock. I knew it was him, but I still stared at the door extra hard until it opened, and I saw his face.

Then I was up and running into his arms. We held each other tight for a long time.

"I'm so, so sorry," he said, sounding miserable.

"It's not your fault."

"Of course it's my fault. All of it is my fault."

"Come sit down."

We sat on the couch, arms around each other. I hated the guilt in his hazel eyes. It was even harder to take than Duke's.

"Stop," I murmured, putting a hand on his chest.

"I feel so awful. Awful about Joe. Awful about what they did to Sam and Lori. The kids. You. Frank and Ferd. It's killing me."

My empathetic heart throbbed for him. It knew what that kind of remorse felt like.

"Take a deep breath," I instructed.

He hesitated, then did as I asked.

I found his hand and squeezed it tight, gazing into his eyes. "Listen: You were just doing your job in LA. You were trying to help people. Honestly, I wish they'd never put you in that position, because you were always going to be haunted by it—by having to pretend and lie to someone. Because that's not who you are. You're a good man."

"I'm not—"

"I'm speaking," I said firmly.

That made Gabriel smile. "Sorry. Go ahead."

I gripped his hand harder. "Whatever happened there, of course it wasn't perfect. No one could be put into that situation and do it perfectly. But that didn't give Joe and Mario the right to come after you like this. It was their choice. That's not on you."

He shook his head. "I thought they'd both died in the fire. If I'd known it was even a possibility that any of the people associated with Vine were on the street and could come after me or Sam or...I would have been on the lookout for it."

"Exactly. You had no reason to expect it."

He sighed and looked at me, still unsure.

"There's nothing to forgive," I insisted. "But I do forgive you if you need me to. Now and forever."

"Thank you." He kissed me softly. But I knew it wasn't that easy. It would take time, maybe a lot of time, for Gabriel to forgive himself.

People, unlike animals, had a hard time moving on.

"Anyway, part of this was my fault," I added.

Gabriel frowned. "What? Why?"

"I'll tell you, but I want some tea first."

I made two cups of tea and settled on the couch with Gabriel's arm around me, Leo in my lap, and the rest of the pack huddled close. The wood crackled in the wood stove and the peppermint tea warmed my hands, and it felt right for the first time in weeks.

I told him everything. About how Joe had been Jim Smith, about the thermos of soup, the dead raccoon, the poison that had been put in the yard in the middle of the night. I described how I'd suspected Troy Hughes, and how I'd taken Duke to town to search for my stalker's scent.

"For God's sake, Tiber, why didn't you tell me this was going on?" Gabriel asked, genuinely upset.

"I knew you were swamped with Sam's case, and you were so worried about it. I thought it was just a bullying thing here. I thought I could handle it."

"Well, that was dumb!" Gabriel growled. "I'm the sheriff, and I didn't even know that someone was targeting my own home."

I felt a little thrill at hearing him call this place *home*. "You didn't tell me anything about Sam's case either. If I'd known more about it, I might have put two and two together."

"I was trying to protect you."

"Ditto."

We stared at each other for a long moment. Then, he pulled me into a deep embrace. "How about we never hold anything back from each other again?" he said in my ear.

I nodded. "Um. Sure. Probably for the best."

He laughed. "Swear?"

"Pinky swear."

He buried his face in my neck. "I love you so much. If something had happened to you, or if you'd decided I wasn't worth the trouble, I wouldn't have been able to go on."

"Yes, you would. But I'm glad neither of us had to face that."

Duke pawed at my leg and Leo whined. So, we parted enough to gather them all in and have a group hug.

With Leo pressed against me, something dug into my chest. Stone Whiteplume's medicine pouch. I'd almost forgotten I was wearing it.

Looking at it objectively, the thing had worked.

I sent up thoughts of gratitude to my ancestors, to the spirits, to God, to all those who had helped us come through this storm. We might be battered and limping, but never once had our love for each other been tested. And here we all were, still standing, still a family.

And that was all an animal whisperer could wish for.

Epilogue

Tiber

***ONE YEAR** and two months later*

They say time heals all things. I don't know if it can heal every raw place of the body and soul, but I do know that habit helps us forget. What we see every day, the love that surrounds us, the simple daily routine that sustains us, forms a groove in our minds that is deep enough to block out the past. Old hurts grow ever more distant meal by meal, chore by chore, calm day by calm day, with each peaceful evening and restful night.

At some point, Gabriel's nightmares stopped. At some point, I no longer checked the yard for footprints or searched the ground for some dark offerings put there by a person with ill intent. And, at some point, the town of Prophet stopped holding its breath waiting for another murder.

I was glad when the *sorrys* eventually dried up from

Gabriel, when the guilt left his eyes. Some of us pay for our sins in the afterlife. And, for some of us, the bill comes due much sooner. But there can be relief in knowing that it's over, that we have survived the worst.

The spring came, and the summer, and then, fall and Christmas. The pack and I took daily walks down to the lake. On the weekends, we drove to the seaside to romp near Neah Bay or La Push. We hiked in the Hoh Rainforest and Hurricane Ridge. We went to Sam and Lori's for barbecues. We hosted Thanksgiving at our house and went to my mom's place in Portland for Christmas. By the new year, my client calls were booking out three months in advance, and I was happy to be so busy. Gabriel and Devin, not so much. They monitored traffic, mediated neighbor disputes, and broke up a few fights.

It was, in a word, an ordinary life, undramatic. And I thanked the heavens for it.

The first of April was an ordinary day too—ordinary in every perfect way.

"Are you ready? Oh! Oh, Tiber. You look so handsome." My mom came into the bedroom as I was adjusting my tie.

"Yeah?" I turned to her, feeling nervous. I held out my arms and posed.

She paused to take it in, her eyes shining. "Very much yeah." She stepped closer and gave me a gentle hug, mindful not to wrinkle anything.

Gabriel and I had picked out the suits. Pure white jackets, black trousers, and white pleated tuxedo shirts. I had a forest green tie and his was gray-blue. They were the colors of this beautiful place where we lived, forest and water.

"I never thought I'd see this day," Mom said wistfully.

I pulled back to give her a stink eye. "Gee, thanks."

She giggled. "You know what I mean. You've always kept to yourself, Tiber. Been your own person. I'm so happy you met Gabriel. He's a good man, and he's good for you."

"I know." The smile on my face felt silly and sappy, and that was all right.

"And, you know, he's a *person*," Mom continued.

"Yes, well, I proposed to Leo once, but he wouldn't have me," I deadpanned.

Mom lightly slapped my arm. "Oh you! I half believe you. Come on. We should get going, or we'll be late. Mom texted to say they were on their way to the park already."

That was my grandmother. She and my step-grandfather had flown in from the rez in Arizona for the ceremony, and I was so happy they were here.

I took one last glance in the mirror and ran a hand through my hair. It had grown out again and was past my shoulders. The product I'd bought for glossy shine had been worth it because it looked and felt like black silk.

Well, if a man couldn't be vain on his wedding day, when could he be?

Gabriel was getting ready at Sam's house, and he was driving their family to the park, as well as my grandmother and step-grandfather, so that they wouldn't have to walk far. So, it was just Mom, me, and the kids in the Subaru. Everyone in the pack had gotten groomed the day before and was wearing a white bow tie around their neck. No way would it be a wedding without them—that was something Gabriel and I agreed upon.

We drove to town, then around the lake. I pulled in at a back gate to the Olympic National Park. There were a few cars waiting there—One-Eyed Jack and Libby. I jumped out and punched in the code, and they followed me through on the forest road.

We'd gotten special permission for this from the park rangers. Since the only way to get close to Sentinel Rocks by vehicle was on private park maintenance roads, it would, by necessity, be a small wedding party. But that was what we wanted anyway.

I parked along the ridge road. One-Eyed Jack and his wife and two kids, and Libby and Susan parked behind me. After hugs and greetings, and many comments on my outfit and the pack's bow ties, we hiked the short, but steep, way down to Sentinel Rocks, an ancient and sacred spot on the shore of Lake Prophet.

A small crowd was gathered there. I saw my Navajo grandmother and step-grandfather, beaming, and Sam and Lori, who was heavily pregnant with their third child. Sarah and Aaron were dressed up and looked so mature. Ezra was there as well. He'd made a special effort to be here for his brother's wedding, taking a few days off from his archaeology gig. Gabriel and I suspected he wasn't an archaeologist at all, and created wild stories where he was off saving the world—doing what we had no idea. Lincoln, Gabriel's friend from LA, Devin and Hen, and park rangers Rowan and Abby were there too. Stone Whiteplume, it turned out, was licensed to officiate weddings, and he'd perform ours today. He stood regal and somber in his buckskin fringe coat.

A flock of crows was also there—perched on the rocks and on the lakeshore. I sent them a silent *welcome*.

But they all faded into the background when my gaze locked with my intended.

I will never forget that moment—Gabriel standing at Sentinel Rocks, so handsome in his suit, the love in his eyes lighting up the world as he watched me come closer. The April day was brisk with a slight wind, and Lake Prophet raised white caps to toast us. White clouds sped through a blue sky as a reminder that time was fleeting, and that each moment was precious.

Though none would ever be as precious as this one. I had to swallow to ease the hot lump in my throat.

I reached him, our hands found each other, and I floated on pure love, drunk with it, as our friends and family gathered close, and the ceremony began, and Stone Whiteplume began to speak.

"*As I walk, the universe is walking with me in beauty. It walks before me in beauty; it walks behind me in beauty; and it walks below me in beauty. In beauty, it walks above me. Beauty is on every side.* As I walk, I walk with beauty. This is Gabriel Thompson, a man with a big heart who faced rejection from his family because of his nature, who left his home to find his own way, and who was given a heavy task that would test any hero. And this is Tiber Russo, who loves animals and found in them his only friends. Now he also loves this one man—loves him more than life itself."

He paused and smiled.

"And together, they will walk."

THE END

How to Howl at the Moon

Sheriff Lance Beaufort is not going to let trouble into his town, no sir. Tucked away in the California mountains, Mad Creek has secrets to keep, like the fact that half the town consists of 'quickened'—dogs who have gained the ability to become human. Descended on both sides from Border Collies, Lance is as alert a guardian as they come.

Tim Weston is looking for a safe haven. After learning that his boss patented all of Tim's work on vegetable hybrids in his own name, Tim quit his old job. A client offers him use of her cabin in Mad Creek, and Tim sees a chance for a new start. But the shy gardener has a way of fumbling and sounding like a liar around strangers, particularly gorgeous alpha men like Sheriff Beaufort.

Lance's hackles are definitely raised by the lanky young stranger. He's concerned about marijuana growers moving into Mad Creek, and he's not satisfied with the boy's story. Lance decides a bit of undercover work is called for. When Tim hits a beautiful black collie with his car and adopts the dog, it's love at first sight for both Tim and Lance's inner dog. Pretending to be a pet is about to get Sheriff Beaufort in very hot water.

Howl at the Moon Series

1. How to Howl at the Moon
2. How to Walk Like a Man
3. How to Wish Upon a Star
4. How to Save a Life
5. How To Run With The Wolves
6. How to Love Thine Enemy

Have You Read from RJ Scott?

What Lies Beneath (Lancaster Falls 1)

In the hottest summer on record, Iron Lake reservoir is emptying, revealing secrets that were intended to stay hidden beneath the water. The tragic story of a missing man is a media sensation, and abruptly the writer and the cop falling in love is just a postscript to horrors neither could have imagined.

Best Selling Horror writer Chris Lassiter struggles for inspiration and he's close to never writing again. His life has become an endless loop of nothing but empty pages, personal appearances, and a marketing machine that is systematically destroying his muse. In a desperate attempt to force Chris to complete unfinished manuscripts his agent buys a remote cabin. All Chris has to do is hide away and write, but he's lost his muse, and not even he can make stories appear from thin air.

Sawyer Wiseman left town for Chicago, chasing the excitement and potential of being a big city cop, rising the ranks, and making his mark. A case gone horribly wrong draws him back to Lancaster Falls. Working for the tiny police department in the town he'd been running from, digging into cold cases and police corruption, he spends his day's healing, and his nights hoping the nightmares of his last case leave him alone.

The **Lancaster Falls** Series

Also By Eli Easton

For a full list of ebooks and links please scan the code above or visit eliseaston.com

Also By RJ Scott

For a full list of ebooks and links please scan the code above or visit rjscott.co.uk/rjbooks

Meet Eli Easton

Having been, at various times and under different names, a minister's daughter, a computer programmer, a game designer, the author of paranormal mysteries, a fan fiction writer, and organic farmer, Eli has been a m/m romance author since 2013. She has published over 30 gay romances.

Eli has loved romance since her teens and she particular admires writers who can combine literary merit, genuine humor, melting hotness, and eye-dabbing sweetness into one story.

Website & newsletter - elieaston.com

facebook.com/100008994061782

x.com/EliEaston

amazon.com/stores/Eli-Easton/author/B00CJUKM9I

bookbub.com/authors/eli-easton

goodreads.com/7020231.Eli_Easton

Meet RJ Scott

RJ is the author of the over one hundred and sixty published novels and discovered romance in books at a very young age. She realized that if there wasn't romance on the page, she could create it in her head, and is a lifelong writer.

She lives and works out of her home in the beautiful English countryside, spends her spare time reading, watching films, and enjoying time with her family.

The last time she had a week's break from writing she didn't like it one little bit and has yet to meet a box of chocolates she couldn't defeat.

www.rjscott.co.uk | rj@rjscott.co.uk

Newsletter - rjscott.co.uk/rjnews

facebook.com/author.rjscott

x.com/Rjscott_author

instagram.com/rjscott_author

amazon.com/author/rj-scott

bookbub.com/authors/rj-scott

goodreads.com/rjscott

pinterest.com/rjscottauthor